D0183319

HEATHER GRAHAM

NIGHT OF THE WOLVES

First published in Great Britain 2012
by Mills & Boon, an imprint of Harlequin (UK) Limited,
Eton House, 18-24 Paradise Road, Richmond, Surrey TW9 1SR

© Heather Graham Pozzessere 2009

ISBN: 978 0 263 89609 1
ebook ISBN: 978 1 408 97492 6

089-0812

Harlequin (UK) policy is to use papers that are natural, renewable and recyclable products and made from wood grown in sustainable forests. The logging and manufacturing processes conform to the legal environmental regulations of the country of origin.

Printed and bound
by CPI Group (UK) Ltd, Croydon, CR0 4YY

To some of my favorite Aussies,
with a bit of Kiwi, too.

Rosemary Potter

Cherie Watts

Christina Tanvadji

Frances Bomford

Monthiti Danjaroensuk

Margaret Bell

and

Mandi Hutton

NIGHT OF THE WOLVES

PROLOGUE

1838
The Republic of Texas

FIRST SHE HEARD THE HOWLING of the wolves. In the West, once you got past the cities and out on the trails leading to the lands of the ranchers and homesteaders, the sound wasn't unusual. It was still eerie, but it wasn't unusual.

But this was so *early*.

And after that, when the air went so very still…

That was when Molly Fox knew that something was wrong, seriously wrong.

Bartholomew, who was generally a fine guard dog, was acting like anything but. He started to whine, tucked his tail between his legs and, keeping low to the ground, crept into the bedroom and under the bed.

The strange silence continued. Molly listened, but she couldn't even hear the sound of the wind moving through the trees.

Taking Lawrence's old rifle, she went out on the porch. As she stood there, she saw the dying sun far on the western horizon.

As she watched, it seemed to fall to the earth like a fiery globe, sending out tentacles of flame to tease the heavens.

It was beautiful, but then, as if it had been enfolded in a dark blanket, it suddenly disappeared as it plummeted to the earth. The last vestiges of pink and pale yellow, mauve and silver, faded from the sky. Even twilight was gone; night had taken over.

Molly stood in the darkness for a moment, then gave herself a shake and quickly retreated inside to light the kerosene lamp on the table.

Bartholomew was still cowering in the bedroom.

"Come out, you ragamuffin," Molly called, though she was still illogically unnerved herself.

She was accustomed to living out here. Lawrence and she had picked up stakes from Louisiana and come here to accept her inheritance from a father she'd never met: a small cattle ranch, but not a very profitable one. Still, they had been able to hire five hands, who lived in the bunkhouse just the other side of the stables, and she even had a girl in from town to help her clean the place and keep up with the cooking, five days a week. They were young; they spent their nights dreaming and their days working hard to make those dreams a reality.

When he was off on a cattle drive, like the one he had recently left on, Lawrence didn't like to leave her alone, and he'd once suggested that they splurge for her to stay in town, but she hadn't wanted to go. He worried about a rogue cowhand or a rustler, or a plain old villain of any variety, who might come along. But she knew how to shoot, and she would hear a horseman coming. Plus she had Bartholomew—who at the very least made a terrible ruckus if there was a stranger around.

He didn't usually hide under the bed.

Molly set about lighting the rest of the lamps in the

parlor and dining area, kitchen, and even her bedroom—
she didn't want Bartholomew spooked any further. Just
moving around and doing something made her feel better.

Then the wolves started howling again, and Molly
heard Bartholomew whining softly in fear.

"Bartholomew, you are not a hound, you are a chicken,"
Molly called to the dog, trying to find a semblance of
inner calm. "Those are just wolves, silly dog. Your cousins,
in the grand scheme of things."

Her own voice sounded unnatural to her.

And even as the sound of her words died, she was listening again. And what she heard—or rather, didn't hear—
was disturbing.

The silence was back. A heavy silence that somehow
just shouldn't be.

She'd left the gun by the door, and she quickly went back
for it. Clutching the rifle with one hand, she carefully
opened the front door again and walked back out on the
porch.

There was nothing out there. The moon was rising high
now—maybe the wolves had known it was on the rise,
climbing up in the sky even as the sun had died in all its
magnificent splendor. She could see the yard in front of
the house, the strong fence Lawrence and the men had
built, and the paddocks beyond. She had gone out earlier
and fed the two horses that remained in the stables, along
with the chickens, and she was glad—she didn't want to
be far from the house now, or even Bartholomew, for
whatever he was worth. She saw nothing, heard nothing,
and yet she was afraid. She wished that she would hear the
sound of hoofbeats or rowdy cowhands—or even outlaws;
she could handle ill-mannered men, despite Lawrence's

fears for her. She blushed. Lawrence was convinced that she was beautiful, and that, surely, everyone saw it. She prided herself more on an admirable sense of honor; she believed in God and believed that He wanted most for everyone to be decent to one another. Whenever she said so, though, Lawrence would shake his head, smiling, rolling his eyes, and tell her that she was naive. But she was still happy. He loved her. And he was such a gorgeous man himself. Tall and strong, and so capable; she even loved his callused hands, because he got those calluses working for her. For their dreams. But he *did* worry.

She had the respect and friendship of most folks in town; she certainly wasn't afraid of them. Not even of any of the local cowhands or farmers; she could quell their bad behavior with one disapproving look.

No, she was never afraid....

Molly went from window to window, making sure they were all securely latched. The house had been built with a breezeway, Southern-style, so she went to the back door and assured herself that it was locked and latched, as well.

All the lamps were on.

The world was still eerily silent.

She set water on the stove to make herself a cup of tea. She had best get over this silliness, she told herself. It would be weeks before Lawrence returned from his cattle drive.

While the water heated, she marched herself into her bedroom.

Bartholomew had come out from beneath the bed, but he was still crouched low, and he was making a strange whining sound.

"Barty, stop it!" Molly implored. She went to her dressing table. The kerosene lamp set strange shadows to dancing around the room, something that didn't help her jitters. Her face appeared gaunt in the mirror, her hazel eyes reflecting back at her filled with a shimmering gold. Her hair caught the light and seemed to spark with fire, appearing more red than usual. She picked up her brush and began to count out a hundred strokes.

Bartholomew barked. She turned to look at him. "Barty!"

He whined, and thumped his tail on the floor.

Letting out a sigh, she turned back to the mirror.

And that was when she saw him.

She let out a startled scream, then turned with a gasp and relieved laughter.

It was Lawrence. Somewhere he had changed from his cattle-drive denims and cotton shirt; he was dashing in a black suit and crimson vest, and a high black silk hat. He was so straight and strong, such a handsome man. Cajun blood ran through him; his brows and neatly maintained mustache and beard were pitch-black, like his hair and eyes. His features were strong and his mouth was generous, his smile filled with a sense of fun and just a shade of wickedness.

She started toward him, then froze.

There was something wrong. His face was so pale. He lifted a hand, as if to keep her away.

"Molly," he whispered. "Molly, I love you."

He was sick or injured, she thought; he looked as if he were about to fall. Filled with her love for him, she went to him.

"What happened? My God, Lawrence, how did you even get in here? I had the place all locked up. Never mind. What's wrong? Where are you hurt?"

She slipped her arms around him, leading him to the foot of the bed. They sank down together, and he turned and stared at her. He had to be fevered, and yet he was cold to the touch. She brought her fingers to his face, tears springing to her eyes. "My love, what's wrong?"

Shaking, he lifted his own hand to her face, his gaze intense as he told her, "Molly, I love you. I love you so much. You are everything that I've lived for, everything that's good and wonderful and pure in life."

Then he kissed her, and though his lips were chilly at first, there was passion in his touch, and he seemed vibrant and vital and…

Desperate…

He kissed her deeply, with a hunger that was seductive all in itself. The way that his tongue moved in her mouth was suggestive and wildly sexual. She felt his fingertips on her shoulder, tugging at the cotton of her blouse, and the fabric that ripped and tore as he removed it seemed of little consequence. He threw off his hat, lifting her higher on the bed, and the fever was in his eyes as he looked down at her, then buried his face against her throat, her breast. "I love you. I love you so much. I shouldn't be here, but I *have* to be here. By God, I won't do another man ill, but I must be here."

She threaded her fingers through his rich dark hair. "I love you—I'll always love you—and you belong here."

He said something, but it was muffled against her flesh as he kissed her breasts, laved them with his tongue, teased them with his teeth, a small pain, but one that was oddly erotic. Their clothing wound up strewn everywhere, and she had never felt more feverishly, thoroughly kissed. He seemed to cover every inch of her body even as she struggled to return the liquid caresses, his urgency streaking through her with the fury of a lightning bolt. Somewhere in the back of her mind she still worried that he was ill. But he couldn't be that ill; no man could love with such steely passion if he were ill....

He paid careful attention to all of her, first the entire length of her back, and then he flipped her over and caressed a slow and lazy zigzag pattern over her collarbone and breasts, down to her navel, her hips, her inner thighs, and then between them. She shrieked and clawed at him, and eventually brought him back to her. She couldn't have felt more loved and sensual and sexual than when he rose above her and thrust into her. He loved her with his body and with his very soul, and she was dazzled and flying, whispering, crying out, soaring higher and higher. When she climaxed, the world seemed to burst like Chinese firecrackers and then tremble as if they'd been caught in an earthquake. Afterward, she clung to him, drifting back to sanity amid the shadows of their bedroom.

She lay still, catching her breath for the longest time, and then she curved into him and said, "Lawrence, why are you back? You're not due for—"

He brought his fingers to her lips. "In time," he whispered. It almost sounded as if he were crying, but she didn't question him. She knew him well enough to know he would answer in his own time. They had grown up together, had spun their dreams for a life with each other forever.

He held her close for a long time, and then they made

love again. Throughout, he whispered "I love you" so many times that she lost count.

And when she slept, it was in the comfort of his arms, basking in the love of their youth and their dreams for the future.

But in the morning he was gone.

She was amazed, disbelieving. She even went into town and asked if anyone had seen him. Sheriff Perkin looked at her as if she were plumb crazy.

"Why, Molly, my dear, you know he's off on the trail with his hands. Honey, the man's barely left. He wouldn't be human if he'd made it back here so fast, now would he? Are you sure you're all right out there? You're looking kind of peaked. You ought to come in and stay with my Susie. With our boys off helping on the cattle drive, she's right lonely."

Molly thanked him but said that she couldn't stay. She went home, completely perplexed. Lawrence had been there on what she'd come to call the night of the wolves, for that eerie howling. She knew it. She could still see his eyes, still hear his words, feel his touch. He loved her; he had made love to her.

It was two days later when Doc Smith came out with the sheriff and his sweet wife, Susie. All three were pale and drawn.

She knew something was wrong. She had actually known it from the moment she heard the horses' hoofbeats. She stood on the porch, clutching the rail as they approached. By her side, Bartholomew let out a low and mournful howl.

Just like the wolves.

She was afraid. More afraid than she'd ever been in her

life. And when the sheriff walked toward her, his old bulldog face filled with grief, she knew.

"No!" she said. "No, he's not dead. Lawrence isn't dead. He isn't, he isn't, he—"

"My poor dear!" Susie Perkin, pretty and round, hurried to Molly, taking her into her arms.

"They were attacked right outside town, just a few days after they left. Cattle rustlers, I'm thinking, 'cause there wasn't sight nor sound of any cattle to be found," Sheriff Perkin said. "Cattle rustlers…Comanche or Apache, most like. We can't rightly tell which. But there are some arrows at the site…some feathers, but—"

"No! Lawrence knew the local tribes and the shamans *and* the war chiefs. He didn't die at the hands of any Indians, I know that!"

Doc Smith was as kind a man as you could ever want to meet, and he took Molly's hand now. "You'll come back into town with us," he said.

"And Bartholomew, too," Sheriff Perkin said.

"But he's not dead. He was here! And he'll be back. Anytime now, he'll be back!" Molly told them. She was falling, but they were there to support her. "He was here, and that's why I asked you if you'd seen him. He was home, but then he up and disappeared. He's not dead, though," Molly told them. "And I won't believe he is. Not unless I see his body, I won't."

"Oh, Lord, she can't be seein' that body," Doc Smith whispered.

"It's not him. I know it's not. I don't care what you say, it's not him," Molly protested.

"There, there," Susie told her helplessly.

In the end, they had to show her what was left of the body.

It was in Lawrence's clothing. It held Lawrence's pocket watch and his billfold. There was a gold chain around its neck with a big locket that carried a picture of her. The matted, bloody hair that remained was black. The body had been found with five others, and those men, she was certain, were their hands. Jody, who laughed all the time. Beau, who was big as an ox. Daryl, Steven and Jacob, too.

After insisting that she be allowed to see them all at the funeral parlor in town, Molly was horrified. At last it was more than her consciousness could bear. She passed out.

As she fell, she admitted that yes, the first man was Lawrence.

Immediately she told herself that no, it wasn't Lawrence. Lawrence had come to her, had made love to her, after this…*thing* was dead.

It was about six weeks later when Molly knew for certain, at least in her own soul, that she had been right. She didn't know how; it was a mystery she would never fathom. But Lawrence *had* come to her that night.

She was expecting.

She rented her house and land to a neighboring rancher, and thanked the Perkins for all they had done for her, then told them that she couldn't stay, that she had to go home to what family she had, back to Louisiana, to the city. They wept when they saw her off in the stagecoach. She wept, too. They had been good friends. She knew they wanted her to stay, to fall in love again.

But she loved Lawrence. He loved her. And she would spend the rest of her life waiting.

He had come once; he might come again.

And meanwhile, she would have her child to raise.

CHAPTER ONE

Summer
1864

DARKNESS HAD COME to New Orleans. Though the detested Union military governor Benjamin "Beast" Butler had been removed from control over the city, the streets remained quiet by night, as if the residents' hatred of the man were an odor, and that odor still lingered in the air. As he approached the office on Dauphine where he'd been summoned, Cody Fox was surprised by the sudden eruption of men, exiting headquarters and hurrying out to the street, rifles in their hands, faces pale, nervous whispers rather than shouts escaping their lips.

He was curious about what was bothering the men. New Orleans was solidly in Union hands and had been for more than a year. As the others hurried out, barely nodding in his direction, Cody went in, wondering what a Union officer wanted from a recovering Confederate soldier. The sergeant behind the desk took his name and bade him sit, then hurried into what had once been the parlor of Missy Eldin, daughter of Confederate Colonel Elijah Eldin, who had died at Shiloh, but was now a Union military office.

Cody had returned from the front lines nearly a month

ago, and as far as he was concerned, he had healed from the wound that had taken him out of the battle and sent him back to the house on Bourbon Street where he had grown up. He was walking fine these days, he had no problem whatsoever leaping up on his horse, and all he had in mind now was getting somewhere far away.

He wasn't afraid of battle; he wasn't even afraid of the enemy, especially since he and his Southern fellows lived side by side with "the enemy" these days. Cody had discovered long before the war that there were good and bad men of every calling, and there were good men and bad on both sides of the present conflict. No, he was simply tired of the carnage, restless, ready to move on.

But he'd been called to the headquarters of Lieutenant William Aldridge, adjunct to Nathaniel Banks, the commander who had replaced "Beast" Butler. Butler had ordered the execution of a man named William Mumford, merely for tearing down the Stars and Stripes when it had been raised over city hall. The act had made him a savage not only in the eyes of the South, but even in the North and among the Europeans. Nathaniel Banks was a decent man, and he was working hard to undo the terrible damage caused by Butler, but it would take time.

"Mr. Fox?" A soldier in a federal uniform, an assistant to an assistant, called him, refusing to acknowledge his rank. He really didn't give a damn. He hadn't wanted to go to war; it had seemed that grown men should have been able to solve their differences without bloodshed. Then again, he had no desire to be a politician, either.

These days...everyone was just waiting. The war would end. Either the Northerners would get sick to death of the toll victory would cost and say good riddance to the South, or the continual onslaught of men and arms—something that could be replenished in the North and not the South—would force the South to her knees. He'd once had occasion to meet Lincoln, and he admired the man. In the end, Lincoln's iron will and determination might be the deciding factor. Lee was definitely one of the finest generals ever to lead a war effort, but no man could fight the odds forever.

"Yes, I'm Fox," Cody said, rising.

"Come in, please. Lieutenant Aldridge is ready to see you in his office," the assistant to the assistant said.

Cody nodded and followed the man.

Lieutenant Aldridge was behind a camp desk neatly installed in the once elegant study. He had clearly been busy with the papers scattered in front of him, but when Cody entered, he stood politely. Aldridge was known as a decent fellow, one of those men who were convinced the North would win and that, when that day came, the nation was going to have to heal itself. It might take decades, because it was going to be damned hard for folks to forgive after Matthew Brady and others following in his footsteps had brought the reality of war home. Brady's photographs of the dead on the field had done more to show mothers what had happened to their sons than any words ever could have. But Aldridge was convinced that healing would come one day, and he intended to work toward that reality.

"Mr. Fox," Aldridge said, shaking Cody's hand and indicating the chair in front of his desk. "Thank you for coming in. Would you like some coffee?" He was tall and lean, probably little more than thirty, but with the ravages of responsibility adding ten years to his features. His eyes were hazel. Kind eyes, though.

"I'm fine, thank you," Cody said. He leaned forward. "May I ask why I'm here?"

Aldridge pulled a file from atop a stack on his desk and flipped it open. "You were with Ryan's Horse Guard, I see. Cavalry. You saw action from the first Battle of Manassas to Antietam Creek, and you nearly had your leg blown off. Doctors said you wouldn't make it, but somehow you survived. You've been back here in New Orleans for a year—got your medical degree up at Harvard, though."

Aldridge paused for a moment, staring at him. "Any corrections thus far?"

"No, sir. None that I can think of," Cody said, still wondering why he was there.

Aldridge dropped the file. "Anything you want to add?"

"Seems like you know a lot about my life, sir."

"Why don't you fill me in on what I'm missing?" Aldridge asked, a fine thread of steel underlying his words.

"What exactly are you asking, Lieutenant?" Cody asked.

"I was hoping you'd be more…forthcoming with the details of your time in the North, Fox," Aldridge said. "Before your state seceded, you were working in Washington. You were actually asked to the White House to converse with Lincoln. You've been involved in solving several…difficulties in and around the capital."

Cody kept his face impassive, but Aldridge's knowledge of his past had taken him by surprise.

"I took part in a number of reconnaissance missions as part of Lee's army, Lieutenant, if that's what you're referring to," he said carefully. "I was given a medical discharge and sent back to New Orleans when I was wounded—initially declared dead, actually. I've been here, helping the wounded of both armies and minding my own business, since my recovery."

Aldridge stared at him and flipped the file shut again. He didn't have to read from it; he apparently knew what it contained. "A series of bizarre murders took place in northern Alexandria in 1859. You were friends with a certain law enforcement officer, Dean Brentford, and you started patrolling with him at night. You apprehended the murderer when no other constable could catch up with him. And when he tore through the force trying to subdue him, you managed to decapitate him with a single one-handed swing of your sword." Aldridge pointed a finger at him. "President Lincoln himself asked you to perform intelligence work for him, but you politely refused, saying your remaining kin were in Louisiana, and you couldn't rightly accept such a position."

Cody lifted his hands. "My mother died the year after the war started, but I'm sure you understand that…I come from here. I was born here. And as to the…incident to which you refer… The brutality of the murders took everyone by surprise, and I'm simply glad I was able to help."

Aldridge leaned forward. "Help? Fox, to all intents and purposes you and you alone stopped them. More to the point, we've just had a similar case here, down on Conti. My officers are at their wits' end, and I don't want this city going mad because the Yanks think the Rebs have gone sick or vice versa. This isn't a battleground anymore, it's a city where people are picking up the pieces of their lives. It may take decades before true peace is achieved, but I'll be damned if I'll allow the citizens to start killing one another because one man is sick in the head."

Cody stared straight across the desk at the man and didn't say a word.

"You got yourself a medical degree, son, then you went off to ride with the cavalry and wound up in intelligence." Aldridge stared back at Cody, hazel eyes intent. "You can help me. I don't give a damn where you came from or what your folks did or whose side you fought on. I just want to catch a killer. Because it sounds like a bloodthirsty madman just like the one you killed is on the loose—in my city—and I want him stopped."

"HOW DID YOU KNOW about the attack?"

Alexandra Gordon was sitting in a hardwood chair, presumably before a desk, but she didn't have any actual idea where she was, since the officers who had come to her house had thrown a canvas bag over her head, and she was still blinded by it. She was stunned by the treatment she had received and continued to receive, especially since she had put herself in great peril to warn the small scouting contingent that there would be bloodshed if they crossed the Potomac.

Apparently she was a deadly spy.

They had tied her hands behind her back, but the officer in charge had whispered furiously to the others, and her hands were once again free. Despite that small courtesy, he seemed to be the descendent of a member of the Spanish Inquisition. He slammed his hands on the table, and his voice rose as he repeated the question. "*How* did you know? And don't say again that it was a dream. You are a spy, and you *will* tell me where you're gaining your information!"

She shook her head beneath the canvas bag, praying for the ability to stay calm. "I merely tried to save Union lives, sir, as well as Confederate. What, I ask you, was gained by this raid? Nothing. What was lost? The lives of at least twenty young men. I went to the encampment to speak with the sergeant and tell him that he mustn't make the foray. He ignored my warning, and now he and his men are dead, along with a number of my Southern brothers."

"I have the power to imprison you for the rest of your life—or hang you," her inquisitor warned.

She heard the sound of a door opening. Someone else spoke, a man with a low, well-modulated voice. "Lieutenant Green," he said, "I would like to speak with Ms. Gordon myself."

"But, sir!" Green was shocked.

"Please," the new voice said politely, but there was authority in the tone.

Alex heard a chair scrape back and was aware of the newcomer taking a seat across from her.

"My wife has dreams," he said after a moment. "In fact, *I* have had dreams. Please, tell me, what did you see in *your* dream, and how did you know when and where the slaughter would occur?"

"I know the place," she said softly. "I used to play in that hollow when I was a child, when we had a farm there. My father worked in Washington then, but we would steal away to the countryside whenever he was free."

She heard someone snort. Green. "Her father was a traitor," the lieutenant said. "He went out West and was murdered. Indians, I heard. Good riddance."

She stiffened at that. "My father was no traitor. He loved the West and chose to move us there to avoid a war he thought unjust. He went looking for a home where everyone was equal. He didn't care about a man's birth or color. He was a brilliant man," she said passionately. "He worked for the government, for the *people*."

"It's all right, I know of him, Miss Gordon," the newcomer said softly, soothingly. "And I was deeply sorry to hear about his death. Now, tell me, what did you see?"

"I saw the hollow in the woods. I heard the horses coming, and I saw movement in the trees. And then the men stepped out, thin, haggard, like starving dogs. And starving dogs can be desperate. When the horses came, the men were ready to attack. And then…it was as if a fog suddenly settled over the daylight, but the mist was red, the color of the blood being spilled.… I saw…I saw them die. Some were shot, others skewered through by bayonets. Then I saw the riderless horses cantering away, and I saw the ground, strewn with the dead, one atop another, as if in death enemies had at last made amends."

"Do you dream often?" he asked.

She longed to see the face of the man who had come to speak so kindly to her. "No."

"But you have done so before?"

"Yes."

"And when you have these dreams, what you see comes true?"

"Unless it is somehow stopped," she said. "I tried so hard…but no one would listen."

She was startled, but not frightened, when he took her hands.

His hands were very large, callused and clumsy, but warm, and offering great strength.

"She's a Confederate spy," someone muttered venomously.

"Gentleman, a spy does not warn the enemy in an attempt to prevent death," he said. "A spy would let the enemy march to their doom. Tell me," he said to her, "do you wish to bring us down?"

"No. I am not a spy. I came home to marry—"

"A Reb," the inquisitor interrupted.

"And instead I watched my fiancé and what was left here of my family die. But I do not pray for either side. I pray for an end to war. I teach—"

"Sedition," the lieutenant stated.

"Piano," she corrected dryly. "And I run a library and bookshop. My father was a great teacher, and I'm proud to say I learned everything I know from him."

The gentle man spoke to her again. "Do you consort with the enemy?"

"If I do, I have nothing to tell them. And I consort with those who are not your enemy, as well," she said, an edge to her tone.

"I believe you," he said. "But now I would like to return to the subject of your dreams."

"I believe that dreams come to warn us, but that if we learn to heed them, we can change the course of events."

She heard the other man sniggering. "Did your dreams warn you about your father's death, Miss Gordon?" the lieutenant asked, mocking her.

"Dreams do not always tell us what we might most wish to know," she said.

"Tell me, Miss Gordon, have you ever changed the outcome of events after you dreamed them?"

"Yes. I…stopped a young man who was wounded from rejoining his unit. I had seen him lying on the battlefield, staring up at the sky with sightless eyes on the battlefield. He has since been reassigned to communications work."

"Spying!" Lieutenant Green said.

She laughed. "He was a Union soldier, so…"

The quiet man spoke again. "What if we are not intended to change fate," the soft-spoken man said.

"We are creatures of free will," she said. "I believe that God helps those who help themselves. We read books. Perhaps we can learn to read our dreams, as well," she said.

"Perhaps." She heard him move his chair back. "It's my belief, Lieutenant Green, that we are violating the rights of this young woman," he said.

She didn't know what she had said, but she had somehow satisfied him.

"What are your plans, Miss Gordon?" he asked, surprising her.

"I've been planning—to head west, to Texas. I want to find out what happened to my father," she said.

"I think you'd do better to stay here," the man said. "Safer."

"I have to go," she said simply.

"Have you received guidance on that matter in your dreams?" he asked.

"No. But I know in my heart that I must search out the truth," she said.

"I understand. At any rate…Lieutenant Green, get that ridiculous hood off the young lady's head."

"I can manage, sir," she said, shuddering at the thought of Green touching her. She quickly pulled the canvas sack from her head.

She looked up and found herself rising. She had never suspected … She had seen President Lincoln many times, and she had heard that he was haunted by dreams and sometimes driven to distraction by his wife's obsession with the occult. But then, the poor man had lost two sons, and the challenge of keeping a nation together did not lessen a father's grief or a mother's desperation.

He stretched out a hand. She accepted it. "You will be in my prayers, young lady."

"And you, sir, will be in mine."

"That is something for which I will be eternally grateful."

"Sir!" Green protested.

"Please see to it that Miss Gordon is escorted home. And if she needs help in any way, I know that you will be kind enough to see that she receives it. Right, Lieutenant?"

Green looked as if he were about to explode.

"Right, Lieutenant?" Lincoln repeated softly.

"Right, sir," Green said.

Lincoln tipped his hat to her. "I wish you could meet Mary. She might be greatly encouraged by knowing you."

"I am here for another fortnight, sir, and it would be my great pleasure to help you in any way."

"Then I shall make the arrangements. You have my thanks."

MARY LINCOLN DID NOT have her husband's calm disposition.

Alex felt she had to be honest and explain that she had

no way to communicate with the dead, but she also found herself desperate to ease the woman's suffering if she could. "Sometimes," she said, "those who have gone before us appear in our dreams, and I believe that is their way of letting us know that they are happy in the next world."

"Has your father, or perhaps your fiancé, appeared in your dreams?" Mary asked anxiously.

"No. But I have heard of it happening. Mrs. Lincoln, I know that your little ones are with God. You must find peace here on earth, and know that you will be reunited with them when the time is right."

She saw a peacefulness enter Mary Lincoln's eyes then, and she left feeling that, in some small way, she had helped.

DAYS LATER, WHEN SHE was actually leaving for her long journey, she saw the president again.

He was riding in a carriage with his wife, as he often did on a Sunday. He didn't see her, though. He was leaning back, his eyes closed, his expression that of a man pushed past the point of exhaustion. As she stepped into her own carriage, she wondered what dreams were plaguing the president as he wearily rested his head. Dreams were such unreliable messengers.

No dream had warned her of her father's death, when she had left him to return to her fiancé in the East.

And no dream had come to alert her to what lay ahead.

CHAPTER TWO

IT WAS JUST SUNSET when Alex started toward the stairs of
the boardinghouse that, following her father's death, was
now hers—despite the fact that he had left behind a new
young wife, a woman named Linda Alex had yet to meet
and couldn't say she thought much of.

She was shaking the dust of travel from her skirt
before heading back up to her room, where clean
clothes awaited after the long trip from the capital. She'd
walked around the house, making note of the changes—
some of them very strange—that had been made in her
absence. Now she was looking forward to cleaning up and
resting.

That was when she heard the shots.

Dozens of them, along with the sounds of horses'
hooves, and the whooping and hollering that came along
with the sudden rush of men into town.

"Oh, no!" Bert, the jack-of-all-trades her father had
hired right after their arrival in Victory, Texas, came
rushing into the entry hall and made his way to the front
window. He peered carefully beyond the lace drapes, the
color draining from his coffee-colored face. "It's…them,"
he said, shuddering.

"What's going on?" Alex demanded, turning. She felt

a surge of fear streak through her, but she headed straight to the gun rack in the library. She had heard strange stories ever since her return, but she wasn't one to put stock in spooky tales, not when she had a gun in her hand.

Her father's Colt automatic was right where it had always been, and it was loaded. She might go down in a hail of bullets, but she wasn't going down without a fight.

Bert turned to stare at her, and she realized she'd never seen him afraid before. "Alex, leave that thing be. It won't help you any. These folks are—they're animals. We've got to get down in the basement and hide. Don't you see? There just ain't no point in fighting these days."

No point in fighting? That was ridiculous. Victory had a sheriff, a deputy, and a town banker, three shopkeepers and a stable master—all of whom had fought in the war or on the frontier and knew how to defend themselves. Not to mention the fact that the saloon had several bartenders and "song and dance" girls who were tough as nails.

Bert turned from the window to stare at her. "We've got to get into the basement. All of us. We've got to hide, and be real quiet. We'll be safe down there."

"I'm not hiding in the basement. This town has guts, and if we fight, others will, too."

Beulah, the cook, appeared, running from the kitchen. "Come on! We've got to go hide." She turned, calling for Tess and Jewell, the maids.

It was crazy, Alex thought, but all this panic was giving her chills.

Fighting her growing fear, Alex strode over and took Bert by the shoulders. "Stop it! We need to stand up and fight."

"No!" Bert shook off her hold and grabbed her in

return. "Alex, you don't know these outlaws. It's the Beauville gang. I've seen what they done, back in Brigsby."

"What happened in Brigsby?"

"They murdered everyone and now the place is a ghost town. Now, you go down in the basement and—"

He never got to finish his sentence. The door to the boardinghouse burst open and revealed three outlaws standing on the front steps, guns drawn.

Alex's heart stuttered, then resumed beating as she told herself that they were just outlaws. Murderers shooting into the air and shouting to create fear and confusion, but men. Just men.

But it was three against one, because only she was armed.

Bert was a courageous man. Despite his fear, he stepped forward, ready to protect her. But the first of the outlaws, a tall man with a gaunt face and black eyes, laughed as, with a single swift blow, he sent Bert crashing against the wall. She heard the crack as his head hit the wood, then saw him slump unconscious to the floor.

"You must be the Alexandra Gordon I've heard so much about," the outlaw mocked, sweeping off his hat and bowing in greeting. The two behind him laughed, and one spat chewing tobacco on her newly swept hardwood floor. "Milo Roundtree, at your service," the first man said, then, "No, that's wrong. I believe *you* will be at *my* service."

"I don't think so." She lifted the Colt. "I know exactly how to use this."

A short man with scruffy, tangled blond hair laughed uproariously. "She'll be at our service? All right! She's a damn sight cleaner than them whores we're always stuck with."

"Didn't you hear me? I said I'll shoot you," Alex announced.

"No, you'll come with us," Milo said, and grinned. It was then she saw that two other men, who must have come in through the back door, had caught up with Tess and Jewell before they could reach the basement and were holding knives at the girls' throats.

Alex was filled with sudden terror, but somehow she managed to stay upright and keep her face as defiant as her words. "Let my friends go this instant, and I won't blow your brains out."

"Aren't you the feisty beauty?" Milo said. "I think you'll be for me. Just for me."

"Not in this lifetime," she said.

"That's all right, too, little darling," he drawled. The words were not reassuring.

"I'll shoot you before I let you lay a hand on me," she said to Milo.

He merely nodded toward the ruffian who held Tess. The man brought his knife closer to her flesh, and a low moan escaped her.

Milo looked at her challengingly, and Alex lowered her gun.

Milo stepped forward and grabbed her, slamming her up against him. She was immediately aware that there was something very odd about the man. He felt…cold, his flesh where it touched her like icy stone. She struggled, trying to wrench her arm away, but she was certain she would wrench it from its socket before she would break the man's hold on her. She looked up and met his eyes, strange eyes, and pitch-black.

More shots, cries and taunting came from the street.

Alex didn't even fight or scream as Milo dragged her out. *Where would be the sense in it?* she thought.

There were eight men in all, she saw once she was outside: three who had remained out on the street with the horses and were the source of the most recent ruckus, the two who had Jewell and Tess, and the three, including Milo, who had accosted her.

"Round 'em up!" chortled one of the men with the horses.

Jewell let out a terrified cry as she was sent flying out the door and into the arms of another man.

Where the hell was the sheriff?

Where were any *of the men?*

"Get them across the street, into the saloon. We've got some more business in town before we leave with our spoils," Milo said to the others.

They were herded into the saloon, where several of the song-and-dance girls were huddled together by the piano.

The only man in the room was Jigs, the piano player.

Milo let go of Alex at last, so he could go behind the bar and open the cash register. Several of his men joined him, breaking open bottles of alcohol and shouting raucously.

Suddenly they heard the sound of clicking spurs.

Someone was coming at last. Alex let herself breathe an almost silent sigh of relief.

The slatted saloon doors were thrown open, crashing back against the walls loudly enough to arrest the attention even of the men behind the bar.

For a moment he was framed there in silhouette, a tall man in a wide-brimmed hat, wearing a railroad duster and cowboy boots, a rifle carried easily at his side.

He hadn't come alone. Behind him stood another man, a shade shorter but otherwise a twin of the dark silhouette in appearance.

The first man stepped closer and nudged his hat up, revealing eyes that seemed to glow with a golden light. He looked around the room and sized up the situation.

His gaze lit upon Milo, who still had his hand in the till. He seemed to be amazed that anyone had had the nerve to enter the saloon. Alex saw his hand inching toward the gun holstered at his waist.

The newcomer with the golden eyes fixed his stare on Milo.

"I wouldn't do that," he said. "I really wouldn't do that."

Milo ignored him.

And suddenly, gunfire blazed.

In seconds the air filled with a fog of gunpowder so thick that it obscured the action. Finally the roar of bullets died, replaced by coughing, followed by…a hard thud.

The smoke began to clear, and Alex saw the man with the shaggy blond hair lying on the floor, dead, blood pooling around his head. The others—outlaws and hostages alike—slowly began to emerge from hiding places behind tables, chairs, the bar and the piano. The sight was surreal, the settling gun smoke wrapping everything in an air of otherworldliness.

Milo was still standing.

And so was the newcomer with the eerie golden eyes.

The two men stared at each other.

Neither one had moved, Alex realized. In the hail of bullets, neither one had moved.

And neither one had been touched.

Milo smiled slowly. "Well, well, what do we have here?"

"That's not really the question, is it?" the newcomer asked quietly. "The real question is, what are you doing here? And the answer is 'running'—because that's the only way you'll leave here alive."

Milo guffawed, but to Alex's surprise, there was something missing now. The absolute confidence the man had emitted before was gone. Even so, he stood dead still—apparently not in the least disturbed by the death of his friend—and continued to stare at the newcomer speculatively.

"I can take you down," Milo assured the man.

"Maybe, maybe not. You just don't know for certain, do you?"

"I can have my men slit the throats of a half-dozen women before you can move…friend," Milo countered smoothly.

"Can you?" the newcomer asked.

Alex never actually saw him move. There was simply a blur in the air, and then the golden-eyed man was behind Milo, holding a glittering bowie knife at the outlaw's throat. "Don't doubt me, friend. I know just how deep I have to slide this blade. Now, tell your men to release the women and step outside."

"Get that knife away from my neck first," Milo said.

"No. When your men are on their way to the door, then I let you go. And then you get the hell out of this town."

"Even with your handy-dandy sidekick over there," Milo said, indicating the older man who had entered behind the newcomer, "you're outnumbered."

"Doesn't matter. If you don't let those women go and get the hell out of here, I'll show you what two men can do."

"The girls will die."

"So will you."

Milo's eyes gleamed with a fury that seemed to glow red, but he was clearly aware of the blade at his throat. He growled a command.

His gang began releasing the women and heading for the door. "Not outside!" Milo bellowed. "Not until I'm with you."

If not for the deadliness of the situation, it might have been amusing to see the way they collided with one another in an effort to stop and turn around. Finally the tall newcomer removed the blade from Milo's throat and pushed him toward his comrades. "Get out now, and leave this town be," he said quietly.

At the door, Milo turned back. "No one tells me what to do."

"No one can stop a man bent on sheer stupidity," the newcomer returned. "But I'm warning you—stay the hell away from here—or else."

"I don't take kindly to threats, friend," Milo said.

But apparently he'd wanted only to get in the last word, because he turned and left, his gang of outlaws following quickly.

For a moment there was dead silence in the saloon. It was as if everyone were waiting, listening for hoofbeats, the assurance that the outlaws were really gone.

When the hoofbeats came, then died away, cacophony followed.

Girls left their hiding places, racing toward the stranger.

"Oh, my God, you saved our lives!" one cried. Alex thought she looked new to life as a scarlet woman. Her hair was naturally red, and she had an innocence about her.

"The Good Lord alone knows what might have happened," another crooned—this one older, harder, a tall brunette, attractive, but with calculating eyes. She didn't look mean, just worn down by life. Alex thought she'd met her a few years back. Sherry Lyn, her name was. Victory was a small town. "Decent" women didn't usually mix with saloon girls, but there was just no way out of the fact that you were going to meet at the general store.

"You can have anything in this place that you want, young man," said a third woman. Maybe she was the madam, Alex thought. She was of medium height, buxom and a bit stout. Her hair was hennaed, and she had the weary look that came from too many years of scraping along in life.

Ignoring the offer, the golden-eyed man said, "Ladies, listen to me. You've got to stay close for the time being. Lock your doors at night, put up a sign saying you're closed to the public, and don't go letting any strangers in."

His words were greeted by silence.

His older friend cleared his throat and nudged him, grinning.

"This is a…funhouse, Cody."

The brunette was the first to speak. She cleared her throat. "Honey, I don't know how to put this delicately, but…if we don't invite people in, this place ain't going to be in business long."

"I see," Cody said gravely. "Well, you're still going to have to be very careful. When you're not…entertaining, you need to lock your doors. And don't fall prey to anyone seeking entrance when they shouldn't be."

"And when would that be, sugar?" the buxom woman asked. "And by the way, I'm Dolly. I keep things running around here."

"Dolly," Cody said, "you have to keep an eye out for things that don't seem...quite normal, for men like that bunch that were in here just now. You have to fight them. All the men—and women—in this town need to learn to fight them." He paused, looking at the bright-eyed female faces staring at him as if he were a god who had come to earth. He shook his head, as if realizing that he wasn't being understood. "I'm Cody Fox, and this is my friend Brendan Vincent. We'll be sticking around for a while. We're going to try to find out what's going on here."

The sound of furniture being shoved across the floor startled everyone, and all eyes in the room were suddenly focused on the piano. It was just Jigs, who had risen from his hiding place at last.

Alex noted that Cody Fox already had a hand on his gun belt.

"You two some kind of lawmen?" Jigs asked. He epitomized the popular image of the perfect piano player with his fine suit, bow tie and misty-gray top hat that nicely complemented his ebony flesh. Tall and lean, he lent just the right touch of class to a place frequented by cardsharps, fast women, ranchers, cowboys and transients.

"Lawmen? No. Just concerned citizens," Cody replied.

Brendan Vincent said, "I had kin who lived out in Brigsby. There's not hide nor hair of them to be seen."

"Well," Dolly said dryly, making no mention of the state of things in Brigsby, "you're mighty welcome here. As you might have noticed, we've yet to see the sheriff or his deputy."

Cody was an extremely attractive man, Alex thought. He had a handsome face, if somewhat gaunt. His eyes were a golden hazel, and when he dusted his hat on his knee, she saw that he had rich wheat-colored hair. Tall and rugged, like many another cowboy, still he had something that was entirely unique. Alex found herself curious about him, and it was no wonder the working women in the saloon seemed about to have the vapors.

"Ma'am, to be quite honest, I think we're looking for a rooming house of some kind, a place where we can have a bit of peace and quiet, a place to think some of this out," Cody said politely.

"Then you want to be staying at Alex's place," Jigs said.

Alex hadn't realized that Jigs had even seen her, but now he stared at her, grinning. "Welcome home, missy," he said softly.

Everyone in the place was staring at her now, and she didn't like the sudden attention. She felt her cheeks grow warm and flushed, though she didn't know why. It must be the stranger, she told herself. Cody Fox.

He looked at her for a long moment. A very long moment. Then a hint of a smile touched his features and he tilted his hat in greeting. "How do you do, miss?"

She had the feeling she looked like a worn-out school marm. Most of the women in the saloon were showing a great deal of flesh and wearing vivid colors.

She was basically wearing travel dust.

"Fine, thank you—considering the circumstances. How do you do?" she replied courteously, feeling inexplicably awkward.

"You own a boardinghouse?" he asked.

"Yes," she said, unable to make further conversation, but then again, it had been a yes-or-no question.

"And might you have a couple of vacancies?" he asked politely.

She started to turn to Jewell to check, then remembered with sudden clarity and horror that Bert was lying unconscious—or worse—back at the boardinghouse. "Oh!" she gasped, and without replying, she raced out the door and across the street to the house. She rushed in, dropping to her knees by Bert's prone body.

She patted his cheeks and called his name, and after a moment he let out a groan and opened his eyes, staring up at her blankly.

"Bert?" she said anxiously.

He blinked, then started to speak, but his words froze in his throat, and he grabbed her arm in a surprisingly strong grasp. She turned to see that Cody Fox and Brendan Vincent had followed her.

"It's all right. They stopped the outlaws," Alex said soothingly.

"Stopped them?" Bert said, staring at the other men skeptically.

"They killed one of them and convinced the others to ride away," Alex said.

"The sheriff?" Bert asked.

"Nowhere to be seen," Alex admitted.

Cody hunkered down by Bert's side. "Looks like you took a hell of a wallop," he said, his eyes sympathetic. "Do you think you have any broken bones?"

Bert looked at him, still suspicious, but said, "I think I can get up."

Cody offered him an arm. Bert got to his feet slowly,

wincing. He continued to study Cody, but he nodded in thanks as he said, "I'm all right."

"Still, you might want to sit for a spell," Cody suggested.

"The library," Alex suggested, leading them toward the comfortable overstuffed sofa in her father's—no, *her*—library.

She got Bert settled, then backed straight into Beulah, who had come in like a whirlwind, followed closely by Jewell and Tess, and Brendan Vincent.

"Oh, Bert, look at you!" Beulah said, taking his hand, along with a seat next to him.

"I'll get him a whiskey," Jewell decided.

"Maybe tea would be better," Tess suggested.

"Maybe we should put the whiskey in a cup of tea," Jewell countered.

"I'm sure that will be fine," Beulah said.

Jewell and Tess turned to leave the room, but not before sighing softly and looking with rapt eyes at Cody Fox. Alex looked at Bert, rolled her eyes and winked, then grew sober again. "Are you sure you're all right?"

"Fine, just embarrassed that I couldn't protect my own household," Bert said. He looked past her to stare at Cody and Brendan. "How the hell did you get that man and his human refuse out of town?" he asked.

"Just threatened him the way he threatens everyone else. Milo wasn't about to lose his own life, and he knew I would take it," Cody said, then cleared his throat. "Brendan and I are looking for accommodations, if they're available?"

"I just got back to town this afternoon, so to tell you the truth, I don't know," Alex said, and looked at Beulah, still at Bert's side. "Do we have any vacancies?"

Beulah let out a very unladylike snort, staring at her as if she had gone daft. "Do we have any vacancies? Child— we have nothing *but* vacancies. No one is coming out this way to stay anymore. No bankers, no railroad men. No new whores desperate to try out the place."

Alex smoothed her hand down her skirt. "Well then, gentlemen, you're certainly welcome to stay."

"It will be right nice to have you here," Beulah added with considerably more enthusiasm. "Breakfast is from seven to eight, and supper is served precisely at seven. If you're here, you eat. If you're not here, we assume you've made other arrangements. I'll just see to your rooms. If you'll excuse me?" She rose and started for the door, then suddenly stopped, a look of horror on her face.

"Levy!" she said. "Oh, dear, where is Levy? I haven't seen him since all this began."

Alex closed her eyes and groaned, hating herself. She'd forgotten the stable hand, as well.

"I'll check the basement," Bert said, rising carefully.

"I'll run upstairs," Beulah said.

"I'll take the stable," Alex said.

As soon as Beulah and Bert were out of the room, Cody Fox caught Alex's arm. Like Milo, he had a grip of steel, though he wasn't using it to hurt her. Still, she stared at him in indignation at being stopped so summarily.

"We're missing a member of the household. Please let go of me so I can go look for him."

"What does he look like? We can help," he told her.

"He's our stable hand, medium height, curly brown hair, thin face, dark brown eyes," Alex said, pulling her arm free.

"I'll head out to the street, see if the outlaws shot anyone we haven't discovered yet," Brendan Vincent said.

"I'll go out back to the stable with you," Cody said. "I think they're all long gone, but just in case…"

Alex ignored him and raced down the hall to the back door. The town had stables and a livery, but they had their own small stable out back, along with a smokehouse.

As she burst outside, the laying chickens began to squawk.

"Levy!" she cried, sprinting past the flustered birds.

Cody Fox ran by her toward the stables.

The outer doors were open and he headed inside without pausing. Alex followed quickly, still calling for the stable hand.

The stalls were to the left; Beau was in the first— kicking at the wall, which was uncharacteristic for the normally phlegmatic draft horse mix that pulled the work wagon. Cheyenne, Alex's palomino, neighed excitedly, pacing the small confines of his stall, and even Harvey, Bert's usually placid gelding, was putting up a ruckus.

"Levy?" Alex cried again.

She felt hay particles falling on her head and looked up to the loft.

And there was Levy. She could just see his face as he peeked down at them.

"Oh, thank God," she breathed, and started for the ladder. Once again Cody Fox grabbed her arm. "Wait."

"Wait? Why?" she demanded, but he was already heading swiftly up to the loft.

Alex followed. "Levy, are you all right?"

When she reached the loft, Cody Fox was already standing over Levy, offering him a hand to help him to his feet.

"Were you attacked?" Cody demanded. "Did those men hurt you…in any way?" he persisted intently.

"No, no, no," Levy said, rising and shaking his head emphatically. He looked at Alex with shame. "I knew they were here. I should have…I should have come out, but I came up here, up in the hay, and I just hid. The horses were going crazy. I…well, we've all heard about what happened over to Brigsby." He took Alex's hand. "Miss Alex, I am so sorry. I don't know what I was thinking."

"You were behaving sensibly and nothing more," she said firmly. "There was nothing you could have done except maybe get yourself killed. I'm just grateful that you're alive and well."

Despite her words, Levy hung his head. She reached out, lifting his chin. Levy was a real asset. He was strong, despite his slim physique, and intelligent; he loved books. The horses responded to his gentle ways, and when he was done with his work, he was a charming conversationalist. As a child, he'd come from Eastern Europe with his parents, who had been running from persecution, and now he was an integral part of the mix of ethnicities that made up Victory.

"I was a coward," he said softly.

"No," Cody said firmly, "you behaved rationally. You would have been able to go for help if Milo and his men had gone on a killing spree. One more body wouldn't have done anyone any good."

Alex found herself grateful for his support, and Levy looked a little less as if he wanted to jump out of the loft.

"Be that as it may, Alexandra, I won't be letting you down again," Levy said grimly.

"Well, thank God we're all fine and the danger is gone," Alex said, smiling.

Neither man offered a smile in return.

"Shall we get down from the hayloft?" she suggested brightly, determined not to dwell on what might have been.

Beulah was waiting outside the back door when they headed up to the house.

She swatted Levy with a dishrag. "You had us scared half to death, Levy!" she said, but then she hugged him. Finally she drew away and looked into his eyes. Something in her expression told Alexandra that the cook was satisfied with what she saw there. "All's well tonight," Beulah said softly.

They had barely entered the house when Brendan Vincent burst through the front door. "You better come, Cody," he said.

"What's happened?" Alex asked.

"Bit of a problem down the road, that's all," Brendan said.

He looked like such a civilized man, she thought, with gentle eyes, yet he was riding with Cody Fox, and Fox handled weapons like a man accustomed to battle. Not that he seemed particularly violent. He just moved with lightning speed and had a strength that was like steel.

"What problem?" she asked.

"There's a fellow...well, the outlaws got him," Brendan said.

"We've got to see who it is," Alex said. "Doc Williamson must be around somewhere," she added, and started for the door.

Brendan looked at Cody and blocked her way.

"There's no reason for you to be seeing this, miss," he said.

"Don't be ridiculous. I might be able to help. I've seen my share of war injuries. I'm not in the least delicate."

Behind her, Cody Fox cleared his throat. "I'm a medical doctor with a Harvard degree. If he needs help, I'll be there to do what I can."

Alex wasn't about to be stopped. "I'm going with you," she said stubbornly.

She saw Brendan look at Cody, waiting for his approval before moving. She wondered what was so powerful about the younger man that Brendan deferred so readily to his authority.

"Whatever you wish," Cody said impatiently. "The situation is undoubtedly dire, so we need to hurry."

With Brendan in the lead, they headed along the wood-plank sidewalk that had been built beside the main street to let people avoid the mud and muck of the broad dirt road. When they reached the end of the walk, they headed out into the street and across to the building that housed the combination dentist and barber shop.

A crowd had gathered there, but no one had approached the man lying facedown on the ground.

"Coming through," Brendan announced.

The crowd backed away, white-faced and tight-lipped.

"Why isn't someone helping him?" Alex asked, looking around the crowd. She saw people she recognized, who quickly lowered their eyes.

Cody hunkered down by the man, turning him over. Alex felt a quickening in her heart, followed by relief when she realized she didn't know the man. He was about forty, and he wasn't going to need a doctor. He had a huge bloodstain on his shirt, and his eyes were open and unseeing.

"Is he from around here?" Cody asked, looking around.

"I don't know him," Alex said.

A man stepped forward. One she did know. Jim Green, the local mortician and photographer.

"He's not one of ours," Jim said. He was a kindly old fellow with silvery hair and matching old-fashioned muttonchops. "He must have come in with the outlaws."

"Who shot him?" Cody asked.

Another man cleared his throat. Ace Henley, who ran the livery. "I was up in my loft, and I got in a few shots when they were whooping and hollering and blowing holes in the sky."

Cody studied him and nodded. "That's good. That's what we're going to need—a plan to get everyone into a position from which to fight, for next time they come in like they did."

"What'll we do with him?" Brendan asked, nodding toward the corpse.

Strange question, Alex thought. He was a dead man. Bury him. Even an outlaw had to be buried. What the hell else were they going to do with him?

"The usual," Cody said, rising, dusting his hands on his jeans.

"It's getting dark," Brendan commented.

"So it is. I'll get him over to the mortuary. Fellows, you got a place we can bury him?" Cody asked, looking from person to person in the crowd. "Might as well get him in the ground tonight."

"There's no preacher tonight," Jim said. "Though I don't rightly know if a preacher would say the words over…such a…one."

The two men exchanged a meaningful look, as if acknowledging a shared but unspoken truth. Alex wondered uneasily what was going on and whether it had anything to do with the strange state of affairs she'd found at the boardinghouse when she arrived that afternoon. Garlands of garlic decorating the windows and wardrobes, and an abundance of crosses hung in every room. Just what was going on here?

"He was a man, a man who had a soul at some time," Cody said. "We can say some words, and when a preacher comes, he can say those words all over again. Now, let's get him out of the street before night comes on."

"Right," Jim said, and cleared his throat. "It's all over town how you two saved the place, mister. We're right grateful." He doffed his broad-brimmed hat in Cody's direction and nodded to Brendan. "I'm Jim Green, mortician and photographer, at your service. We're mighty glad to have you."

"Thank you," Cody told him. "Anyone seen the sheriff yet?"

"Him and the deputy went off just about an hour or so ago—there was talk of some cattle rustling out at Calico Jack's. That would be John Snow's trading post," Ace clarified.

John Snow-on-Leaf, now known simply as John Snow, was part white, part Mexican, part Apache and all entrepreneur, Alex thought. He and his current wife and twenty of his children—a brood whose color went from sable to snow—managed the trading post where the tribes and white folk alike came and went.

Cody nodded, glancing at Brendan Vincent. "All right, anybody sees the sheriff, tell him I'd like to meet him come the morning. Now, let's deal with the dead."

He reached down and grabbed the dead man under his armpits as Brendan went for the man's ankles.

"Lead on, Mr. Green," Brendan said.

"Right this way," Jim said.

The crowd broke apart and began to disperse, everyone looking uneasily at the sky, as if they were desperate to be off the streets before dark.

Alex stood there, watching the townspeople and frowning.

Strange—no, bizarre—the way people were behaving.

As if he sensed she was still standing there, Cody paused and turned back. "Go home, Miss Gordon. Please."

Then he started walking away again, the weight of the dead man suspended between him and Brendan Vincent. Either one of them might have thrown the body over a shoulder and carried it easily.

They didn't seem to want to touch the blood.

Spooked by the intensity of his insistence that she go home, but too stubborn to just run away without knowing what was going on, she decided to pretend to obey his directive. She walked away and stepped up on the sidewalk, then paused and looked around.

No one was left on the street. It was as if the town were deserted. When she saw Fox and Vincent follow Green into his place of business, she stepped back off the sidewalk and walked swiftly and as silently as she could in their wake.

The door to Jim Green's photography studio and mortuary was closed by the time she got there, but the curtains were still open at the windows, and kerosene lamps were lit within.

The front room held the photography studio; the mortuary was in the rear. Someone had neglected to shut the door between the two, so she stood to one side of the big front window and peered in.

The men had carried the body through to the back and placed it on a long oak slab—a rudimentary embalming table. Green's instruments were laid out on a small cart nearby. Since the war, she knew, the art of embalming was in demand.

There were a lot of dead boys making the long journey home.

She continued to stare through the window, carefully trying to shield herself from the men within.

They were examining the body and talking, but she could only catch snatches of the conversation.

"I don't think so. I really don't think so," she heard Cody say.

"We have to think about safety," Jim said.

"He's right, Cody—better safe than sorry," Vincent added.

Cody studied the corpse, turning it, touching the throat and studying it, as if he might find a pulse.

Doctor? Educated at Harvard? A farm boy could see there was a massive shotgun hole in the man's chest.

"Better safe than sorry," Cody agreed.

Jim Green handed him a long knife with an edge so sharp it glittered like diamonds in the lamplight.

Cody took the knife.

She nearly gasped aloud as she saw him position himself—then sever the corpse's jugular.

She clamped a hand over her mouth and leaned against the wall, stunned. Then she turned back to the window again, thinking that her eyes must have deceived her.

Now only Jim Green was standing over the corpse. Or rather, the pieces of the corpse.

There wasn't all that much blood, but then, the man had

already bled out all over the street; a shotgun blast could do that to a fellow.

But now… Now the dead man's head had been severed cleanly from his body. The face was turned toward her, the eyes staring out at her.

Caught in the glow of the lamplight, they seemed to be alive.

They seemed to be staring straight into her soul.

CHAPTER THREE

ALEX HURRIED BACK to the boardinghouse, deep in thought, the image of the dead man's eyes burned into her brain. She opened the front door and stepped inside, thinking that the world had gone mad.

Of course, in a way the world had gone mad the day the first shot of the war had been fired. But this was something worse. Worse? What could be worse than a war that was exterminating half the young men of a divided country?

Losing all sanity and all souls.

The thought came to her unbidden, and she shook it off. But what was happening here *was* strange. People were behaving *differently*.

Cody and Jim had literally severed the dead man's head.

"There you are, Alex!" Beulah chastised her as she came through from the kitchen, clasping a hand to her heart. "Don't you go round worrying me so now, young lady, do you hear?"

Alex stared at her. "Beulah, I was right down the street."

"Maybe so, but you need to be inside now. It's dark, and the moon…well, the moon is out."

Alex smiled, giving her a hug and wondering what the moon had to do with anything. "I'm fine. The bad guys got sent away with their tails between their legs. Tonight we're all safe."

Beulah drew back, shaking her head sadly. "Honey child, no time is safe anymore. But darkness? It's not safe at all."

Alex stared at the older woman.

"Beulah, what's going on here?" she asked.

"Evil," Beulah said sagely.

"Evil?"

"Bad things, very bad things. It's like the devil himself is trying to take hold here. Oh, honey, I don't know everything. But it's like an evil disease. So we just stay inside. Oh, Lordy! Brigsby gone. And Hollow Tree, too, I hear tell…and now Victory. Maybe we thought we'd be spared. Maybe we felt we couldn't do a thing about it 'cept run, and for too many folks, this is all we have and there ain't nowhere to run *to*."

"Beulah, I don't understand you," Alex said impatiently.

"I don't rightly understand it myself," Beulah said, then smiled suddenly, her eyes lighting up. "But tonight…well, that was a miracle, it was, those two fellows turning up when they did. And now they'll be staying here. What a fine thing that is."

Beulah made the sign of the cross over her ample chest as she spoke.

Alex nodded. That much was true. She would definitely feel safer with the men who had successfully defied the outlaws staying in her boardinghouse.

Suddenly her smile of agreement froze on her face.

She had just watched Cody Fox decapitate a dead man.

With the blessing—no, at the insistence of—of Jim Green.

She realized she was exhausted. No doubt the world would look normal again after a good night's rest.

"I think I have to go to sleep," she told Beulah.

"You need to have something to eat, child," Beulah said.

Alex laughed. "Beulah, you're a sweetheart, but I'm too tired to eat. I'm going to go up to bed now, and I'll worry about what's going on in the morning."

"It's the devil," Beulah said, nodding sagely.

Alex took Beulah's hands. "I saw the devil's work when anger and hostility entered the hearts of men and sent them to war." Her eyes grew sad. "I guarantee you, God has no part in the carnage of war. Whatever this is, we can fight it, and we will."

"Maybe. Now that they've come," Beulah agreed, then added, "But maybe not. This evening they came in a roar of gunfire. But sometimes they come in stealth and quiet, slipping into our lives and our souls—like the devil. Please, Alex, you heard what Cody Fox said to them fancy girls. It's time to be smart and careful."

Alex gave Beulah a hug. "I'll be careful, I swear," she promised, and headed for the stairs. Just dragging herself up the steps suddenly seemed like a tremendous effort.

She made it to her room. Her father's room. No, her room now, as he would have wanted it to be.

One of the girls had laid out her nightdress, and left her a basin of water on the washstand. By rote, she carefully removed and hung her clothing, washed up and slipped on the nightgown. She dipped her hands into the water again to refresh her face, and caught her reflection in the mirror. In the white gown and the lamplight, she appeared gaunt and pale. As if she were some kind of wraith. Despite herself, she found herself thinking of the women in the saloon. Dolly, who was so…assured. That new girl, oddly pretty and fresh. She paled in comparison. She winced. How odd! She wasn't accustomed to feeling insecure.

She turned again to her reflection and realized she was comparing herself to others because…

Because of Cody Fox.

A flood of red heightened her cheeks as she continued staring into the mirror.

She took her towel and patted her face dry, and turned quickly away from the mirror, feeling ridiculous. The world had gone crazy—and she was worried about being noticed by a man. She definitely needed sleep. Ever since Grant's death, she hadn't even thought about men except when she'd volunteered at the hospital, where they'd simply been sad and scared human beings longing to die with the warmth and comfort of a woman's hand clutching their own.

Maybe that was it. It had simply been so long since she had buried her fiancé, so long since she had even thought about appearances, attraction…and then a man like Cody Fox came along and suddenly she was seeing herself as a woman again.

Alex let out a sigh of irritation, blew out the lamp and crawled into bed.

Darkness, exhaustion. They would surely allow her to rest.

But she found that her eyes were drawn to the double French doors that led from the master suite to the balcony. The moon wasn't full, but still there was a flood of light falling to earth from the heavens, a yellow glow permeating the world beyond her windows, making its way through the drapes.

Bathed in that glow, shadows moved. They looked like the wings of birds, giant birds dancing in the air beyond the window. She almost thought she could hear the rush of wings, but she knew it was only the sound of the wind as it rushed over the plain.

She forced herself to close her eyes, and at last she slept.

THEY WERE IN THE ACT of burying the decapitated man when the sheriff and his deputy made it back into town at last.

The sheriff, Cole Granger, was a tall, hard-muscled man with sharp blue eyes and hair so dark it had a blue sheen in the moonlight. His deputy, Dave Hinton, was smaller, but he had a solid handshake and steady eyes.

Jim Green explained what had happened when Milo and his band of outlaws had come to town.

"These fellows saved us, and that's a fact," he said, then cleared his throat, kicking at the freshly dug mound of earth below his feet. "Honest, Cole, we weren't being cowards—we just didn't know what to do, you know? Ace Henley got this fellow, though. We don't have a name for him, don't know nothing about him. But we've taken care of him—and we've buried him deep."

"Damn it, damn it all straight to hell!" Granger said, sounding disgusted with himself. "I shouldn't have ridden out, and I sure as hell shouldn't have taken Dave with me." He looked Cody and Brendan in the eyes. "Thank you. I don't know how the hell you did it, but thank you. There'd been trouble out at John Snow's trading post—and I had to get out there, see what was going on. But I didn't count on getting back so late."

"We hit some trouble on the return," Dave said.

"Trouble? What happened?" Cody asked.

"Darnedest thing," Cole said, shaking his head. "We were coming through a patch of brush and trees about five miles from here when the horses just went crazy. Go figure. We've both been riding since before we could walk, and first we lose Dave's horse, and he's running around like a headless chicken till I can catch him and start to get him settled. Next thing you know, my Titan is rearing and snorting, and starting Dave's horse going again. There was something out there, but damned if I know what. Wolves, coyotes, something. All I know is, I've never seen horses acting up so badly." Cole stopped speaking and looked Cody in the eye again. "Everyone is saying the devil is loose in these parts. I don't know what the devil is, but there's sure as hell something going on. Something that lets Milo and his crew annihilate whole towns. I figured they'd be coming for us sooner or later. It's just sooner than I expected." He looked from Cody to Brendan, and back to Cody. "How the hell did you stop him?"

"I know Milo's type," Cody said. "I know how to make him believe that he'll lose his own life if he doesn't listen to me. I know this kind of enemy."

"We finished decapitating the dead man," Jim Green put in nervously.

Cole set a hand on Jim Green's shoulder. "If you feel it was necessary, Jim, then that's fine."

"Absolutely right," Dave agreed, shaking his head strenuously. Cody and Brendan exchanged a look. It was obvious that Dave thought the very devil was walking the streets.

Cole Granger was a harder man altogether, and his attitude

said he'd seen his share of vicious men. He clearly still believed that he was dealing with something real and tangible.

"With everything going on out here," Cody said, "haven't you gotten any help from the army or the U.S. Marshals?"

Cole Granger shook his head. "If we'd ever suspected we could all be wiped out this way, we might have gotten together and mustered up a militia. As to government help…Texas is part of the Confederacy, and the Confederacy has lost too many men to have any left to send out here. Our only help might come from Chief Tall Feather and the Apaches, and maybe some of his Comanche friends. At least we don't have problems with the Indians out here. They live their lives, we live ours, and we trade. They say an evil spirit has come to earth and possessed the souls of men. I don't know what it is, only that I'm not running and I *will* see these killers stopped."

"How'd you know about the trouble out here?" Dave asked suddenly.

"I have family out here—or I did," Brendan said, correcting himself. "And Cody's folks lived in these parts. His father died out here."

Cody shrugged.

"My mother went home—back to New Orleans— before I was born. But the important thing is that we're here to help you fight. Tomorrow, as a matter of fact, if it sits well with you, Sheriff, I'm going to go out and meet that Indian chief. You say his name is Tall Feather?"

"That's right. He's a good man, even though the Apache are a warrior clan. Tall Feather sees the way the world is going. He says the Spirit Fathers have told him that the white man will not go away, that he will come in greater numbers. If you can't fight them, in his opinion, you should study them and figure out how to use them. Go ahead and talk to him—he'll tell you what's been going on."

"What did you find out at the trading post?" Cody asked Cole, changing the subject.

Cole shook his head. "Two of John Snow's children have gone missing, both of them beautiful young girls. But I couldn't find a trail, not a drop of blood, not a broken branch. It's as if the girls wandered into another dimension."

"I'll try to get out that way, too," Cody said. "So where do Milo and his band hole up during the daylight hours?"

"No one knows," Dave said.

"Brigsby, I'm thinking," Cole said. "But I haven't had a chance to get back out there to check. We had a gunslinger go through here a few weeks back, and he thought he was tougher than solid stone. He went out to Brigsby. We found what was left of his body on the ground out by where the horses went crazy on Dave and me."

"We need to get out there as soon as we can manage it," Cody said. "I'd like to be sure what we're up against. Men like Milo…they can deceive, build traps. We need to find out everything we can if we're going to fight them. Anyway, Sheriff, what you and your deputy here need to be doing is warning your townsfolk not to open their doors to strangers—and especially not even to be on the streets at night. I tried to tell the girls at the saloon that it was important to be…cautious, but that may have been a lost cause. Thing is—" Cody broke off, hesitating. The thing was, Cole Granger was going to have to accept some of the truth of the matter—or else the sheriff would be running him out of town before he could count to three.

"Inviting folks in just leads to danger," Cody finished lamely. "This place needs to be locked up tight at night. We'll talk more in the morning, if that's all right with you, Sheriff. I think we're all worn to the bone right now."

"Good night, then," Cole said, and Cody and Brendan started out of the graveyard. "Hey," Cole said, calling them back. "Where are you staying?"

"Miss Alex is back in town. They're over at the boardinghouse," Dave said.

"Right. Alex is home," Cole said thoughtfully. "Good night, then. And thank you for your help this evening. I offer you a true welcome to Victory."

Cody waved a hand in acknowledgment, wondering at the sheriff's tone when he'd mentioned Alex's name. Was something going on there? Long-ago lovers? She had gone back East to marry, so the story went. But now that she was back in town, maybe things would be rekindled out here. Why not? The sheriff seemed like a good man, young, good-looking. And Alexandra Gordon was...beautiful. More than that. She was a fighter. There was a life inside her that was like a shimmering flame, beckoning everyone to her.

Even him.

He tamped down the thought. He'd decided long ago that his life was meant to be a solitary one.

"You think the boardinghouse is safe?" Brendan asked as they walked together along the street.

Cody shook his head. "It's a boardinghouse. Its business is opening its door to strangers."

"Someone in there knows something, though. There are

crosses all over the place, garlic festooned around the window."

"Doesn't matter. Milo has already been in there," Cody said.

"Maybe we need more crosses," Brendan suggested.

"What we need is to kill Milo," Cody said, and kept walking.

Brendan looked after him. "Right. And then pierce his heart, chop off his head and burn the body to ash."

AS THE TWO OF THEM walked back to the boardinghouse, Cody thought back to how he and Brendan had met. It had started with the murderer Aldridge had needed his help in stopping. He could still remember bending over the first two bodies....

The first of the two latest victims was lying on his back, a look of abject terror on his face. His wife was in worse condition. Her tormentor must have played with her first, because her eyes were closed, as if she had clenched them hard against the sight of her impending death.

Both bodies bore stab marks about the chest and abdomen, but neither was lying in the expected pool of blood, and both were curiously white.

"It beats everything I've seen," Aldridge said quietly, watching as Cody moved the woman's hair aside to reveal the marks he'd been sure he would find. Cody hesitated, wondering just how much of the truth Aldridge might be able to accept.

The evidence was actually encouraging, at least as far as putting an end to the killing spree went. He was pretty sure he was looking at a rogue killer, someone who was trying to blend in with the population of the city. The stab marks had been made to fool whoever found the bodies, and it was only luck—good for Aldridge, maybe not so good for Cody himself—that someone had connected these killings to the case Cody had put an end to.

Cody looked up at Aldridge. "I'll go after your killer, sir, but it's unlikely I'll be able to bring him in for trial. This…person will fight to the death."

Aldridge stared at him. "You do what you have to do. I need you to catch this man."

"I can't be held to any curfew."

"You'll have free rein," Aldridge promised.

That night, Cody prowled the streets.

He tried the bars first, but found nothing unusual. Then, as he walked along Dauphine Street, he noticed a gate standing ajar. Curious, he pushed the gate open and stepped into a dark courtyard.

He scanned the courtyard quickly, then winced, seeing what looked like a pile of clothing off to one side. He hurried over and found the body of a young woman, still warm to the touch, but dead.

Quite, quite dead.

Still warm, he thought. Which meant the killer might still be near.

He heard piano music and a songstress at work coming from one of the nearby restaurants, so he walked over to see what he might find.

He stood by the bar and sipped bourbon as he looked around the room. Several soldiers were at a table close to the piano, where they watched a dark-haired and quite beautiful woman as she played and sang, all the while flirting openly with them.

As he watched, the songstress rose, whispered in the ear

of one of the men, then left him sitting and staring hungrily after her as she walked toward the back and the alley Cody knew ran behind the building.

As subtly as he could, he followed.

He had to stop the death toll. Now.

She was waiting, leaning against the wall, a wicked smile upon her face as she waited with supreme anticipation. He stared at her for a moment, realizing with a sick feeling that she wasn't the intended victim at all.

"Excuse me?" she said, surprised when she saw Cody, and not the young man with whom she'd been flirting.

"Good evening," he said.

She smiled and shivered, though it was far from cold. "Lovely night, actually. I'm Vivien La Rue. How do you do?"

She stretched out a hand, and when he took it, she allowed her fingers to wander over his flesh.

"You shouldn't be out here," he said, playing along. "There's a killer loose in the city."

He glanced toward the door. The young soldier had yet to emerge, but it might not be much longer until he showed. This would have to happen quickly.

"Are you interested in other sorts of…entertainment?" he asked softly.

She laughed and sized him up. "What might you have in mind? And what are you offering?"

She moved closer and slid her arms around his neck, gazing up into his eyes. Something she saw there seemed to startle her, and she started to pull away.

He didn't let her. She let out a hissing sound and threw back her head, lips receding, teeth extending. She started to aim for his throat.

But he was ready. And he was extremely strong. He slit her throat, instantly severing the jugular. Trying to avoid the spilling blood, he worked relentlessly, sawing, finally dropping both the body and the head to the ground as he made the final cut. In moments, nothing was left but a pile of ash.

Grateful that the soldier had not yet made an appearance, he hurried out of the alley and straight to Aldridge's office, where the lieutenant had promised to wait for word.

Cody informed him that the killer had been found and, as he'd predicted, been killed.

"Where's the body?"

"I'm afraid you won't find it." Suddenly, Cody realized Aldridge was looking at someone who was seated behind him, and he cursed himself. He should have sensed the other presence.

He turned quickly to see a lean, dignified man of middle age. Cody recognized him as Brendan Vincent, a one-time brigadier general in the Union army, discharged on medical grounds, who had made his reputation in the Mexican War and was now honored by both sides in the current conflict.

Vincent stood as Aldridge made the introductions and smiled grimly as he shook Cody's hand. "I'm pleased to meet you, young man. I need you desperately."

"Oh?"

"We've been having some trouble out West. In Texas."

Startled, Cody looked at Aldridge.

Aldridge nodded grimly. "Yes, Texas, still a Southern state. But murder is murder, and Brendan is my cousin. He's made Texas his home since his discharge, and…well, I'll let him explain for himself."

"We've had a few…incidents recently. Whole towns disappearing, and I think we're looking at the same kind of killer my cousin tells me you've now defeated twice. I'm desperate, Mr. Fox. I need you to come with me."

Cody winced, looking downward for a moment. Did he really want to go back there? Out West? Where he'd been conceived?

"All right," he said after a moment. "When do we leave?"

"First thing in the morning."

"Exactly where are we going?" he asked.

"We're going to Victory, my boy."

At first he thought Vincent was trying to be poetic. Then it hit him.

"Victory, Texas," he breathed, and the other man nodded.

Cody swore under his breath, cursing fate.

If there was any place he hated, it was Victory, Texas.

THE DREAM CAME UPON Alex as if she were watching a play. It was as if velvet curtains opened and stage lighting slowly illuminated the scene, a scene she went from watching to starring in. She was lying in her bed at first, but then she rose.

The moonlight outside the window was so tempting. Or it might have been the shadows, like wings, like beckoning arms.

They'd been warned to keep everything locked, but it was such a beautiful night. The outlaws were long gone, had ridden out of town, and the sound of the breeze against the windows was enticing. She wanted to feel the wind. Feel it lift her hair and caress her cheeks. It would be soft and balmy, as gentle as the moon glow. The breeze would lift the soft cotton of her gown, and she would feel its cool sensation on her flesh.

For a few moments she hovered by her bed, but then, almost as if she were floating, she moved toward the French doors that led out to the balcony and pushed them open.

And there was the moon. Not yet full, but it was a cloudless night, so perhaps that was why the moonlight seemed so strong. From her balcony, she could see virtually the entire town, except she couldn't really see most of the houses, only the lights here and there where someone was keeping a lantern burning through the night.

She saw the trees, the branches that had created the beckoning shadows she had been unable to resist. Though the breeze was gentle, the branches bowed and waved as if they were in fact greeting her. She slid her hands over the rail at the balcony's edge and felt the wood beneath her hands, warm and supportive, as if it were something living. The air moved around her, and she blushed, even though she was alone, at the way she was seduced by the erotic feel of it. The fabric of her gown, like the shadows, seemed to touch her, to stroke her with arousing fingers.

She needed to turn away.

To go inside, to lock the door.

To close away these feelings.

But even as the thought gained a foothold in her mind, the shadows continued touching her, their touch palpable, sensuous. It was as if they had substance, as if they could take her and whisk her away into the night. The shadows were taking form, as if they were giant birds, or even bats, as if they had talons and could pluck her up from where she stood and fly with her, their prisoner, into the night.

Into true darkness.

A scream froze in her throat. The dream had become a nightmare. She reminded herself that she was strong, that she knew how to fight, how to shoot. But she had no weapon, and even if she did, shooting a shadow would be of no avail, and fighting the wind was a futile task.

And then *he* was there.

Just as suddenly as he had appeared that day. The tall man in the railroad duster and the hat dipping low over golden eyes.

He stood straight and firm against the wind, defying the darkness.

He closed his arms around her and swept her close, and she was uncomfortably aware of the intense way he was looking down at her. His eyes, which in reality were hazel, were glowing with a true golden splendor against the night. It was like being touched by the sun, and heat coursed through her, warming her face, her limbs, and stirring an arousal she'd never experienced before.

He walked with her into her room and gently set her down on the bed. Then he touched her cheek with a tenderness that made her catch her breath, but when she would have stroked his face and drawn him to her, he rose.

"Always fight the shadows, and never listen to the wind," he whispered. "And don't worry. I'll be here," he added, as if it were a vow.

Despite the words, though, he stepped away from her and stood at the foot of her bed. "Never open your door. Believe me as you believe in God, Miss Gordon, and do not open your door," he warned her.

She wanted to speak.

She wanted to draw him back to her.

She wanted to forget that her father had been killed, that there had ever been a past and would ever be a future.

She wanted him back.

But she couldn't form words. It was a dream, of course. A dream turned nightmare, turned dream again. Because she was safe, and she knew it.

Because he was there.

"Sleep now, Miss Gordon."

"Alex," she managed to say.

"Sleep, Alex."

And so she did.

WHEN SHE OPENED her eyes, she was alone.

Of course.

And yet she could remember every detail of the dream.

In the cold light of day, she groaned aloud, wishing she didn't remember with quite so much clarity.

She rose impatiently and turned toward the doors to the balcony. They were closed, the curtains drawn. And it was the light of day seeping in, not moonlight punctuated by dancing shadows.

Then she noticed the door that connected her room to the one beyond. Once that room had been the nursery, but it had long ago been converted to a guest room.

She hesitated, her heart thundering, then set her hand on the doorknob and slowly turned it.

The door was unlocked.

She pushed it open.

The bed was unmade, as if awaiting the maid's attention. And lying on the bench at the foot of the bed were saddlebags. Saddlebags engraved with a name. Cody Fox, M.D.

CHAPTER FOUR

BEULAH WAS SINGING when Alex went down to the dining room.

"Good morning, Miss Alex," she said happily.

Alex cast her a curious glance. She wasn't feeling quite as chipper as Beulah. She'd arrived in town to discover that vicious outlaws were decimating the region, she'd nearly become a victim herself, and then there had been that truly bizarre dream. "You're certainly cheerful this morning," Alex said to the older woman.

"Honey, I'm alive and kicking and breathing. That makes for a good morning in my book. And not only that, but I see hope for the future." Beulah grinned, pulling out a chair for Alex. "Come on, sit down, honey. You're still tired from the journey out here, that's what's bothering you. Didn't you sleep well?"

Despite herself, Alex was certain she was blushing again. It was absurd—she knew the strange events of the night before had been all in her mind. And yet…he'd been right there. The door between the rooms hadn't even been locked.

But she knew the difference between a dream and reality, and she had been dreaming, as strange as it had been. Then again, what *hadn't* been strange since she had arrived?

Until now, she'd never seen anything odd about unlocked doors.

This had always been a trusting household. Her father had liked people and possessed a natural ability to size them up. No thief had ever come in and stolen anything.

The thieves terrorizing their little piece of the West right now didn't seem to be interested in the usual ill-gotten gains. They were after souls, it seemed.

Where on earth had that thought come from?

She dismissed it quickly, shuddering despite herself.

"I slept okay," Alex answered at last. "Maybe coffee will make the world look brighter," she added hopefully.

"Right here, honey," Beulah said, setting a cup in front of her. Her father had chosen wisely. No delicate china here. Their dinnerware was attractive, but of a thicker mold. The cup she lifted was sturdy, and the coffee was delicious.

"Beulah, you perform wonders out here," Alex said, the compliment heartfelt.

"Well, thank you, child. And what, may I ask, are you planning to get up to today?" Beulah asked, eyeing the tailored shirt, riding breeches and boots Alex had chosen.

She meant to see where her father had died, but she decided not to mention that fact to Beulah.

"Oh, I just want to do a bit of riding."

"Riding," Beulah said, disturbed. "Now, Miss Alex, you've seen what can happen around here."

"I'm going to coerce Deputy Hinton into being my escort, and I'll be careful," Alex promised.

Beulah pointed a finger at her. "You promise me, you swear on the souls of your blessed parents, that you'll be back before sunset."

Outlaws could and did attack by daylight as well as in the dark, Alex thought, but she decided to humor Beulah. "Yes, ma'am."

Beulah sat back, eyeing the compact Colt six-shooter, caliber .58, that Alex had strapped around her hip.

"You didn't forget how to shoot while you were off in the big city, did you?" she asked.

"I swear I remember how to shoot, so you mustn't worry," Alex assured her.

Beulah poured herself a cup of coffee and took a seat at the table, smiling slowly. "Just so long as you're careful. You're all we've got now, and keeping you safe is mighty important to us. Your father was a wonderful man. He was always so wise and so clever—" her smile faded "—until Linda."

"Where *is* my father's widow, anyway? Did he really marry her? Legally, I mean. According to his letters, it was quite a whirlwind thing."

Beulah let out a sniff. "First time I ever saw your father thinking with his pants."

"Beulah!"

"I'm sorry for the indelicacy, but it's true. No sooner had he met her than he stopped coming home—he'd be sleeping over at the saloon every night."

"So she was…working there? What was she? A pianist? A hostess, or maybe a bartender?"

"Whore," Beulah said flatly.

Alex digested that for a minute before speaking. "Beulah, we've both learned over the years that everyone has to survive somehow. My father was a good man, and if he fell in love with Linda, she's probably a fine woman. But where is she?"

Beulah snorted. Alex lifted a brow, and Beulah told her, "Your father weren't never a complete fool. He left her a little bit of money, and she took it and moved out. He made sure with a big Eastern lawyer that the property and everything else went to you. Linda found out just how ironclad your father's will was, and she didn't stay to butt her head against any walls."

"All right, the property is mine, but she *was* married to my father," Alex said. "Surely, she must know she's welcome here anytime."

"Speak for yourself, Miss Alex," Beulah said. "That one—she's a tough cookie. I don't know what went on while your father was alive. Maybe she really loved him— he was certainly worthy of love. But since he died…well, here it is. Some women are whores because they like being whores. It's addictive. They like pretty things. And they like men."

"Linda is back working at the saloon?" Alex asked.

"When she's in town. She comes and goes," Beulah told her.

"Oh, I see."

In fact she didn't really see at all. She thought of her long journey out, the train cars crammed with people that began to reek after the first hours, followed by the stuffy jolting carriage and the chubby banker who had passed gas all the way. She thought of the men fresh off the cattle drives, mud-encrusted and sweaty, and the nasty way some of them had of not seeming to know there was such a thing as a toothbrush. How could women choose to sleep with such men? Were whores allowed to force their customers to bathe first?

"She wasn't there—yesterday," Alex noted.

"I told you. She comes and goes," Beulah said.

Alex started to rise from the table.

"And where do you think you're going, young lady?" Beulah asked.

"I told you, I'm going to ride around, just get the feel of being home again," Alex said. "It will be fine. I'm going to walk down to the sheriff's office and get Dave to go with me."

"Not until you've had breakfast. You just relax. Tess is in the kitchen, and I'll have some eggs out for you in a flash. I made corn muffins this morning, too, and you are not leaving until you've told me just exactly how delicious they are. That nice Mr. Fox and his friend Mr. Vincent said they'd never had better."

Alex frowned, looking at Beulah. "They are up already? Where are they now?"

"Honey, they were up bright and early. But I don't know where they are now."

"You didn't ask?"

"I don't put my nose where it shouldn't be," Beulah told her firmly. "What those fellows choose to do is their business. I have no right to pry."

Alex had to laugh. "You don't mind grilling me as if I were a prisoner!"

Beulah looked at her sternly. "Honey child, *you* are my business. And bless the Lord, those fellows are like manna from above, the first paying customers in weeks, so don't you go questioning them, either, missy—we want those men around here just as long as we can get them to stay. Now, sit tight. I'll have your breakfast in two shakes, and then you can hurry down to see Dave and get up to whatever *extremely careful* adventure you've got planned for the day."

CODY AND BRENDAN were both well aware, as they neared the Apache camp, that they had been followed for a long time.

Victory, like its now ghost-town neighbors Brigsby and Hollow Tree, sat near the winding Little Red River. An offshoot of the Little Red, Dead Man's Creek, meandered north through the plain and on into brush and forest land, to the sudden outcrop of cliffs that surrounded Tall Feather's main camp. In the past, the Apache people had been known to move, following the buffalo trails, and sometimes they still did. But Tall Feather's main camp, here in the cliff country, had been established for decades. It was a perfectly secure setup. Tall Feather's warriors could see for miles around and were stalking them now from the heights.

Cody had expected the escort, but he wasn't expecting any actual trouble, even though the Apache were generally regarded as warlike, and they had a complex social network. According to Brendan, who had spent time in Texas and knew the man, Chief Tall Feather was part of the Jicarilla tribe, the Llaneros band and his own clan, which he had named for the area in which he chose to live; in English, it translated as the Cave Warriors, and he was their supreme authority.

These days, Tall Feather had chosen the richness of life over the glory of warfare. In fact, from all that he had learned, Cody didn't believe that Tall Feather had ever been responsible for cold-bloodedly murdering anyone, including Alex's father. If he went to war, if he attacked riders or a wagon train, he would not deny what he had done.

"There," Brendan said quietly, nodding in the direction he meant. "The chief is waiting to meet us."

They were nearing the vast array of deer- and buffalo-skin tents, many adorned with antlers, feathers and other trophies from the hunt, that marked Tall Feather's camp. A path led through the camp, and at the end of the path stood an extremely large tepee.

A man stood in front of it, as still as the cliffs themselves, his face set in an expression that told them nothing of his feelings.

Cody noted that the warriors who had watched them from above had descended a path down the face of the cliff and were now following them, six men on horseback, silent and orderly.

Tall Feather did not have an intermediary speak for him. He waited for them to dismount directly before him, by which time the entire tribe had gathered around. Warriors, stone-faced, stood without hostility, but at the ready should there be any threat to their chief. Women hovered behind the men; children looked out around their mothers' knees.

"Tall Feather," Brendan said, "I have brought you my friend Cody Fox, who has come to help us all with the evil that has invaded this land we share so peacefully. May we speak with you?"

At last the chief moved, merely inclining his head. That seemed to be the signal for two of his warriors to take their horses as they dismounted. Cody nodded his thanks, and the young warrior who took the reins gave him a slight smile in return.

Tall Feather preceded them into the tepee, where a central fire burned, the smoke escaping through a shaft at the peak. Tall Feather's tent was large, and Cody saw sleeping pallets and skins all around the edge. Tall Feather had many children, it appeared.

He sat before the fire, indicating that they should join him. Something bubbled in a pot that hung over the fire. It smelled oddly like coffee, Cody thought.

The chief was dressed handsomely in hand-sewn and beaded buckskin, a band around his forehead keeping his long braided hair from his face. Cody estimated that the man had to be in his sixties, but his posture was so erect and his muscles so honed that they were at odds with the reality. His face, however, was deeply lined, and there were many gray strands in his long black hair.

"We are living in grave times," Tall Feather said, staring at Cody. "I am anxious to hear what you can do to help."

The man definitely didn't need an interpreter. His English was perfect.

Cody spoke carefully. "Chief, what I hope to do is root out the evil that my friend Brendan has spoken of. To do that, we must first find the heart of that evil. It's my belief that this man, Milo, is more than your usual outlaw. So no matter how brave, strong and selfless your men may be in battle, they simply aren't prepared to fight this particular enemy."

To Cody's surprise, Tall Feather smiled. "You need not be so careful in your words, Cody Fox. You are not speaking to one of your reporters."

Cody smiled in return. "I'm talking about a different kind of being. Something diseased and…not human."

Tall Feather nodded. "In our culture, the Black Sky and the Earth Mother came together and created our Great Spirit, who we call Hascin. When a man or maid is ill, ghosts will offer them fruit, and if they accept, they will go on and enter the new world. If they do not, they will return to us. If they eat of the fruit and die, we take them carefully to their burial place. The dead are tended reverently, clad in their best. The horse of the dead man is slain, and his belongings are dispersed. The funeral party takes a different route back from the burial site, because we believe in ghosts, and our ghosts do not always come to plant a gentle kiss on the cheek of a loved one. Our ghosts sometimes come with vengeance in mind, angry over some wrong that was done to them in life, and they can take many forms, perhaps the coyote or the bear or the mountain lion."

Tall Feather paused, and Cody nodded silently, certain that it wasn't his time to speak yet.

After a moment Tall Feather nodded, as well, satisfied that Cody accepted the way of the Cave Warriors. Then he went on.

"At first I thought that ghosts had come in the form of these outlaws, an army of ghosts, our enemies from years gone past," he said.

"So you fought with them?" Cody asked.

Tall Feather nodded gravely. "Many of our maidens were at the stream. They were set upon by the outlaws, and our young warriors heard them screaming and ran to save them. We killed several of their kind, but they killed one of my warriors, as well. He was buried in the caves, as is our custom. But soon after that, my daughter Gentle Doe, who had loved the warrior and awaited his payment of ponies for marriage, began to see him by night. Then, last week, Gentle Doe vanished into the darkness. I will not see her again."

Cody hesitated. "How do you know that?"

Tall Feather offered a sorrowful smile. "We smoke the pipe, and the dreams and visions come to us, Cody Fox. We see what others cannot. My daughter is…dead. At least to me. This I know." He hesitated. "Now I fear for another warrior, for he has been ill. He tells me that he has visions of my daughter. He fears to tell me the whole truth, but I believe that the vision attempts to seduce and lure him from his resting place."

Cody said, "I believe everything you have told me, and it fits with what I know of the evil terrorizing this land. The monsters must be found and routed out, and I believe you will understand my methods more than many a white man would. There are men like you and I who ride with those who are…diseased, because the diseased men need the help of those who are not tainted. But it's often difficult to tell the difference between them. This is a Spirit World enemy, Chief Tall Feather. Brendan and I have brought you some new weapons that you and your men must use. We have stakes as sharp as spear points—and your own lances must be made equally sharp. A single bullet, even in the head or heart, will not kill the diseased men—or women— though many bullets or arrows will wound and weaken them. Once they have fallen, they must be destroyed completely. The head must be severed from the body, the heart cut from the chest. We have brought you army swords, to make this task easier for you, and knives that work just as well. It is not easy to sever the head from a body, but it is necessary. Also, the enemy may come in daylight, but they are far more powerful at sunset and by night."

The chief gave him no argument, simply nodded gravely.

Cody hesitated, then went on. "When someone has… disappeared, he—or she— cannot just be welcomed back with open arms. You will know if they are…infected. Their eyes will be different. They may look perfectly normal otherwise, but their eyes will give them away. But when the infection is new, as it is…with any of your people, they will not know how to handle it. They will not be good at guile and pretense, and you will know they are not…as they were. Do you understand?"

Tall Feather stood stiff and straight as, again, he nodded. Then he spoke.

"An Apache warrior knows that he may die in battle, whatever that battle may be. A diseased warrior who fell in battle against evil will still be accorded the honor of one who fought well, even if he lost."

Cody was aware that someone else had come into the tepee. He turned and saw a young maiden in bleached white buckskin, her hair arranged in shiny black braids, bearing pottery cups. She dipped liquid from the pot above the fire.

"I will accept your gifts, but first we will share a welcome drink," Tall Feather said.

"Thank you," Cody told him gravely. He was anxious to get started, and worried about what might be in the pot. The Apache were not averse to hallucinogens.

"There is more, Chief Tall Feather. You must take us to the grave of your fallen warrior."

Tall Feather frowned, about to argue.

"Chief, we believe he may have been tainted. He will not be strong yet, but in time, he might taint your entire clan," Brendan said gently.

The young woman handed Cody a steaming cup. He

smiled his thanks, and she blushed. "This smells like coffee," he said.

Tall Feather grinned. "It *is* coffee. We knew you would come, and we wanted to make you welcome."

They drank the coffee, praising its taste—despite the fact that they ended up chewing on the grounds. When they had finished, Cody rose. "Tall Feather, forgive me, but it's imperative that I see your dead warrior. He is a danger I can stop."

"It will be as you say. Come. I will send for the horses."

IT WASN'T EASY FOR ALEX to get Dave to ride out with her.

He and Cole were talking when she got to the sheriff's office, but he made himself scarce when she entered. Cole greeted her with a hug, offering his sympathies on her father and her fiancé. She hugged him back with equal warmth. A lot of people, including her father, had always thought that she and Cole should get together, that they would have made a perfect couple. What they didn't understand was that, though she and Cole loved each other, it wasn't a romantic love. They were both only children who had lost their mothers when they were small and grown up lonely. He was like her brother, and you didn't marry your brother.

She sat down across from him as he went back behind his desk, grinning pertly as she threw her legs up on the desktop and eased back.

"I must say, Miss Gordon, that all that time you spent back in Washington didn't do much for your manners," he teased. "What are those feet doing on my desk?"

"Resting," she said with a laugh, but then she grew serious. "I need one of you to take me out to the place where my father died," she said.

Silence greeted her words.

"I won't be leaving the limits of this town again," Cole finally said. "Not anytime soon. I leave, and that band of filthy thieves comes in. Thank God for those two fellows from back East. And speaking of them, I sure hope they get back from wherever they went in time for the town meeting I'm planning for tonight. The men in Victory can't be cowards. They have to step up and fight."

"I'm sure they'll be back. The trouble out here seems to be the reason for their appearance in town, after all," Alex said.

Cole nodded. "And that trouble means this isn't the time for you to be running around out there. Can't you go…bake a cake or something?"

"Cole Granger, how dare you?" she demanded as she swung her legs off the desk and stood. "I'll find the place by myself."

"Damn it, Alex!" Cole said, rising as well. "Look, right now it's daytime—"

"And everyone knows the danger comes by night. So instead of arguing with me, have Dave take a quick ride out there with me now. Cole, you know me, and you knew my father. I have to see where he was killed…where he was found. I have to know what happened to him. I don't believe it was Indians, but I need to be certain."

Cole thumped his fist on the desk, staring her in the face. "Alex, God help us all, I know who killed your father. The outlaws. Milo and his crew. And I mean to bring them to justice. So you need to stay here and stay safe, and let me do my job."

She turned away from him. "I'm going now. Great to see you, Cole."

"Alex!"

"Cole?" She turned back.

He was frustrated. "I'll put you in a cell," he threatened, pointing toward the two rarely used cells at the back of the room.

"No, you won't."

"If your father were alive…"

She smiled sadly. "That's just it, Cole. He isn't."

As she had expected, Cole let out a growl of irritation. "Dave," he called, and the deputy appeared from wherever he had been lurking.

"Yeah, boss?"

"Alex wants to see where her father was killed, and I need you to—go with her. Just make sure she's back by sunset. And then…hell, make her bake a damned cake!"

THE WARRIOR HAD BEEN called Running Cat. He had been buried with honor, dressed in his finest buckskin and plumage. His body had been wrapped in buffalo hide, and he'd been placed on a natural shelf within the cave, then covered with rocks.

Only the chief had come with them, but Tall Feather had not helped them remove the stones.

Nor did he speak when they stared down at the corpse, though despite the absolute composure of the older man's features, Cody knew that he was surprised to see no sign of decay on the body.

"Chief, you won't like what I have to do next," Cody told him.

"I will like whatever saves my people," Tall Feather said gruffly.

Cody looked at Brendan, who nodded.

Quickly, Cody drew a stake and hammer from his pack, then drove the sharpened stake into the warrior's heart. There was a horrendous sound, a loud, ghastly hissing, and the warrior shot up, his eyes flying open. They were the color of glittering onyx, but scarlet fire gleamed in them.

Those eyes fell on Cody, and a few soft words escaped the warrior's lips.

Then he fell back.

Cody finished his gruesome work, severing the head. It was enough. He didn't cut out the heart.

Through it all, Chief Tall Feather stood stoic and silent.

"It is done," Cody said, standing over the body, which would now begin to decay as it should have days ago.

Tall Feather nodded.

"What did he say?" Brendan asked.

"He said 'thank you, by the Great Spirit,'" Tall Feather answered.

They turned to pick up the rocks and replace them over the body, but Cody heard a rustling from the far side of the burial ledge and turned swiftly, the stake, still bearing a trace of blood from the warrior, at the ready. He saw her, and his heart sank.

It was a maiden, a stunning Apache maiden with huge dark eyes and gleaming black hair. She had strong, beautiful features. All that marred her beauty was the look of madness in her eyes, the fire that burned at the back of them—that and the contorted twist of her features, which spoke of nothing but rage and pure hatred. She bared teeth that came to a fine point.

Tall Feather turned then, too, staring in horror. He cried out in pain and misery.

He spoke, and though Cody didn't know much of his

language, he understood the man's meaning. This was his daughter, his lost daughter Gentle Doe.

And she was indeed lost to him forever.

There was no help for it; she was about to attack, and she was fueled by full-blown rage. She had lain silent during the staking and decapitation of her lover, but in the end it had proved to be too much for her. She wouldn't have understood that he had already been dead—that she herself was no longer among the living. The word "vampire" didn't even exist in her language, much less her mind, and she had become one without knowing that the hunger it created would drive her to murder her own people.

There was no choice.

In another second, Tall Feather would be taken, or killed.

Cody spun, the stake pinning her directly in the heart.

Tall Feather let out an anguished cry. There was nothing Cody could do to save the chief from having to watch as his daughter reached out to him while death throes racked her body and her face contorted further in pain. Her death had been so recent that she wouldn't crumble into dust and ash, but, like the warrior, would begin to decay naturally.

Tall Feather reached out to his daughter, his expression both beseeching and welcoming.

The innocence and beauty of youth were back in her eyes, along with recognition and pain. And love.

Then her eyes closed, and Tall Feather howled, the sound deep and shattering.

Cody stepped between him and his daughter, then eased her down to the pallet where the warrior she had loved in both life and death still lay. He quickly drew his knife and severed her head. Then, while Brendan set his hands on Tall Feather's shoulders and forced him outside, Cody respectfully arranged the remains of the lovers, ensuring that they would go together into the next world.

He hadn't known either of them or, until this morning, Tall Feather, and yet he felt great sadness for the father, a compassionate man in a world of violence, who had lost both a daughter and a man who would have become a son.

He replaced the stones that sealed the burial place.

When he stepped out of the cave, the other two men were mounted and the sun was just beginning its descent in the west. The first glorious streaks of sunset were already painting the sky.

"I must hurry back to my people," Tall Feather said, his expression stoic and his back straight atop his mount. "And you must return to yours." The Indian nodded gravely to them and turned his horse's head toward his village.

Cody climbed quickly into the saddle. They did need to return to town. When the sun fell, the heat of the day disappeared with surprising speed, and the pink-and-gold-streaked sky would turn to darkness—and shadows.

A sudden sense of urgency filled him, and he kneed his mount into motion.

"The chief is right—it's time to get back," he said to Brendan, and their horses began a swift thundering across the plain, the animals' hoofbeats matching the pounding of his heart.

CHAPTER FIVE

A CHILL WIND SEEMED to sweep the plain as they reached the spot where her father had breathed his last.

They were just east of the woods. A hard ride down-river led to John Snow's trading post, while bracken, brush and pine forest led off to the west. They could see the cliffs that shielded the Apache camp but not the camp itself; they might as well have been in the middle of nowhere. Truthfully, even in the center of Victory, Alex reminded herself, they actually *were* in the middle of nowhere. Here, alone, with the whisper of the trees in the background, the sky overhead and the plains seeming to stretch forever, a waving sea of tall grasses, the world seemed a vast and mysterious place.

"There," Dave said, and pointed to a spot where the grasses seemed deepest. "Right there is where we found him." He looked away from Alex. "He was cold, Alex. We couldn't tell when he had died."

She dismounted and walked to the place Dave had indicated, where she sank down to her knees. She had been afraid she would burst into tears, wondering how he had ended up dying here, all alone. He should have grown old; she should have been there to hold his hand at the end. It hadn't been his time.

She didn't cry, though. Instead she felt the breeze touching her cheek. A wave of nostalgia swept through her, and she just wished she could let him know how much she loved him, what a fine man and fine father he had been.

She looked up at Dave. "How did he die?" she demanded.

Dave dismounted and came over to sit across from her. He looked at her gravely. "We don't know."

"What do you mean, you don't know?" Alex demanded. "Was he shot? Stabbed?"

Dave shook his head. "No."

"Then what happened to him?" she persisted. "Dave, come on, help me. You're not making sense. Please, Dave, he was my father!"

"His horse was gone, his personal effects were gone. He might have had a heart attack, and then someone came by…or…someone might have scared him into having a heart attack. Cole thinks it was Milo and his gang, but the truth is, we just don't know. Things were happening…. Brigsby was dying, and…we didn't even know what was happening until it suddenly became a ghost town. And your dad…there wasn't a mark on him. Weren't no doctor in the town at the time. Jim Green, over at the funeral home, was the closest we had to a medical man. Anything serious, we sent for Dr. Astin over in Brigsby or Dr. Peters in Hollow Tree, but now…" He shook his head as if to clear it of thoughts too terrible to dwell on. "We brought your dad home. We prepared him for burial. And we mourned him. And then we got the news to you as quick as we could."

She nodded, then looked out across the plain. "Not a mark on him," she repeated.

"Not that we could see. Jim bathed him and embalmed him for viewing, and he didn't see a thing. Everyone loved him, Alex. No one in town would have wanted to see him dead."

They sat in silence. Then, just as she was about to speak, the comfortable quiet between them was shattered by an earsplitting howl that seemed to shake the very earth.

"My God!" Alex exclaimed.

Dave had started, too, and he laughed ruefully at himself. "It's just a wolf."

"I've never heard a wolf sound like that," Alex said.

"It must be wounded," Dave said, and shrugged. But then he looked past Alex and hurriedly got up and headed in the direction of the horses, which had been grazing untethered. They had been lazily grazing, but now both animals were prancing and snorting, disturbed by the cry of the wolf.

"Quiet down now, you two," Dave said, walking toward them.

But as he spoke, the howling began again, so eerie and high-pitched that it was painful.

It wasn't a single wolf anymore. It was many wolves, and as they let loose their mournful wail, it was almost as if they were giving a cue for the sun to fall.

The sky had been blue. Now, pink and gold streaks suddenly started shooting across it. Then pink darkened quickly to purple, gold to amber.

"Hey!" Dave cried. He'd been trying to soothe his horse, but the gelding was not about to be soothed. It reared, and Dave backed away. "Hey, who feeds you, you bastard?"

Alex hurried toward her own horse, but the palomino mare was backing away. "No, no, not you, Cheyenne," she said. "Please, come on, baby, it's all right, it's me. I'll protect you." What a lie. She? Protect the horse from a wolf? Not even if only one wolf was on the prowl. And if a group of hungry wolves were on the hunt…?

She realized she was letting fear set in and forced it back and focused on trying to catch her horse. She had a gun, and she was a damned good shot. She hated killing a creature as beautiful as a wolf, but if it meant survival, she would do it.

"Stop!" Dave cried, and she looked up to see his horse racing off—heading like a maddened being into the woods.

"No," Alex whispered desperately.

Too late. Her mare looked at her with wide eyes, then took off after Dave's gelding.

Alex stared after Cheyenne, then turned to stare at Dave, guilt filling her. They were there because she had insisted, and now night was coming. Night, when the evil everyone was afraid of came out to play.

She sighed. "I'm sorry—I didn't figure on wolves."

"Think we can catch the horses?" Dave asked worriedly.

"I think we have to. Maybe they stopped once they made it into the woods."

"Unless the wolves set them off again."

"Well, let's go look. We can't wait here forever for them to come back," Alex said.

Together, they started walking toward the trees. There were pines and wild oak, with shrubs and an occasional flowering bush. There were trails, because the Apache sometimes came here to hunt, but they were overgrown and narrow.

As they started down the trail the horses had taken, Alex found herself looking up at the sky, catching glimpses through the trees. Already the pastel colors were fading to darkness. Pink had become magenta, and now even that magenta was darkening.

"Stay by me," Dave commanded.

"Oh, you can count on that," she assured him.

He stopped and motioned her to do the same, listening. Earlier a gentle breeze had stirred the air; now it was as if it rustled through the trees with an edge of warning.

She spun around when it sounded as if something large had moved in the brush behind her. "Cheyenne…?" she said tentatively.

"No horse could hide in that bush," Dave said worriedly.

Simultaneously, they drew their guns.

A black shadow swept across the trail ahead of them, a shadow like the wings of some immense bird. It had to be her imagination, she told herself, a trick of the dying daylight, the time when the sun wasn't completely gone and yet the moon was rising.

"What the hell was that?" Dave asked, demolishing her hope that it had been only a figment of her imagination.

"I don't know…. An owl, maybe, or some kind of bird," Alex said, trying to come up with a rational explanation.

But she didn't feel in any way rational. It was as if something in the woods had awakened every primal fear that had been lurking unacknowledged within her.

"A trick of the light," Dave said, sounding as if he was trying to convince himself as much as her.

The wolves began to howl again, the sound more high-pitched than she had ever heard, and as loud as if every wolf in Texas had joined the chorus.

Instinctively, Alex whirled around, so that she and Dave were back to back. She held her Colt firmly, her finger on the trigger.

The shadows began to rise and fall around them. She heard a strange swishing sound, as if giant wings were beating unseen just above their heads.

Soon there would be no more shadows, though. For soon the darkness would fall, and the light of the moon wouldn't be strong enough to penetrate the canopy created by the great oaks and pines.

"Be ready," she said to Dave.

"I am."

The sound, like the *whomp, whomp, whomp* of beating wings, was suddenly very close.

Dave fired, then fired again.

"Save it until we can see something," Alex said. "I have a feeling we'll be needing all our ammo."

"Save it until we can see something?" Dave protested, as the light continued to fade around them. "It's like we're fighting…invisible birds!"

Alex felt her muscles contract. She could hear those wings again, coming closer and closer. And again that sound.

Whomp, whomp, whomp.

The air around her was moving. Whatever it was, it was coming. She could already feel the caress of the air against her cheek, as if it was about to touch her.

THEY WERE GALLOPING flat out, and Cody thanked God that his horse was sound and healthy. And fast.

Brendan raced close behind him.

They could hear the wolves, and Cody knew it was not the ghosts of long-dead Apaches inhabiting the creatures and crying out in hopes of revenge. These wolves were howling in fear. They were predators, and they knew another predator was loose in the wild, trespassing on pack territory, and the scent of the intruder was driving them insane with terror.

Suddenly he reined in.

"What is it?" Brendan asked, jerking his own mount to a stop.

"A horse—there!"

Cody started forward at a more cautious pace. The animal didn't move. It stood, trembling, in the tall grass, facing the edge of the forest. He could see the broken brush where it had crashed through from between the trees. Even at a distance, with darkness falling, he could tell that the animal was trembling. It was amazing that the creature's heart hadn't burst from exertion.

"Hey there…" Cody said soothingly as he approached the horse.

His own horse was starting to prance nervously, as if he scented something frightening.

Brendan rode up beside him. "That mare is from the boardinghouse stable," he pointed out.

"I know." Cody was already leaping down. He unstrapped his large bow from the saddle, along with his quiver of arrows. Brendan followed suit, choosing a sharply pointed stake.

At the edge of the trees, Cody paused. He let the breeze surround him, and he felt the movement of the descending night. Her scent came to him before the sound of her voice.

"Dave, you're shooting too wildly. We have to hold!" she cried.

"But it *touched* me!" Dave replied.

"We need to make our shots count, Dave," Alex replied.

Cody could tell that she was close, and even now, with the monsters all around, something about her seemed to call to him, arousing a soul-deep longing in him. She was in danger, but she would never give up without a fight, even though she had no idea what she was fighting and would never believe him if he told her.

What the hell was she doing out here?

He dismissed the thought and called her name.

"Alex?"

"Over here!" she shouted back.

He and Brendan raced in the direction of her voice and found her in fine defensive position, standing back to back with Dave, which might be what had saved them thus far. It was easier for the creatures to pick off a single man or woman, to swoop down and avoid the bullets. Bullets that wouldn't kill them, of course, but would certainly hurt, causing damage that might last for hours or even days, depending on age and other factors.

He and Brendan hurried to help the others, taking up their own positions. While Brendan fell to his knees, stake held firmly, his arm steady, Cody focused on listening. His hearing was acute, and he quickly located his target and sent the first arrow flying. He was pleased to hear a shrill scream and an erratic flapping as his shaft found its target. The shadow veered off, and he heard it crash somewhere far away.

Again he listened, took aim and fired.

And again.

And then the wolves went silent and the beating of wings stopped. The shadows were gone.

They all went still and silent for several seconds, instinctively waiting to make sure that the danger was truly gone.

"Thank you for another timely arrival," Alex said. She sounded assured and unafraid.

Damn it, he thought. What was wrong with the woman? She should be terrified.

"What the hell were those things?" she demanded.

Cody didn't answer her at first. He was too stunned by the strength of his response to her, and finally he swung around to stare at her, shaking with the desire to take her by the shoulders and emphasize his point. "What were they? They were death, that's what they were. What the hell are you doing out here?"

"This is where my father was killed and I wanted to see the place where he died, not that it's any of your business," she responded quickly. She had stiffened like a bowstring and was staring back at him, eyes narrowed, everything about her announcing that he had brought out her defenses—and hostility.

"Cody…" Brendan said warningly, but without effect.

He couldn't control the anger he was feeling, and though he managed to keep himself from grabbing her, he couldn't control the fury in his words.

"You're a fool. I thought you were supposed to be an educated young woman. An intelligent one. Last night, you might have been raped and murdered, and yet here you are, prowling around in the dark and—"

"Now, Cody," Dave protested weakly. "She asked me to come with her for protection. We were heading back when the wolves spooked the horses, who ran off. That's the only reason we're still here."

"Right. The horses," Brendan said. "Let's get to them before they decide it's safe to head home without us. Miss Gordon, your horse is out there just beyond the trees. Dave, we haven't seen yours, so you can double up with me. Cody?"

Cody knew that he was still staring angrily at Alex. And she was staring back at him, her fury the equal of his.

"Mr. Fox," she said, as if the discussion of the horses had never happened, "I am a free agent and over twenty-one. And I am not stupid. Not even my father raised his voice to me in such a manner as you just did, and I will thank you not to do so in the future. I'm not going to ask you to move out of my boardinghouse over this one incident, especially since your arrival has now proved useful not once but twice. But while your presence is deeply appreciated, your opinions are not."

With that, she spun around and strode past Brendan and Dave, who was standing openmouthed after her outburst. The three men quickly followed her, Cody swearing beneath his breath.

Once they left the thick darkness under the trees, the world felt familiar and safe again. The moon shone down with a gentle benevolence, and the breeze whispered softly, cool and fresh and smelling of the wildflowers that dotted the plain.

In silence, Cody mounted his horse. Alex needed no help to mount her still-quivering mare, who at least responded to her crooning tone, growing calm at her owner's soothing words.

Dave leaped up behind Brendan and Cody urged their horses toward Alex.

"I hope you'll forgive me, Miss Gordon, if my concern for your life caused me to lose my temper and offend you. There's a serious danger to be fought here, and it will be far easier for Brendan and me to root it out and put an end to it if we're not constantly worrying about your safety."

He didn't give her a chance to respond. After the tongue-lashing she had given him, he was determined to have the last word. He nudged his mount around and started loping smoothly back toward Victory.

As they neared town, he slowed his horse, and Brendan moved up to ride by his side. Cody saw that the older man was smirking at him knowingly, but he just shook his head and continued on toward civilization.

THEY ALL RETURNED TO the boardinghouse together, Alex dreading the thought of having dinner in his company. Yes, she had perhaps spoken more harshly than she should have, but he had insulted her first, so really, it was all his fault. Levy quickly came over to tend to the horses, telling them that Cole Granger was inside pacing, after Dave's horse had returned without him.

"Thank God you're back!" Cole said as they trailed in. He immediately gave Alex a huge hug, and she hugged him back. She felt his heart pounding and knew he was especially grateful for her return. He went on to clap Dave on the back, and pump Brendan's and Cody's hands with enthusiasm. "I don't mind telling you, I was terrified. After what happened last night, I couldn't leave this town unprotected again, but when Dave's horse came back… What happened?"

"Something spooked the horses," Dave said. "And…I

think we have some kind of giant birds in the woods," he added, shaking his head, knowing his words sounded irrational. "Giant birds—they got the wolves howling like I've never heard before, and then they started swooping down on us. Alex and I were barely holding our own, and—then Cody and Brendan found us."

"Giant…birds?" Cole asked doubtfully.

"I swear, that's what they seemed like. Giant birds— and I think they're what's killing everyone around here."

Cole stared at the four of them.

"Cole," Alex said, "I don't know what was out there— but they flew, and they would have killed us." She hesitated, trying to keep her voice level. "I think Cody hit one of them, but it flew off before it fell, and it was too dark under the trees for me to see anything. Finally they quit attacking us and we got out of there as fast as we could. So now…"

Her voice trailed off as Beulah, Bert and the girls came running in, kissing and hugging everyone with unbridled enthusiasm. Alex couldn't help but notice that Cody had an awkward grin on his face, as if he were glad of the warmth being shown him on his return.

She remembered the bizarre dream she'd had about him, but insisted to herself that that was all it was, just a dream, nothing she needed to be concerned about.

But she couldn't help being scared. Too often in the past, her dreams had been a forewarning of what was to come.

"All righty now," Beulah said firmly once everyone's return had been celebrated. "You folks get on to the dining room right now."

"Not me, thank you, Beulah," Cole said. "I called a

town meeting for just about an hour from now, and I ought to be getting over to the saloon to get ready for it."

"We'll all be going to the meeting, Cole Granger," Beulah said firmly. "And you've still got to eat. Now, get in there, everyone, and don't forget to wash up first. Then you'll all eat a nice, civilized dinner, before we get back to making plans so we can stop being so afraid."

No one was about to dispute Beulah when she was so determined, so Alex hurried upstairs to her room. Her washbowl had been filled, and it felt delicious to dip her hands into the cool water and scrub the dirt and sweat off her face. She didn't have time to change, much less for what she wanted—needed—which was a bath. A long, hot bath. Maybe after the town meeting.

She hurried back to rejoin the others. Just as she left her room, Cody Fox emerged from his. He stiffened at the sight of her.

She stiffened in turn.

They stood that way for a split second, then he held out an arm politely. "After you, Miss Gordon."

She nodded in acknowledgment of the courtesy and swept by him, but she felt him behind her every step of the way to the dining room.

Brendan had apparently washed up with Cole and Dave in the pantry, because all three men were already seated at the table. They rose quickly at the sight of Alex, who murmured a thank-you and took her place as Cole pulled out her chair for her. When he set his hands on her shoulders for a moment, she reached up and gave them a squeeze. He took the chair to her left, and Dave slid into the seat to her right. Cody and Brendan took the chairs across from them.

Beulah, Tess and Jewell served, hurrying back and forth with bowls and platters. Beulah had outdone herself, concocting a creamed chicken dish with tiny peas and onions, fresh sautéed greens, and a mound of mashed potatoes. Bert brought in water and wine.

Civilized.

Yes, it was an amazingly civilized dinner. Alex might have been dining in a fine mansion in Washington. They might have been planning to discuss the races, the weather, or even politics, in a measured and courteous manner.

In fact, at first they *were* quite courteous.

"Beulah, this is amazing," Dave said as the cook hovered nearby, like a mother hen protecting her chicks.

"Thank you, Dave," she said.

"This is truly a fine meal," Cody told her. "Thank you."

The words were perfectly innocuous, Alex thought. So why did she want to hit him?

"Ditto," Brendan said.

"You didn't have to go to so much trouble, Beulah," Dave said.

"Cooking took my mind off worrying about you," Beulah told them.

"Miss Gordon," Cody said, "would you kindly pass the peas?"

"I'd be delighted, Mr. Fox," she assured him, fighting to keep herself from throwing the bowl across the table at him.

After that they ate in silence for a while, until Cody—of course it would be Cody, she thought—brought reality crashing back in.

"Pardon me for asking, Cole," he said, staring intently across the table at the sheriff, "but just what do you intend to say at the meeting tonight?"

Cole set his fork down, seeming a bit startled. "Well, I'm going to point out that these outlaws are now making a play for Victory. We didn't see what was happening when they went in and destroyed Brigsby and Hollow Tree. God knows what they've done to all the people, if they've fled, or if they've been—" He broke off and hesitated, looking around, clearly uncomfortable. Alex knew that Cole had been raised to believe that certain conversation was indelicate and not for the company of women.

"Cole," Alex said quietly, "is 'slaughtered,' or maybe 'massacred,' the word you're looking for?"

He looked down, sighing. "All right, Alex, I guess I do have to speak plainly. Slaughtered," he said, then turned back to Cody. "And what scares me most is that I wasn't here when they attacked Victory, and this whole town might have been lost if you and Brendan hadn't been here. Tonight I'm going to tell people that they can't be cowards. We have to fight together, we have to look out for one another."

Cody nodded. "It's a good start, but it isn't going to be enough."

Alex felt another surge of irritation rise. Was it because he had no right to lecture Cole, who had lived here all his life? Or because, dream or no, she was fascinated by him—and afraid at the same time...?

"Mr. Fox, as I've said, we're all extremely grateful to you and Mr. Vincent. But Cole is an excellent sheriff and a very courageous man," she said.

Not only didn't Cody take offense, he didn't even glance her way, only grinned at Cole. "I don't doubt that. In a pinch, Sheriff, you're one man I'd like fighting at my side. But I'm afraid that Miss Gordon isn't likely to understand what I'm about to say. And I'm rather afraid, as well, that if I stand up at your town meeting and try to explain what's going on around here, a few folks are going to know in their hearts that I'm right, but all the rest are going to tell you that I'm a madman."

"I'm lost myself," Cole said. "What on earth are you getting at?"

Cody looked across the table to the corner of the dining room where Beulah stood, half hidden by shadows.

"Beulah knows," he said softly. "And I'm certain that Tess and Jewell believe, as well. This boardinghouse has been protected, not just decorated. The garlic fronds, and all those fine crosses."

Cody glanced at Brendan, then went on. "We are facing true evil here. Those men are not just outlaws. Not all of them, anyway. Some are…diseased. The disease is terrifying and transmissible. Sometimes it's transferred by an act of pure terror, sometimes through seduction. Sometimes, rarely, if a person has only just contracted the disease, they can be cured. But there is a point of no return, and it comes quickly."

"What the hell are you talking about?" Alex demanded bluntly.

"What you and Dave saw in the woods tonight—I did bring something down with an arrow, something against which your bullets were worthless," Cody said. "We're fighting an ancient evil, something unlike anything you've ever faced before that can be fought only with specific weapons, kept at bay only by specific precautions."

"What weapons?" Cole asked. "What precautions?"

"The weapons are arrows, stakes, knives and swords. And holy water, but you don't seem to have much of that around here, though I have a small supply. And the precautions—let no one in. No one. The enemy can enter only if asked."

"This is insane," Alex said. "Do you think I asked those men in last night?"

Cody shook his head patiently. "This is a boarding-house. Open to the public, just as the saloon is. Such places need more protection than anywhere else."

"This evil?" Dave asked. "Does it have a name?"

Silence fell as Cody met each of their eyes in turn.

"Vampires," he said at last.

CHAPTER SIX

"HERE, HERE, NOW!" Cole roared out above the din in the saloon.

Alex, sitting in the front row, sat back and sighed. Cole was getting irritated, while Cody, standing beside him, remained impassive.

It was just as Cody had expected. Half the town already believed that something evil and beyond anything they had ever thought of as normal was going on.

The other half thought the first half was crazy.

She saw Jim Green, the photographer and undertaker, who had insisted Cody lop the head off the corpse the night before, sitting quietly, as if oblivious to the commotion going on around him. Others, men and women, husbands and wives, friends, associates, and would-be lovers, were all arguing with one another at the tops of their voices.

"I suggest you all shut up and listen," Cody said suddenly. He didn't shout, but his voice rose above the sound of the crowd. "Your lives are at stake."

Silence fell. People stopped speaking and stared at him as if they'd been frozen in place. It would have been comical if the situation hadn't been so dire.

Of course, the whole meeting had been bizarre from the onset. It was taking place in the saloon—the brothel. Most of the women, the "ladies" of the town, were respectfully garbed, many in homespun cotton, their necklines high, shawls around their shoulders against the evening chill. The saloon girls, however, were in their working attire: dance hall dresses, plumed hats and very, *very* low décolletage. One woman—a blonde Alex hadn't met yet, a bit older than the others—was obviously wearing nothing more than a corset and garter belt beneath the velvet robe she had wrapped loosely around herself.

"The Yankees brought this down on us!" someone yelled. "They couldn't beat the Southern boys, so they came up with this instead...."

Cody's look changed to one of such incredulity that the room fell silent again. "The Yankees did not bring this down on us. But since there *is* a war in progress, and Texas is a Southern state, we have to realize that there will be no U.S. troops rushing down to help us, and the Confederacy hasn't a man to spare. But that doesn't matter. Whether you want to believe my words or not, I suggest you listen to what I have to say. Learn how to fight what we're up against. Never invite a stranger into your place—and be careful even when inviting friends in. Beware of changes in people's behavior, and above all, beware of dreams. Loved ones may come to you, trying to coax you out in the open. Don't go. Fortify your houses with garlic and crosses. And remember—"

"Are you saying those bandits are...vampires?" someone interrupted suddenly. Alex looked around the room and saw that it was the blonde in the robe she had noticed before.

"Not all of them, but I believe that, yes, some are. Vampires need the help of the living, because they are weak by day. They draw their strength from darkness and shadows and, of course, the blood of the living," Cody said.

The uproar started all over again.

Cody continued to speak, his voice once again ringing loud and clear above the din. "Bullets will wound them, but not kill them. To destroy this enemy, sever the head, and either impale the heart or cut it out."

"Oh, God!"

Mrs. Madry, a widow who ran a small dress and tailor shop on the main street, cried out—and then swooned.

The men rushed around her.

But not one of them chastised Cody for indelicate speech.

"Lock your houses at night," he went on. "Stay in after dark. Hone stakes and keep them nearby so you're prepared for an attack. You can make stakes out of broom handles, rake handles, anything wooden. Gentlemen, practice your archery. Solid, sharp-tipped arrows well aimed can maim and even kill. Holy water—should you have any—is a premier weapon. It scalds and blisters the vampire's skin. If a known vampire doesn't react, that means he—or she," he added, his experience in New Orleans still fresh in his mind, "hasn't yet crossed the divide. It means he hasn't yet died and returned, and that there is a chance for his salvation."

The blond saloon girl spoke again.

"Is there any such thing as a good vampire?" she asked sweetly.

To Alex's surprise, Cody hesitated. "Not that I've come across," he said at last. "Certainly not Milo and his gang. It's a question I can't really answer, but for now, remember

Brigsby and Hollow Tree. We all have to assume that anyone bearing the taint of vampirism is evil, and out to devour everyone around them." He paused and stared from person to person around the room.

"It's night now, and while you're all welcome to ponder my words, to believe or disbelieve everything I've said, whatever else you do, lock your doors—and prepare to fight."

He nodded to Cole, then walked toward the back of the room, where Brendan was leaning against the wall near the door—as if standing sentinel, ensuring that only those who'd been invited could enter.

"That's it, folks," Cole said. "Either Deputy Hinton or I will be in town at all times. Tomorrow we'll all start practicing our archery and taking shifts patrolling the streets in pairs. I'll have a schedule drawn up by ten."

The blonde stood. "What do you think about this ridiculous theory about vampires, Sheriff?" she asked.

"I think that Cody Fox and Brendan Vincent were the salvation of this town last night, and I'm willing to follow their directions until proved wrong," Cole said.

Alex found her eyes straying to the back of the room and Cody Fox. He was far too lean and rugged-looking to be considered beautiful, she thought. And yet, in her eyes, he was. His beauty was in his stance, his strength of character and his eyes, golden and hypnotic.

Too bad he was crazy.

She looked away.

Vampires?

She remembered peering into the mortuary last night, seeing the head of the dead man.

Still…vampires?

She felt numb. She didn't know what she believed. She herself had been arrested because of her visions. Most people didn't believe in visions any more than they did in vampires.

She wished she could have a vision now. See the future, see…salvation. Or…

Damnation.

Beulah was coming for her, with Bert keeping pace at her side.

"Come on, Miss Alex," the older woman said. "We're going to get inside right now and lock up, just like Cody said to. It may be a boardinghouse—but we're not letting any strangers in tonight, no sirree."

Alex rose to accompany her. At the door they met up with Levy, Jewell, Tess—and Cody and Brendan.

"Come on, all together now," Beulah said firmly.

"Yes, ma'am," Brendan said, grinning and tipping his hat to her.

As they walked, Alex caught Beulah's arm and leaned close to ask, "Who was that, Beulah? The blonde who kept speaking?"

Beulah started. "Oh, child, that's right. You don't know."

"Don't know what? Who is she?"

"That's your step-ma, Alex. Mrs. Linda Gordon. Looks like she made it back into town—and the saloon—just in time for the town meeting."

"THINK IT WAS TOO SOON?" Brendan asked Cody as they sat alone in the dining room. Having secured the boardinghouse for the night, they were sipping Beulah's coffee, laced with good shots of whiskey.

"Probably," Cody said, "but after today… Tall Feather is an Apache, and they believe in a ghost world, but even he didn't know how to prevent that young warrior from coming back to take his daughter. Now he will. Next time the townspeople here will conduct a more organized battle when Milo roars into town. Trouble is, we both know that there may be…folks out there who are tainted. Friends and relatives from those other towns who may be able to infiltrate here. Not everyone believes what I said tonight, but at least those who do will be on the lookout."

Brendan turned away, nodding, and Cody winced. They were here because Brendan hailed from Hollow Tree.

"I'm sorry," Cody said.

Brendan's jaw tightened, but he nodded, and turned back.

"We'll stop it. We'll put an end to it." He shook his head. "I'm not even looking for revenge. I simply want justice, and a return to a world of sanity." He let out a long sigh. "There's been too much insanity. This war… I joined up with the Union because I thought it was the right thing, even though I was from the South. Sorry—I know you're a Reb."

Cody shook his head ruefully. "I'm done with war, that's what I am. I grew up in a city where there were free men of every color, and good and bad doesn't have anything to do with the color of someone's skin. Slavery is wrong, no matter how you look at it. States' rights to make choices, well, that's another issue. It doesn't matter to me, though, because I was telling the truth when I said I'm done with war. I went to Harvard, I'm a doctor. I'd like to get into healing again, rather than killing. But…I guess we have to save folks before we can heal them."

He rose, gave Brendan a squeeze on the shoulder and started for the stairs. He had a feeling that Brendan needed some time alone.

Cody went on up the stairs feeling exhausted. It had been a long day. And a perplexing one. His mother had lived in Victory—or on her property not far from town, anyway—years ago, and then something had happened. She had always called it *the night of the wolves.*

But he knew—or at least he was pretty damned sure— what had happened.

So why had so many years gone by before things had gotten to this point, where whole towns were being attacked and wiped off the map?

As he neared the second landing, he felt a change in the air. Subtle, but there. He hesitated. He might be wrong.

But this wasn't the time to take chances.

He strode down the hall and threw open Alex Gordon's bedroom door.

The French doors to the balcony were open, the curtains billowing inward with the breeze. Alex, clad in a shimmering white nightgown, was standing out on the balcony. The night air lifted the gown so that it danced around her ankles, then fell back to hug her body. Her hair waved softly behind her, glowing in the moonlight.

He went to her as quickly and quietly as he could, then stopped behind her. Just then she lifted her arms, as if embracing the wind or perhaps something she saw within it, whatever power of matter and mind that was calling to her.

He was just in time.

"Alex!" he said sharply.

She didn't even seem to hear him.

He slipped his arms around her, pulling her back. She was compliant, as if she had no strength left, as he lifted her into his arms, then closed the doors carefully, rearranging the strings of garlic around them.

Garlic couldn't keep her inside, and it didn't even work to keep all vampires out, being most effective against the young.

But something told him it was no young vampire coming after Alexandra Gordon, though from what Brendan had told him and what he'd seen the other night, Milo did like to send his underlings to carry out his orders. Especially if he sensed danger to himself.

He carried Alex to her bed and laid her down. Her eyes were open, though still a little glassy. She smiled at him, a beautiful, full-blown, seductive smile. Irresistibly erotic. She squirmed on the bed, arching her back, thrusting her hips.

Her gown was far too thin.

And then she wrapped her arms around him.

Her eyes were open, but she was in a trance of some sort, he thought. Hypnotized, seduced—definitely not awake and conscious and acting of her own free will.

And her arms were still around him.

Tempting, so tempting…

"Alex, go to sleep," he said.

Her arms tightened and she drew him downward. He tried to keep his balance, but as he braced himself, his hand brushed her skin, and then her breast. He was made of flesh and blood, just like any man, and a jolt went through him, wicked lightning, an arousal like nothing he had felt in years…or maybe forever.

He straightened quickly. He was who he was, and he

was on a mission. And if she couldn't accept the truth he told her about others—she was certainly never going to understand who he was.

What he was.

Swallowing hard, clenching his jaw, he straightened. "Alex, you need to sleep. I'll be right next door to keep you safe."

He made it to the foot of the bed, then paused, looking down at her. Her eyes had closed. The strength of his will had penetrated her mind. In this, at least, he was more powerful than Milo.

He couldn't help but linger for a moment. She looked like a princess from some fairy tale, caught in the pale moonlight that sifted through the fabric of the drapes. Her hair was strewn about the pillow, and though her expression was angelic, her body, every curve outlined by the delicate white fabric of her nightgown, was anything but.

He turned away and opened the connecting door to his own room. After a long last look, he stepped through and lay down, fully clothed, on his own mattress. When at last he slept, it was only lightly. True, he needed rest.

But he needed to listen more.

Alex believed that she was strong. And she *was* a fighter, beyond a doubt. She just didn't yet know how to fight a battle that had been begun without her knowledge against an enemy she didn't even believe in.

ALEX AWOKE WITH THE oddest feeling. As if she had been…active during the night.

Active?

She sat up, looking around the room.

The garlic strands were in place, the curtains hanging

undisturbed. The French doors were closed—but then, she had seen to it herself that they were closed and locked.

She rose, stretched, and then noticed her feet.

They had been clean when she'd gone to bed. And now...

She lifted her right foot. It wasn't filthy—not as if she had been walking out in the garden. But there was dirt on it, and she never went to bed with dirt on her feet, because—she hated to get it on her sheets.

A sense of dread filled her, along with a full body blush as someone knocked on the connecting door to the next room.

Someone?

It could only be one person.

She dived toward the trunk at the foot of her bed and the dressing gown that lay there. She slipped the gown around her shoulders just as he called out to her, his voice holding an edge of anxiety.

"Alex?"

"Yes?"

She smoothed her hair back as the door opened and stared at him, wondering just what had gone on during the night.

Her dream *hadn't* been a dream. It had been a vision. But visions were always of what *might* be. They were a warning, and the future could still be changed.

Had it changed?

"We have to talk," he told her gently.

"Oh?"

He took a seat at her dressing table, staring at her. "I'm truly sorry if I was harsh with you yesterday. I was frightened."

"You? Frightened? I don't believe you. I don't believe you're *ever* frightened," she said.

He smiled. "Am I afraid of death? Not particularly, though I do love living. And am I afraid of facing my enemies? No, because an enemy must always be faced or the battle is lost before it begins. But I can be afraid, I assure you."

She was still for a moment, and then nodded. "All right, apology accepted. I suppose I might have been a bit hostile in return."

"A bit."

She lowered her eyes but allowed herself a careful smile as she sat at the foot of the bed to face him.

"Do you know what happened last night?" he asked her gravely.

She felt as if her stomach were falling to the floor.

Oh, dear God, no!

She looked up at him with dread. He was waiting for her to speak. "I—I might have an idea. I—" She broke off, wincing. "I sometimes…have visions of…things that will happen, *might* happen. I was arrested once because of them. Although, I met President Lincoln because of that, and he's a wonderful man. I feel so sorry for his wife, though. She's—"

"Alex," he interrupted softly.

She blushed and stopped talking. She didn't normally babble, but she certainly was babbling now. She forced herself back on topic.

"I have an idea, and it has something to do with what you were saying at the town meeting. I confess, I'm not sure I believed you then, or maybe even now, and I don't remember anything that happened last night after I went to bed. But the vision I had before…it was beautiful. The night was so perfect. I got up and went out on the balcony, as if someone had entered my mind the way you said…*they* could, and even though all I was doing was standing there, I felt as if I were being caressed, as if I were somehow being…I don't know, cradled, cared for…I can't really explain." She paused and saw that he was watching her gravely. She couldn't tell if he believed her, but at least he wasn't mocking her.

"Then you were there," she said. "You drew me back into the bedroom, and you told me to go to sleep."

"You can't let him into your dreams, or your conscious mind, either," he said.

"I…never meant to. And by him…you mean Milo?"

"Yes, that's who I believe is behind all of this."

She let out another breath, looking downward once again. "So you…saved me from him last night?"

"Yes," he said calmly.

"Thank you."

"My pleasure. Truly."

The intensity with which he said it scared her a little. She looked up at him again quickly and cleared her throat.

"You, um, brought me in and told me to go to sleep, right? And…I did."

The slow grin that teased his lips was genuinely charming, and yet it made her want to smack him. She realized immediately that he wasn't going to give her a straight answer.

He wanted to see her squirm a bit.

Surely that meant that everything that had happened was innocent, didn't it?

"Yes, you slept," he said. "After the incident, of course."

"I mean, I didn't…you didn't…"

"Didn't what?" he asked innocently, but then he turned serious. "Here's the thing that you need to think about, and I hope it scares you, because it should. He was out there somewhere. His power was working. You were his for the taking. You would have done anything he told you to do. Anything. The only reason you are still here and still *you* is because I found you and brought you back inside before he could take full control of you."

Alex crossed her arms defensively over her chest. "I understand. And I *am* afraid. I need…I need you to teach me how to be strong."

"You already know how," he said. "You're already strong, and now that you've seen and you believe, your mind will take over and fight. You'll be all right. And I'll be here to make sure of it."

She blushed again, looking away. "But—"

He rose, cutting her off. "I'll let you get dressed. I'm afraid it's going to be another long day."

He started for the connecting door. He was already dressed—down to the gun belt riding low on his hips and the railroad duster that discreetly held a variety of weapons.

And he was smirking.

"Bastard," she told him.

His smile broadened, and he left her.

BEULAH HAD SET UP BREAKFAST in the kitchen, and everyone sat down to eat together. The meal started off grimly, with everyone focused on the dangers they had escaped in the night and those that were yet to come.

But Jewell and Tess were too full of life to stay depressed for long, and they quickly grew flirtatious and silly. Beulah looked on like a proud mother, Bert shook his head in wonder at the craziness, and even Levy smiled now and then.

Poor Levy, Cody thought. He still looked like a haunted man.

At one point Cody glanced over and met the stable man's eyes.

"You doing okay?" he asked.

Levy nodded and straightened his shoulders. "I'm going to practice my archery today. I never was much of a shot with a gun, but when I was a boy, we actually hunted with bows and arrows. I was decent as a child, and now I'm going to learn to aim true."

"Good for you," Cody said. "I'm sure you'll do fine."

He smiled at Levy, who trembled slightly but managed to smile back.

It was while they were all sipping the last of their coffee that the knock came at the front door.

Every one of them froze, and Cody thought they were all a lot more spooked than he had imagined.

"I'll go," he said.

He strode down the hallway, looking through the glass pane in the top of the door before opening it.

"Dave," Cody said. "Come on in. We're just finishing our coffee."

"Can't come in, Cody," Dave said. "Sheriff Granger needs you over at the jail."

"You've got someone in jail?" Cody asked.

Dave shook his head. "Sorry, I mean the office. No one in jail. Not even the usual drunks. But Dolores Simpson is there, with her husband, and she's acting weird, and he's upset, and…well, you've got to come. I just don't know how to tell this story."

"Just give me a minute to tell the others where I'm going," Cody said, and turned to walk back to the kitchen, then stopped short. The others had followed him en masse and were hovering just a few feet away.

"Brendan, would you come with me? Everyone else, please go about your lives normally. Just be careful who you let into the boardinghouse, and make sure you're inside by sunset." He stared at Alex, who blushed prettily, but nodded.

"Who is Dolores Simpson?" Cody asked as he and Brendan accompanied Dave down the street.

"She and her husband, Bill, have one of the larger farms, just a few miles outside town. They've taken in orphaned children for years, not to mention they've had just about a litter of their own. One of their daughters died recently—consumption, we're pretty sure. She didn't come out once her folks decided they knew what was ailing her."

They had reached the door of the sheriff's office, and Cody stopped and looked meaningfully at Brendan.

Brendan arched an eyebrow and asked Dave, "How long ago was this?"

"A month back, maybe. They're still mourning, that's for sure. Anyway, Cole thinks you've got to hear the Simpsons out. He seems to think it's mighty important."

They entered the office. A thin woman was sitting in the chair next to Cole's desk, a handkerchief in her hands. It was evident that she had been crying. She was probably about forty, and once she had been very pretty. Her hair was streaked with white, but rather than detracting from her appearance, it only seemed to add to her character. Cody thought she had the look of a gentle soul who had lived a life of hard work, only to reach a place of terrible sadness. A man who had to be her husband, Bill, was perched on the edge of Dave's desk, across the room. He, too, was thin. He had a bulldog face, pleasant, worn and, now, concerned.

"Ah, Cody, Brendan," Cole said, rising. "I'd like you to meet the Simpsons, Dolores and Bill. Bill caught Dolores out on their front porch last night. When he asked her what she was doing there, since everyone had been told to stay inside at night, she said she had gone out because Amy, their daughter—who passed away recently—was calling to her."

Cody shook Bill Simpson's hand, then hunkered down by Dolores.

She looked at him with tear-reddened eyes.

"They think I'm crazy, but I'm not. I heard her calling to me."

Cody took her hands. "Mrs. Simpson, lots of folks think *I'm* crazy, too, but I'm not. And you have to listen to me. I warned you last night that you might hear loved ones calling to you, didn't I?" When she nodded, he went on. "If it happens again, you mustn't listen."

"Our daughter is dead," Bill Simpson said harshly. "Our beautiful daughter is dead. And that's that."

Dolores started to cry again. "You don't understand. It was Amy, and Amy is *not* evil. By the grace of God, Amy is out there somewhere, and I have to find her and let her in. Maybe she's cold and lonely, afraid. Maybe the evil men are after her."

Cody stood. "Mr. Simpson, I'm a medical doctor. I'd

like to give your wife a small dose of laudanum. She needs some rest, to sleep long and deeply."

"Thank you," Bill Simpson said gratefully.

"I'll get your bag from the boardinghouse," Brendan said.

Cody nodded his thanks to Brendan, then knelt down by Dolores again. Instead of trying to convince her that she was mistaken about Amy, he asked her about her other children. They had two boys and two girls of their own, and four more they'd adopted after most of the travelers on a wagon train died of smallpox.

Brendan returned with the bag, and Cody gave Bill a small bottle of laudanum and instructions for dispensing it.

Bill thanked him, then said, "Come on, Dolores. We have to get home. And you need to think about the other children. They need us, and our strength, right now, too. All right, dear?"

Dolores looked at him vaguely. "I'm so tired, Bill."

"I know. But Dr. Fox here has given us something so you can get to sleep."

Dolores looked over at Cody. "You're very kind."

"And you're going to be fine," he assured her.

Bill Simpson took his wife's arm and led her to the door, while Cody warned him that the laudanum was just to help her through this troubled time, and that he should watch for signs of growing dependence on the drug.

When the door closed behind them, Cody turned to the sheriff.

"Where is Amy buried?" he asked.

"In the cemetery just yonder, of course," Cole told him, then frowned. "Why?"

"Because we're going to dig her up," Cody said.

"What?" Cole demanded, shocked.

"Don't worry. It should be easy. I'm willing to wager that the ground will be soft—and that her coffin will already have been opened."

CHAPTER SEVEN

FEELING AT A LOSS as she wandered the boardinghouse, Alex decided this was a fine time to indulge in a long, hot bath in the kitchen tub. Beulah was a wonderful watchdog, keeping the room clear of anyone else, and Alex was so delighted to have the time to indulge that she delighted in the soap and shampoo until her skin pruned.

But after her bath she grew restless again. Cody hadn't come back, though Beulah said that Brendan had come by for his medical bag, assuring her it was for a minor situation, and that they had everything under control.

Alex helped with household chores for a little while, then wandered into the parlor and sat down at the piano.

She thought about the times she had come here and played for her father. Even as a child, she'd been gifted, or so her father had said. She'd never parlayed her talent into a performing career, but she *had* discovered that she loved to teach, and had done her best to infuse her own love of music into children, and even the occasional adult, she had taken on as students in D.C.

But as much as she loved playing, and as passionate as she usually felt about music, today her études and sonatas fell flat on her ears. She switched to battle songs, and let her pent-up energy and anger run through her fingers onto the keys. When she at last grew weary and restless, she turned to see that the household had gathered behind her to listen. Only Levy was absent.

Her little audience clapped for her—just as they had done whenever her father had dragged them in to listen to her.

She stood, thanking them. "Where's Levy?" she asked.

"Target practice," Beulah said, then gave Bert's shoulder a swat with her dust cloth. "Let's get back to work. Soon enough Victory is going to be booming again, and we need to be ready."

As they left, Alex smiled. She wasn't sure that Victory, Texas, had ever actually "boomed."

Beulah might have been a mind reader. She suddenly stuck her head back inside the room and said, "You mark my words—that war will end, and displaced people will be heading West. Victory is destined to boom—if we can just keep it alive long enough."

After Beulah disappeared, Alex ran her fingers over the keys again and then rose. She couldn't stand being housebound. She had no intention of behaving foolishly, but it was broad daylight, and she couldn't bear the thought of being locked away from the sun. And not even Cody had suggested that everyone stay locked up by day.

She wondered what was going on down at the jail that was still keeping him busy.

Just as she started from the room, Bert came in. "Someone to see you, Miss Alex."

"Oh?"

"An old friend."

She walked out to the entry, and there, standing straight and unwavering, not a glimmer of expression in his eyes to give away the reason for his visit, was Chief Tall Feather. Behind him stood two of his warriors.

"Chief Tall Feather," she said welcomingly, then walked over to him, and, despite the fact that he was standing so stiffly, she hugged him, just as she'd done since the first time she'd met him as a child.

She felt him soften as he held her briefly in return, before drawing away.

"What are you doing here?" she asked, looking past him to smile at his companions. "I thought you hated coming into town?"

"I had to see you," he said.

"Well, you're always welcome. What can I get you? I know you like coffee, and Beulah made some wonderful muffins this morning."

She saw one of the young warriors cast a hopeful glance, quickly concealed, in Tall Feather's direction. She took the chief's arm. "Please, come on back to the kitchen."

He went with her, saying something to his companions in swift Apache that Alex couldn't follow, but they, too, headed for the kitchen.

To Beulah's delight, they made swift work of the muffins. Then Tall Feather spoke to the warriors again, and they nodded gravely and went out to the front porch, apparently intending to stand sentinel until Tall Feather was ready to leave.

Alex led Tall Feather to the parlor so they could discuss the reason for his visit in private. There, seated in comfortable brocade chairs, the coffee service on a small table between them, Tall Feather at last seemed to relax.

"I'm delighted to see you here," Alex said. "My father

valued your friendship, and you've always been like an uncle to me."

The chief let out a sigh. "I know there are those who claim that I or my men killed him, or perhaps a band of rogue Apache, but I have come to tell you that we loved him. We called him Thinking Owl, and we would never have done harm to your father."

She set a hand on his. "I know that. I never believed such tales. And now, I'm afraid, we know what kind of monster *did* kill my father."

Tall Feather looked away for a moment, and though he rarely betrayed emotion, she could tell that something was hurting him almost unbearably now.

"I have lost both a child and the fine warrior who loved her," he said.

"I'm so sorry."

He met her eyes then, his expression intense. "You must never go out at night," he said. "And you must believe what Cody Fox tells you. I have seen, and I know."

She nodded. "I'll be very careful. I swear."

"Good. Then I will leave you. I look forward to the time when you will come to us again. Head Woman is anxious to see you, as are all who know you."

"Soon," she promised him.

He rose, and she followed suit. As they walked to the front door, she asked him, "Have you seen John Snow and his family recently? I know the sheriff went out to his place, but so much was happening here that I never got the chance to ask if everything was all right."

"I haven't been there, but John Snow is no fool. Still, perhaps he needs to be warned of the danger. Talk to your new friends. Perhaps they should visit him."

"I'll do that, Tall Feather. I promise."

He left, and after she watched him and his warriors disappear down Main Street, she realized she could no longer stand to stay in the house.

It was time to get to know her stepmother.

THE CEMETERY WASN'T EVEN a mile from the town, inland from the river on high ground, and it rarely saw any excitement.

But when they arrived later that morning, it was obvious that something had been going on.

Staring at the cemetery with its poor wooden crosses and the scrub that passed for ornamentation, Cody felt a sense of dismay. Several graves looked as if they had been dug up again mere hours ago. And Amy Simpson's was one.

"Cody, over here."

Cody turned to see what Brendan was referring to and saw the scattered remains of a half-dozen small animals.

Some had been…gnawed down to the bone. Others were freshly decaying.

"What is it?" Cole asked, coming forward to join them.

"Milo is being…selective," Cody said, indicating the disturbed graves. "Bringing those he chooses into his fold, allowing them to join the band, if you will. When his chosen few awaken here, they do so with a hunger that burns inside them so fiercely that they can't stand it, but they don't know how to hunt. They have to learn. They might have devoured any innocent soul walking out here at night, but luckily, that hasn't happened—yet. When the dead awaken, they're disoriented. They start feeding on small animals, but they're afraid, so they either stay close to their graves or go looking for where they used to live. Evidently Amy has been wandering home, crying out for her mother. She was a child when she was taken, so she believes her mother can help her."

"Lord," Cole said softly. "Amy was a beautiful little girl. Sweet as sunshine. It broke her folks' hearts when she died. So how…how did he get to her?" he asked.

"I don't know. When we're done here, Brendan and I will pay a call on the Simpsons and see what we can find out," Cody said.

"Well, then, let's get started," Brendan suggested.

"Yes," Cody said. "Looks like we've got five of these things to deal with, so let's each take one and get this over with. I want to finish this business while the sun is high."

The disturbed graves were scattered, so Brendan headed to the west side of the cemetery, Cody to the south, and Dave and Cole toward the center.

Cody started digging. As he had expected, the earth was soft, and it wasn't difficult getting down to the coffin. He lifted the lid, which wasn't difficult, either. The seals had already been broken.

He found himself staring down at the face of an elderly man. He looked as if he had just died, and been laid out for his viewing. Cody could see why people had assumed the man had died of natural causes; he must have been over ninety. The rudimentary etching on the stone at the head of his grave read "Arthur Connelly, Revolutionary War, a True Hero."

At least the man had lived a long life after having fought for his country's independence, Cody thought as he reached for his stake and hammer.

Now the man would have his soul returned, as well.

He drove the stake into the man's heart. Arthur Connelly's eyes opened for a split second but never even had a chance to focus. The creature didn't cry out, only closed his eyes and began to decay.

Cody felt numb as he leaped out of the grave and closed the coffin.

"Cody!"

Brendan's voice wasn't loud, but it still managed to sound urgent.

Cody stared in the direction Brendan indicated. Cole Granger had finished digging out Amy's grave and opening her coffin, but he clearly hadn't been prepared for what he had to do.

The sheriff was down in the dark earth with Amy and had taken the little girl into his arms.

Cody looked up to the sky. Old vampires could function in sunlight, though they weren't at their most powerful and were far more vulnerable than in the dark. But they could still rip out the throat of an unwary soul. Amy was a new vampire, but she had been made by one of the most powerful vampires Cody had encountered to date, so…

"Cole!" Cody shouted, and raced across the graveyard.

"She's so precious," Cole said, holding her as if to defend her from Cody. "Couldn't there have been a mistake? Maybe…she was buried alive and somehow managed to crawl her way out. Maybe—"

"Cole!" Cody yelled again.

Amy had awakened. Blue eyes instantly took on a burning red cast, and a look of vicious pleasure curved her lips. She started to draw them back, revealing her fangs.

Cody leaped down into the grave, ripping the girl from Cole's arms. Then he threw her down, pinning her with his foot, realizing suddenly that his stake and hammer were at the other grave. The girl thrashed with surprising power beneath him.

"Cody!"

He turned. Brendan was hurling a stake in his direction. Cody caught it and slammed it into the girl's chest with all his might.

Little Amy Simpson went still at last.

Cole stared down at her with horror, then turned to Cody, his eyes wide with horror. "Sweet Jesus, this is all for real."

Cody gripped the sheriff by the shoulders. "You're a good man, Cole. You don't want to see evil in what was once innocent, but this is turning into an epidemic. You can't let them trick you, can't let your heart take over from your mind. This is going to be hard on you, because—you know all these people. But God help me, Sheriff, I don't want to be staking you, but if I have to? I won't hesitate." He met Cole's eyes and held the stare until the other man stiffened. "This can't happen again."

Cole stared back at him, green eyes flashing. "It won't. I'm the sheriff, and I know my business, but you'll have to forgive me for finding it hard to stake a child in the heart. You may have nothing but ice in your veins, but that was a child I knew."

Cody nodded. Cole Granger was as tightly wound as a piano wire, and his jaw was locked hard.

It was like the first time the friend next to you on a battle line was suddenly blown to bits, Cody thought. You'd have to be made of stone to take it in stride.

Cole bent down and severed Amy's head. Proving his point, Cody thought, and looked down at his boots, wincing. He shouldn't have allowed Cole to be the one to dig up Amy's grave.

No, maybe it was better this way. Now Cole would be prepared for anything. And anything just might come their way.

"Oh, hell!" Dave suddenly cried out.

He was standing by the last of the disturbed graves and looking over at them with his face a sickly shade of green.

"What is it?" Cole demanded, leaping out of Amy's grave and rushing toward his deputy, though he looked as if he'd been run over by an entire wagon train himself.

Dave didn't answer, so Cody walked over to join the two men.

The customary wooden cross had been erected over the grave, along with a stone marker—in this case a large rock, probably dredged up from the river—with crude writing on it.

Cody looked down at the grave marker, and his heart sank when he saw the name scratched on the stone.

Eugene Alexander Gordon.

And below that:

Beloved Father, Best Friend and Philosopher
Dearly Missed, But God and His Angels
Shall Shelter Such a Man

Cody nodded. "Let's hurry this up and get things over with."

They worked together to quickly widen the hole, and then Cody jumped down to stand beside the coffin.

The seal was broken, as he'd expected.

He threw open the lid and was hit by an almost physical wave of shock.

The coffin was empty.

ALEX DIDN'T EVEN CONSIDER telling Beulah where she was going. The other woman wouldn't have been happy about her visiting the saloon, stepmother or not.

It was past midday, but as she entered the room and waited for her eyes to adjust to the dim light, it seemed to her that both the dining area and bar were empty, very strange for that time of day. Jigs was not at the piano, and none of the girls were around.

Suddenly a head popped up from behind the bar. It belonged to Roscoe Sheen, the bartender. He had been there for as long as she could remember.

Except that he hadn't been around the other night.

"Roscoe," Alex said, trying to cover the fear that had jolted through her at his abrupt appearance.

"Why, Miss Alex. I heard you'd come home. Welcome home." Roscoe was old, tawny-colored and strong. She was pretty sure that he was a mix of every race known to man. He had a broad smile and kind eyes, and he worked the bar so Gerald Sweeney, who owned the place, could spend his time "auditioning" the girls.

Roscoe came out from around the bar and shook her hand, but she stepped back as soon as she could. "Good to see you, Roscoe. I've been in here twice since I got back, but I hadn't seen you yet."

He didn't blush or look away. "I wasn't here the night the outlaws came. I was out at my daughter's farm for a few days. Just got back in town this afternoon." He scuffed his shoe along the floor. "I heard about the town meeting, and I have to say, all this talk of vampires sounds plumb crazy to me. But I'm fond of living and willing to do whatever it takes to keep this place afloat, on account of I'm hoping to buy it from Sweeney one of these days." He rolled up one of his sleeves. "As glad as I am to see you, Alex, I don't think you came over here to have a chat with me. What's up?"

"I heard my father's widow works here," she said.

Roscoe's smile froze in place. "Linda."

"Right. And I'd very much like to meet her."

"Hey, honey! Good to see you," someone called from the upstairs railing. Alex looked up as Sherry Lyn, the tall brunette who had been there for years, waved down to her.

Sherry Lyn had evidently just woken up. She was in short silk pajamas that revealed the shapely length of her legs and had thrown a feathery robe around her shoulders. Clearly she didn't much care who saw what part of her anatomy.

"Hi, Sherry Lyn," she said.

"What are *you* doing here?" the other woman asked.

"She came to meet Linda," Roscoe answered for her.

"That makes sense," Sherry Lyn said, still staring down at Alex.

"Is she here? I saw her last night, but I didn't find out who she was till after we'd left."

"I think she's around," Sherry Lyn said, shrugging. "I don't rightly know for sure. We've all taken to locking our doors after…after our gentlemen callers have left," she said. "Come on up. I'll show you to Linda's room."

"Thank you," Alex said. She had been in the saloon several times before, but she'd never climbed the stairs to the quarters where the fancy ladies conducted their business, and she felt awkward and just a little bit excited to be doing so now.

"Come on, sugar," Sherry Lyn said, smiling broadly, and for a moment it was as if she'd become a young and mischievous girl once again. "We don't bite, Alex, you know that." She frowned. "Sorry. Bad choice of words."

Alex shook her head and smiled, wondering why, if her father had to fall in love with one of the girls at the saloon, it couldn't have been Sherry Lyn. The brunette had a gentle soul. She'd once used her savings to help out a young man from a nearby ranch, and people had speculated that they might marry.

But Alex had heard that he'd gone off to war and hadn't come back. Not even in a box. His remains were lying somewhere in Northern Virginia.

Sherry Lyn shivered when Alex reached her. "Vampires... Do you really think Milo is a vampire? I mean, trust me, honey, you don't need to be a vampire to be a monster. I've met my share of folks through the years, and I've known some real monsters who were pure human."

"I believe you," Alex told her.

"Right there, honey. That's Linda's door," Sherry Lyn said, then knocked loudly on it.

A voice responded imperiously, "Yes? What is it?"

"Visitor for you, Linda," Sherry Lyn said.

"I don't receive visitors at this time of day," Linda called back.

"It's your stepdaughter," Sherry Lyn said dryly.

A second passed, and then the door flew open. Linda ignored Sherry Lyn and stared at Alex, then smiled slowly.

"I'll leave you two to get acquainted," Sherry Lyn said.

Alex murmured a thank-you as the other woman walked away with a swish of silk.

Linda was attractive, she had to admit. Older, like Sherry Lyn, but tall, shapely, and with a handsome, character-filled face. Alex wasn't certain that Linda would ever be considered beautiful, but, beyond a doubt, she was interesting.

"So you're Eugene's daughter, come home from the big city," Linda said, standing in the door of her darkened room, the only light sifting past the edges of the heavy damask drapes. Like Sherry Lyn, she was dressed in a robe, hers decorated with pink-dyed plumage, and very little else. She didn't seem the least bit embarrassed about her skimpy attire, either, as she flung out an arm dramatically and said, "Come on in, have a seat."

The only possibilities were Linda's bed—quite rumpled—and the chair sitting in front of her dressing table.

Alex chose the chair.

"I'm sorry. I didn't mean to impose, or to arrive too early," Alex said.

Linda sat on the bed. "I've always been a late riser—always. I've hated mornings for as long as I can remember. But then, my mother was a whore. I was born in a whorehouse just outside of Dallas, and I've always kept whores' hours. I managed to get some education because my father was in the city government, and paying my mother kept her from telling his wife about me."

"I see," Alex said.

"Oh, I doubt if you see anything at all—no offense." She looked up at the ceiling for a moment. "Your father was quite a man. I can only imagine what it was like, growing up as his child, in a world filled with respect."

"Did you love my father?" Alex asked, deciding that the other woman's bluntness gave her carte blanche to be equally blunt.

"Did I love Eugene?" Linda repeated. "Yes. Does that make you happy? I mean, you can hardly be angry that he married. He left an ironclad will. The house is yours. His effects are yours. He did leave me a little money, though. He wanted me to choose a different lifestyle," she said with a sad smile.

"Did he not leave you enough?" Alex asked. "He left me the boardinghouse, but surely you know, as he would have, that I'd be happy if you made it your home."

Linda laughed, but not unpleasantly. She actually reached out and stroked Alex's face. "You truly are his child. So earnest and compassionate. Alexandra, your father left me enough money to make a choice, and I've made my choice. While he was alive and we were together, I did my best to live the life your father chose. But he's gone now, and though you may not understand it, I like this life, Alex. I like men. While your father was alive, I was content with him. But I have no intention of being an upright and lonely widow, trying to fit in with the so-called decent folk, all the while knowing they're talking about me behind my back."

"Linda, I would never let anyone—"

Linda burst into laughter, then sobered quickly. "I'm so sorry—I know you mean well. And I see that you are outraged by injustice, just like your father. Thing is, I'm reckoning the North will win this war and laws will change, but not people. It takes decades for people to change. And you know what? They may accept white, black, any religion, Northerner, Southerner—but the world is never going to accept whores into the ranks of decent folks. My time with your father was good, but it's over and I've made my choice. But I thank you, and I'm glad to have met you."

Alex stood up. "I'm glad to have met you, too. And if I can ever do anything..."

"Thank you, but you go on now. This isn't a fit place for you to be."

"Just remember that you're welcome at the boarding-house anytime."

Linda nodded, and Alex decided she had gone as far as she could go. She hadn't much liked the woman the night before, but now she was far more impressed. And happy. At least she felt that her father had enjoyed Linda's com-panionship—and, though she certainly didn't want to dwell on it, Linda's sensuality—during his last days.

But how the hell had he died?

The door to the boardinghouse was locked when she got back, but she had brought her key and let herself in.

The house was quiet. She could hear the old grandfa-ther clock in the parlor ticking away the time, but nothing else.

"Beulah? Bert?" she called as she made her way to the back of the house and into the kitchen.

"Oh!" she exclaimed.

The bathtub was occupied once again.

Cody Fox was staring at her. His head leaned easily back against the wooden rim, and his knees were bent, allowing his long frame to fit within the confines of the tub.

The heat of the water created a rising mist of steam around him.

His flesh was deeply bronzed and sleek. Moisture shone on the muscled contours of his chest and arms.

She should have apologized for her error, and backed away, but she didn't. Couldn't. She simply stood there, staring, her mouth frozen in an O.

He stared at her, then smiled slowly and said, "I gather you're enjoying the view. In any case, this is your house, after all, so please do come on in. Don't mind me."

She knew he expected her to blush and go running. Well, it wasn't going to happen. Something about his superior tone really irritated her. He'd enjoyed taunting her this morning, making her wonder just exactly what had occurred during the night, and now it was her turn to make him sweat.

She wasn't easily cowed. After all, she had just paid a visit to the whorehouse.

She shut her mouth and sauntered on in, taking a glass from the cabinet and setting it down while she primed the pump over the sink. "Mr. Fox, I hope you'll excuse me for saying so, but you do seem fond of flattering yourself. I can't say I'm all that interested in your…natural state."

She filled her glass and turned casually, leaning back against the counter and staring at him with casual disinterest. "I trust you had a good day?"

His smile seemed sad for a moment. "I believe we're moving in the right direction, yes."

She grew serious herself, frowning. "How do we make a move in the right direction? Help will never come from anywhere else. And Milo Roundtree and his group of…of vampires will be back, won't they?"

"Yes, eventually, they will."

"So how on earth do we ever stop them?" she asked.

"Perhaps, my dear Miss Gordon, you'd be kind enough to pass me a towel," Cody said.

She saw the towel Beulah had apparently left for him, lying on the table. She reached for it and handed it to him, trying not to look down and to keep her gaze casual.

She wished that her heart weren't beating quite so hard. Or that she didn't feel so tempted not only to look at him but to touch the sleekness of his skin.

Honestly, it was his eyes, she thought, that she'd first found so arresting. And then, of course, the lean contours of his face, the strength of his jaw. And she found his grin charming, despite herself. Not to mention that he was strong and brave and had twice saved her life.

His muscles rippled as he rose, discreetly wrapping the towel around his waist as he did so.

She was unsurprised to see that her assessment had been completely correct. He was a handsome man, deeply tanned, tall and ruggedly muscled.

And she was standing too close.

Far too close.

Not to mention that she slept far too near him...

Suddenly she was overwhelmed by longing. She wanted to be held by him, and she wanted...more.

But just what "more" consisted of, she wasn't sure. She barely knew him, and yet she had never met anyone— even her fiancé—who fascinated and compelled her more.

"Excuse me," she said, her tone as dignified as she could make it. "Please excuse my intrusion. I'll leave you alone to dress."

With those words, she mustered her pride and departed

at last. As she walked out, she was afraid that she would hear him laughing at her.

She was relieved when she didn't.

And somehow she knew that he watched her until she shut the door and he couldn't see her anymore.

CHAPTER EIGHT

THAT NIGHT, Sheriff Cole Granger and Deputy Dave Hinton joined them for supper. Alex noticed that Cole was having a hard time meeting her eyes, but she attributed it to the stress everyone was under and turned her own attention to Beulah's delicious cooking.

It was interesting, Alex had to admit. Men had a tendency to band together based on their vocations: ranchers with ranchers, farmers with farmers. And they customarily maintained a certain ego-based distance, as well. Most men, whether in small towns or big cities, liked to swagger. Unless they were shy and made every effort to blend into the background.

And those men, she thought, could sometimes be far more dangerous than the swaggering kind.

Maybe it was the fact that all four men were joined together by their pursuit of Milo and his bloodthirsty gang—she almost smiled at her own choice of words—but they seemed to have formed an easy camaraderie, which she had to admit was nice. As they ate, Cole asked Cody about his past, which he ran through in an oddly cut-and-dried manner. His folks had owned land out this way, he said, but his father had been killed many years ago, and his mother had returned to her home in New Orleans. He'd grown up there, then gone on to Harvard. He'd found work in the capital and then in Northern Virginia, until war had broken out and he'd joined up with a Louisiana unit. Wounded and discharged, he'd been practicing medicine in New Orleans before he'd come west.

Brendan Vincent sat forward. "I actually went to New Orleans to find Cody. I'd heard word that he'd faced a killer like Milo before, and I needed his help out here."

"And how did you know there was trouble in Victory?" Cole Granger asked.

"I had family once in Hollow Tree," Brendan said. "A while back, they wrote to me about strange goings-on out this way. Then I met a soldier in New Orleans who had been through these parts, and he told me Victory was the only town still hanging on, that Brigsby and Hollow Tree were ghost towns."

Alex hesitated, then asked, "Trouble? Did other people tell you about the vampires?" she asked.

Cody looked at her. "No one believes in vampires— until they become one, or are killed by one and there's no coming back."

"Enough of this," Dave said suddenly. "We've still got to live like civilized people, and in my book that means no talking about murder at the dinner table, all right?" When no one challenged him, he went on. "Miss Alex, you've got to play for these folks. You never heard anything like her," he added to Cody and Brendan.

Alex laughed. "If we're being civilized, you gentlemen are supposed to move into my father's library for brandy and cigars."

"We'd rather hear you play," Cole told her.

"Perhaps Mr. Vincent or Mr. Fox would like a brandy

and a cigar, and then I could help Beulah clean up after dinner," Alex suggested, suddenly feeling self-conscious and trying to get out of playing.

"A cigar over the company of a beautiful young woman?" Brendan asked, smiling. He reminded her of her father, though he was younger, maybe because he'd been regarding her sympathetically all evening. He was dignity made flesh, his voice gentle and kind. She knew he had been an officer, and she imagined he had commanded the respect of his men.

"You folks go on," Beulah said. "Bert and I can get this place picked up neat as a pin faster without none of you trying to help."

"So you play the piano?" Cody asked Alex.

"A bit," she admitted reluctantly.

As they moved to the parlor, she finally remembered to ask Cole, "Is John Snow all right?"

The sheriff nodded grimly. "He was missing livestock, and his oldest son—who has children of his own now—was worried about *his* eldest son. But the boy seemed fine when I was there. Thing is, now we have to get word to him, let him know what's happening. I should have had someone on that today, but things in town were—well, let's just say the day was full. It's important that we be prepared here first, then we can help others."

"Brendan and I will go first thing in the morning," Cody said.

"Enough of that kind of talk. Play something for us, Alex," Dave said.

"What would you like to hear?" she asked, wondering why Dave kept trying so hard to force the conversation away from their situation.

"Anything but a funeral dirge," he said.

She sat at the piano and played a Chopin prelude, followed by a reel.

"We ought to be dancing," Dave said.

"Hard to dance when the only woman in the room is at the piano," Cole pointed out.

To Alex's surprise, Cody suddenly smiled broadly and said, "That's because you never served under the right commander during a long campaign. Brigadier General Vincent, sir, may I have this dance?"

"Indeed, soldier. At ease," Vincent replied, grinning back. Then the two men began to whirl around the room, much to the delight of Dave and Cole. Beulah slipped her head in to see what was going on, and before she could retreat, Cole had pulled her into his arms for a dance.

Dave suddenly slipped onto the bench next to Alex. "Go rescue one of the men, Miss Alex. My playing isn't as good as yours, but I can still manage a reel."

She allowed him to take her place and rescued Brendan Vincent. She danced with him for a bit, swapped with Beulah and danced with Cole, and then found herself with Cody.

She was both exhilarated and afraid.

It was just dancing, she told herself. But there was something different about dancing with Cody.

He held her the same way Brendan and Cole had held her, but she could *feel* the way Cody held her, and when she looked into his eyes, something about the golden fire she saw there seemed to steal her breath away far more effectively than the speed of the reel.

At last Brendan cried, "Mercy!"

Dave stopped playing. "Thank God you caved in first,

sir. My fingers couldn't have gone on much longer. I'm not much of a musician, as you could probably tell."

"Why, Deputy," Brendan protested. "That was absolutely fine, and deeply appreciated. Though Cody may do as a partner in a pinch, Beulah and Miss Alex made far finer companions on the floor—no offense, Cody."

"None taken," Cody assured him.

"Well, ladies and gentlemen, that was quite enough exercise for this old gent," Brendan said. "If you'll excuse me, I'm off to bed. Cody?"

"I'll be seeing to the house," Cody assured him.

Brendan nodded and went upstairs, and Cole and Dave announced that it was time they headed out.

"Why don't you go on upstairs?" Cody suggested to Alex. "I'll see them out and lock up."

"Thank you," she said. A few minutes later, as she stood in the privacy of her room, she could hear him walking around below, checking the windows and doors.

She slid into her nightgown and brushed out her hair, all too aware of his footsteps as he climbed the stairs and of the opening and closing of his door. A moment later there was a tap at the connecting door, and she froze. She'd never felt so torn. She wanted him to come in and do something as ridiculously dramatic as sweep her into his arms. And yet she was also afraid that he would do exactly that. She wasn't afraid on moral grounds, but because she thought she could so easily lose her heart and soul to this man. There was something about Cody. He was restless, not the type to stay in any one place for long. He came from Louisiana. If he had a home, that was it. No matter what happened between them, he wasn't the sort to stay around. Touching him, she was certain, would make her long for more. And that way lay heartbreak.

The tapping came again.

"Come in," she breathed, wondering if he could even hear her.

He could.

"I'm going to check your doors," he told her as he opened the door.

"I locked them," she told him.

"I'll just double check. If you don't mind."

"I don't."

She realized that she was sitting frozen at her dressing table, her brush still in her hand and raised halfway to her hair.

Cody checked the windows and French doors, then returned to the connecting doorway and paused. She heard the ticking of a clock, and then, when it speeded up, she realized she was listening to the beating of her own heart.

"Good night, Alex," he said at last.

And then he left, closing the door between them.

THE DREAM CAME SOMETIME in the very early hours of the morning.

Once again she knew it was a dream, that it wasn't real, but perhaps it *was* a vision of what might be….

She had ridden out to the plain. She knew there was danger, but something was driving her to go. She had no choice.

She rode hard, and Cheyenne, her mare, was swift, seeming to fly over the ground.

As she rode, she became aware of a silhouette in the distance. A man was standing there, facing away from her, and he was wearing a railroad duster and a hat, common attire out on the plain. But he stood tall and straight, and she knew him, though she couldn't see his face.

She reached the place at last.

The place where her father had died.

She dismounted. The man's back was still to her as she started to walk toward him. She had no choice; she was once again compelled. She had to see his face, though she knew in her heart who he was.

He turned to her, and her heart seemed to flip in her chest.

It was her father.

He stared at her, and his face twisted in agony, tears filling his eyes.

"Alex," he whispered.

He reached out to her, and she went to him.

"I love you, Dad," she whispered as he embraced her.

"Alex, I know you love me. And I love *you*, my dearest child. You have to know, you have to believe me when I say…it isn't me."

His arms were solid and real, and she felt the power of his love, but she drew away from him slightly and reached out, trying to smooth the lines of pain from his face.

"What's not you, Dad?" she asked, confused.

He paused, and she realized he was listening for something. And then she heard it, felt it, herself: the trembling of the ground that meant that riders were near.

"We have to go," he said. "Quickly. We have to go!"

"I have Cheyenne," she said, and he nodded, leaping up on the horse behind her. They started to race, but when they reached the base of the cliffs and stopped, he dismounted, pulling her down after him. He gave Cheyenne a firm slap on the rump, sending her home, and he grasped Alex's hand, drawing her forward along the towering stones.

They passed the burial caves of the Apache and kept running, until he finally drew her into a dark cavern.

She started to speak, but he lifted a finger to his lips to silence her.

She heard movement, laughter, and then she heard Milo call out orders to his men. "Search the place, and be thorough. She won't get away from me. I *will* have her, do you understand?"

Alex inhaled sharply. Did he mean *her?*

Footsteps came near, hurried footsteps, as Milo's men searched intently for her. Her father pressed her behind him, warning her again to silence.

"Wait!" Milo cried out. "I know where they've gone. He's taken her to Hollow Tree. Come on. Let's ride."

Alex waited for the footsteps to recede. "He's gone," she told her father. "Dad, we're safe. Oh, my God, they told me you were dead, but I knew it couldn't be true."

"Shh," he said again.

She didn't hear anything. Not a footfall, not a breath of air. But she froze, anyway, at her father's command.

"You have to let her be." It was the deep, calm voice of Cody Fox.

"She is my daughter," her father said, his voice strained.

"And Milo is using you," Cody said.

"I would never hurt my daughter," her father insisted.

"Cody, this is my *father*," Alex said, trying to make him understand.

But Cody didn't pay any attention to her; he was

looking at her father, and the men were exchanging a look full of meaning that she couldn't begin to fathom.

"You have to believe me. I'm hiding. I am not a part of the horror," her father told Cody.

"Then send her back to me. She can't be part of this. Milo has a connection, and every minute she's with you, she's in danger."

Her father inhaled and exhaled deeply, then looked down at Alex. "Go with him. You have to."

"No! I've just found you again. I won't leave you," Alex protested.

"You must. I'm begging you, Alex, go with Cody."

Her father pushed her away and started to turn toward the deep darkness at the back of the cave.

"No!" she cried, then sat up in bed, trembling, and realized she'd cried out in truth, not just in the dream.

She blinked and told herself that was all it had been: a dream. Not a vision of a future she might prevent, because her father was dead and she would never see him again in this world.

"Alex!"

Cody Fox called as he burst through the door that separated their rooms.

She was still too shaken by the dream to be hostile or play flirtatious games.

"Oh, Cody," she said, and tears welled in her eyes.

He rushed to her side, taking her into his arms, and though she was still trembling, his embrace felt so good. He held her close, and she felt as if she were on fire, her breasts and every inch of her skin tingling with an awareness of him. Despite her fear, she was aware that he aroused her in a way that was raw and undeniable.

"What happened, Alex?" he asked, pulling back to smooth her hair.

"I had a dream."

"A dream? Or a vision?" he asked carefully.

She shook her head. "No vision tonight. Just a wall of sadness, and I should have expected it. You were there." She smiled ruefully, seeking his eyes. "Trying to save me, as usual. But I didn't need to be saved."

"What was the dream about? Tell me," he insisted softly.

Her smile deepened. "It was a dream of the heart, I suppose. I miss my father…so much. I dreamed that I rode out to the plain, to the place where he died. But he wasn't dead. He was there waiting for me. But he knew the outlaws were coming, and that they were looking for me, and he made me ride to the cliffs with him. Milo and his men came, and they were searching the caves, looking for us. For me. But my father hid me, and they went away to Hollow Tree, and then you were there and…and you talked to my father. And he made me go back with you."

He didn't laugh at her dream, only studied her gravely and smoothed her hair back again. For a moment she thought that he was going to speak, but then he pulled her against him, soothing her again.

After a long moment he eased away from her, lifting her chin with one hand as his other palm slid over her cheek. She didn't know if she moved or he did, but suddenly their lips met. It was only a touch at first, and then it was a tangle of hunger and passion, their arms crushingly tight around each other, their mouths fusing, and their tongues hot and wet and seeking.

When he broke the kiss, Alex knew that her lips were

wet and swollen, that she was panting, and that…her eyes were staring into his, lost.

"I'm not what you want?" she whispered.

"No," he told her, then took her face between his hands and spoke vehemently. "You're everything any man could want, and it's killing me to let you go. But I am not the man you want, and you can't even begin to understand why. But I'll be here to keep you safe. I promise before God, I'll be here. But I'm not what you want. I can't be."

His hands fell, and she saw the way his fingers curled, his nails digging into his palms.

Then he turned and left her.

And once again the door closed between them.

CODY KNEW HE SHOULD expect the unexpected from Alex, and she proved him right the next morning, at the breakfast table.

She was cordial to everyone, including him. But as soon as she had finished eating, she dabbed at her lips, turned to him and said, "I'm going to take a ride out to Calico Jack's. I want to see John Snow and his family."

He sat back and looked at her speculatively. True, someone needed to ride out to Calico Jack's, but he and Brendan should go, or the sheriff or Dave, paired with one of the men from town.

"We'll check on him, Alex."

"No, I want to see him. It's important."

"Alex—"

"It's broad daylight, and you're welcome to come with me. If you're busy, I'll ask someone else. But I *am* riding out to Calico Jack's," she said determinedly.

"Fine," he said. "Let's get saddled up and go." He glanced over at Brendan, who nodded.

The two of them had decided that it would be a good idea if one of them stayed in town at all times over the next few days, because trouble was bound to come soon. With Brigsby and Hollow Tree turned into ghost towns, he had no idea where Milo and his gang were feeding, nor even how big the gang had gotten. Milo was experienced enough to know that the food supply had to be monitored, so creating too many of his own kind to be fellow predators in one area was definitely a mistake. But the younger vampires wouldn't have the same knowledge or the self-control to be careful in choosing who they transformed and who they brought over. His experience at the graveyard yesterday had been proof of that.

They needed to round up a group of the locals and find Milo's hideout. It had to be in the caves, or in one of the deserted towns.

There was another problem, though.

Alex's dream was troubling, especially since her father's grave was empty. He had to find Eugene Gordon. He'd never heard of a new vampire, like Eugene, fighting the hunger. All vampires fed off animals when they couldn't find their prey of choice: humans. But the temptation to take human life was forever there, fused into their makeup. It took years to learn to control that hunger. Few had ever managed the feat, because few even cared enough to try.

Eugene was out there, and what was truly terrifying was that Milo had a mental connection with those he created, allowing him to bend them to his will.

It was frightening to think of Alex standing out on that balcony the other night. Milo had been the one calling to her, but he had tapped into her love for her father to disguise his call, forcing her father to lure her outside, where Milo could get to her.

But how could he tell her what was really going on?

He was talking about her father, after all. She would fight tooth and nail against the reality that her father had become a vampire. And she would never believe that he could have become evil, even if he revealed his fangs and sank them straight into her throat.

"Cody?" she said, and he realized that she was standing impatiently by the door.

"Sorry. Just wool gathering," he said, and rose to join her.

"I'll keep watch around here, help folks get ready, set up an archery range…and take stock of what weapons we have," Brendan said. "Cole's going to send Dave and some men and stop by some of the ranches where folks might not know yet that…they're in danger."

Or might already be dead, or turned into soulless creatures of the night, Cody thought, but he only nodded and said, "Good." Then he turned to Alex and said, "I'll see you out back in ten minutes."

Without waiting for her response, he headed up to his room. He had a feeling that today he would need both his medical supplies and his weapons.

Levy saddled the horses while Alex waited, ready to go the minute Cody appeared. Which he did, and well within the ten minutes, his saddlebags thrown over his shoulder.

She was surprised by her own ability to behave civilly and calmly toward him as they mounted and headed out. She had never imagined putting her honor on the table, only to have it refused. But something in the way he had spoken last night had touched her.

I am not the man you want.

The words had seemed to come from his soul, filled with something that sounded very much like pain.

"So how are you with a bow and arrow?" he asked a few minutes later as they rode through town.

"Well, I'm a crack shot with a gun, but to tell you the truth, I've never even held a bow and arrow."

"I see. Then you, young lady, have target practice tomorrow," he said, his pitch-black stallion prancing under him, until he easily brought the animal back under control with the slightest command.

"I'm impressed," she said, looking admiringly at the horse.

"Taylor was a gift from Brendan's cousin, back in New Orleans. The man was crazy about President Zachary Taylor, and thus this fellow's name."

They fell silent after that, as he led the way through town. As they neared the edge of civilization, Alex found herself lagging for a moment.

Looking.

She half expected to see her father standing there, looking toward the horizon, his hat lowered against the sun, his duster billowing in the breeze.

But there was no one there.

"Alex?" Cody said a little sharply, turning back to look at her.

"Coming!" she called.

They continued to ride in silence until they reached Calico Jack's.

Calico Jack's appeared to be deserted.

There were no wagons standing out front, whose owners might be inside buying supplies. Nor were there any Indian ponies about, or a single saddled horse.

"Don't get down," Cody told Alex, dismounting.

She waited and watched while he stepped carefully up on the porch and walked to the door. One hand on the gun in the holster at his hip, he used the other to throw open the door.

He strode inside, and Alex waited with her heart pounding and her breath held.

It was only seconds before Cody reappeared.

"Come in," he told her.

She slipped down from Cheyenne and tossed the reins over the hitching rail, then hurried up the steps. John was there, along with Mina, his mixed-blood wife, and they both greeted her with hugs and grim expressions.

"Let me get you some coffee," Mina said.

She was a striking woman, a perfect match for John. There must have been Scandinavian blood in her background, or perhaps Germanic; she was tall, at least five foot ten inches, and her hair was still a shimmering blond color, even though she was at least forty. Her bronzed features were Apache, but her eyes were green.

John Snow was a mix himself, though he had grown up among the Apache. He always said that though his mother had been a white captive, she had loved his father. He hadn't wanted to be part of any band, and he liked his trading post—and his relatively solitary existence—quite fine. Mina was his third wife, and he'd had children with each of his wives, creating his own band, in a way.

"Coffee would be wonderful, Mina, thank you," Alex said. Both Mina and John Snow seemed on edge. She glanced at Cody. "I'll go help Mina."

John and Cody sat down at the big rough wooden table standing in the middle of the room, a place for customers to sit down and chat, drink coffee and compare wares. She and Mina brought the coffee and joined them.

"There is evil afoot," John said. "Not the Apache, and not the white man. Evil from the bowels of the earth."

"I know," Cody said. "Sheriff Granger came to see you the other day, but when he came, he didn't understand. He thought his only problem was outlaws."

"Outlaws don't kill this way. I found carcasses…deer, cattle. Ripped open. Drained of blood. And then I knew. Evil has arisen from the earth, and it is not a ghost. This is different. This is the thing the Great Spirit Father and Earth Mother deplore. An abomination."

"We call them vampires," Cody said.

"Vampires," John repeated. "I have not heard this word before."

"John, I need to know—what about your family?"

John inhaled deeply and looked at his wife in misery. "April," he said.

"April?" Cody repeated.

"My son's daughter. Beautiful, and just sixteen. She is dying."

"Where is she, John? I need to see her," Cody said. "I'm a medical doctor. Please. There's a chance I can save your granddaughter."

"My son's land is just behind the trading post," John Snow said.

"Let's go," Cody said.

Coffee was forgotten. The four of them hurried out the back door and down the slope that led to his son's ranch.

When they entered the house, they found that most of the family was already gathered there. Alex recognized most of the older children, and surmised that some of the younger ones were Mina's and the rest were John's grand-children.

"She is worse, Father," Jeremy, John's eldest son, said sadly, coming forward to meet them. He greeted Alex with an emotion-filled hug, then looked at Cody warily.

"Cody is a doctor," Alex said. "He believes he can help your daughter."

"Come, then."

He led them into a typical young girl's room, with frilled curtains and dolls on shelves. The girl herself had sable hair and pale skin. She was lying still when they entered, but when Cody leaned down over her, she began to toss.

"You're making her worse," Jeremy said with dismay.

Cody ignored him and sat down on the bed, holding her wrists easily in one hand, opening her eyes one at a time, then parting her lips with his fingers.

Alex let out a gasp.

The girl's canine teeth had grown. They were…fangs.

The girl's mother cried out, and suddenly the girl's eyes flew open. She tried to bolt up and began gnashing her teeth, trying to bite Cody.

"We may not be in time," he said.

Alex flew across the room to him. "You have to save her. You have to!"

He looked back at her and sighed. "I'll do my best. Open my bag. You'll find needles there, and some tubing."

"Needles?" John Snow said worriedly.

"She needs blood," Cody said. "Believe me, it's very important."

Alex brought him the supplies he'd requested, and he looked down at the girl and murmured beneath his breath. It looked as if she heard him, though it was hard to be sure.

"I'm going to give her some of my blood. It's the only prayer we've got."

CHAPTER NINE

APRIL WAS SLEEPING PEACEFULLY. She looked younger than her sixteen years. She was a stunningly beautiful young woman, and Cody was certain that Milo had come after her himself. At one point she had even opened her eyes to smile at her mother, and Cody knew he had gained the trust of the Snow family.

They left her mother and several of her siblings to sit with her as she slept, and the other adults had gathered in the main room of the trading post. Coffee was served, and Mina insisted that they have a late luncheon, as well.

"John, Jeremy," Cody said at last, "I believe it will be best if we bring April into town for a few days."

The father looked at the son, and the son looked back at the father, so Cody was startled when John Snow didn't respond to what he said, but said, "Fox, Alex said you were born here, and I remember your family now."

"My parents had property here," he said. "But it was a long time ago."

"The property is still yours, Cody Fox," John Snow said. "It is long abandoned, but it is still yours."

Cody shrugged. "I don't believe I'll start ranching anytime soon."

"That was the first night of the wolves," John said gravely. "The night your father died."

Cody shook his head. "I'm sorry?"

"The first night of the wolves," John repeated.

He knew exactly what John Snow was talking about, of course, but he had to feign ignorance. Though the dishonor of a lie pained him, he'd lived a lie all his life.

"Whatever happened then, it was a long time ago. It doesn't have any bearing on what's happening now and the evil that must be stopped before it claims April."

"We will see that it is stopped in her," John said.

Cody shook his head. "She'll still be susceptible to Milo's influence. She will try to escape you."

"There are many of us, and we will never leave her alone. Two of us will sit with her through the night," John assured him. "We can guard her."

"You must be certain Milo never gets near her," Cody said. "I don't think she can be brought back again. And if you lose her, she will become a vampire, and your only choice will be to kill her."

"You will tell us what we must do," John said.

Cody told them, cautioning them not to let anyone in, not only a stranger, but not even someone they might think of as a friend, not once the day had begun to die. He found all the garlic in the trading post and showed them how to gird the windows with it to repel the creatures. He explained that if they were attacked, they needed to forget about their guns and fight back with lances and arrows, and he told them that they had to sever the heads of the fallen or cut out their hearts.

They listened to him intently.

No one suggested that he was a madman, and when he'd told them all he could, he and Alex left.

She glanced at him as they rode. "You didn't tell them to hang crosses," she said.

"If you noticed, John and his son had pipes and eagle feathers and other items sacred to the Apache. They have no crosses to hang, nor do I think a cross would do John's family much good." He met her eyes. "Every people, every race, has its own beliefs. What matters is a man's heart, and John and his family have good hearts and a strong belief in a higher power."

"I see," she said.

He shook his head. "I don't think you do. I'm still not sure you believe me."

She looked away, half smiling. "You have to admit, it's not easy to accept the fact that vampires roam the plain, as abundant as the buffalo."

"You saw that girl," he said.

She nodded. "Yes, I did. What would have happened if we hadn't come?"

He shrugged. "He would have come back for her."

"Milo?"

He nodded.

"But how did he get to her?"

"He called to her, in her sleep, in her dreams, and she went to him."

"The same way I went out on the balcony. But I didn't hear voices. I went out because the breeze was soft and the moonlight was beautiful."

"The method of seduction doesn't matter," he said. "Come, let's ride harder. The dark comes quickly, and it's been a long day."

IT WAS BATH DAY at the boardinghouse, and the tub, freshly scrubbed, awaited Alex and Cody, so they could take their turns in the relaxing hot water.

Cody deferred to her, and Beulah sat sentinel as she bathed. Once Cody, too, was clean, everyone set about the task of setting out the stew Beulah had been cooking all day. As they ate, they talked.

Brendan was quite pleased with Levy, who was proving to be an excellent archer. He'd repeatedly hit the bull's eye, despite never having picked up a bow and arrow until that day.

After the meal, Alex went up to bed early. She was exhausted and was sure she would fall asleep easily, given how much had been going on.

Instead she tossed and turned, thinking of April and how she had bared her…

Fangs.

Cody hadn't lied. Vampires were real. Cody had likened vampirism to a disease. Apparently a disease that first killed, then reanimated the body in a dreadful way, with a burning hunger.

And a desire to kill.

She thought she heard the front door opening, so, both curious and afraid, she leaped out of bed and raced to the head of the stairs, but she saw no one. She hurried downstairs to look out a front window and saw Cody and Brendan headed across the street. To the saloon.

And brothel.

She felt a wave of anger sweep through her, though she knew it was irrational. Maybe something important was going on there. Maybe something had happened there.

Or maybe something was *about* to happen there.

She groaned and forced herself to head back to her bedroom.

She *was* going to sleep, she told herself.

But she didn't. Instead she waited. And she listened.

THE SALOON WASN'T CROWDED. A few of the townspeople were there, but no one from the outlying ranches and farms. Very wise of them to stay home, Cody thought. Sheriff Granger was playing cards with his deputy, and the girls were sitting around talking, as if the place were a social club rather than a brothel.

Brendan ordered two beers, while Cody took a seat near the girls. Sherry Lyn, Dolly and the younger girl, Liz, were together at a table, poring through *Godey's Lady's Book*, oohing and aahing over the fashions, though it appeared the issue was several months old. They looked up from the book to greet him.

"Mr. Fox," Sherry Lyn said. "Welcome. Can we get you anything?"

"Anything at all," Dolly said with a knowing smile. "On the house, of course."

Dolly might be a bit older than the other girls, and a bit stouter, but he had a feeling she had a few tricks up her sleeve. He smiled back. "I'm just checking in to see how things are going. How is everyone? Anything unusual happening?"

"Not a thing," Sherry Lyn said. "In fact, if we don't solve this problem soon...well, we won't be buying food, much less fashion."

The caustic blonde who had seemed to mock him at the town meeting was sitting at the bar, watching the others but not taking part in the discussion. She seemed amused.

"Linda?" Dolly said, turning to her. "You've been quiet all evening. You doing all right?" Dolly turned back to Cody and said conspiratorially, "Linda wasn't here when Milo and his gang showed up, so she doesn't really understand how bad they are."

"I make house calls," Linda said sweetly.

"Humph," Dolly snorted. "Looking for another wedding ring, I'll warrant."

He frowned. "A wedding ring?"

"Didn't you know?" Dolly asked, bright-eyed at the thought of passing on such a juicy piece of gossip. "Linda was hitched to Eugene Gordon, Alex's father."

He hid his surprise and only looked at her curiously, and she went on.

"She could have stayed over at the boardinghouse if she'd had a mind to. In fact, Miss Gordon came over here the other day and told her as much. But that one—" she inclined her head toward Linda "—well, she's always moving on. She doesn't intend to be a black-clad widow, no sirree."

Dolly shut up when she saw that Linda was on her way over to the table. The other woman had a slow, sultry walk; she moved with the certain knowledge that she was attractive, even if her appeal might not be considered decent.

She watched Cody with the sensual eyes of a cat and dipped low over the table to speak, showing ample cleavage. "Now, Dolly, don't go telling tales about me when I can speak for myself. Eugene Gordon was a fine man. But I like it right here, Mr. Fox, right where I am. In fact, I'm downright fond of men. And you…well, you do look like a lovely example of virility, so speaking for my—sisters—and myself, of course—anything at all that might strike your fancy would certainly not be too much to ask. I might not have been here, but even so, you have my absolute gratitude."

"The offer is greatly appreciated," Cody said, grinning. After all, it was a saloon girl's job to solicit men. "I'd like to introduce you to my friend here," he said as Brendan appeared with their beers. "This is Mr. Brendan Vincent. And I'm afraid we're keeping vigil over at the lodge, so we're not going to be here long. But I thank you for the offer."

Linda seemed momentarily annoyed, but she greeted Brendan with a pleasant-enough smile, and he replied with his customary courtesy. Linda, apparently bored now, yawned and excused herself, telling Dolly that she would be just upstairs—should she be needed.

Dolly rolled her eyes.

"Oh, Linda's all right," Sherry Lyn said, whispering, even though Linda was halfway up the steps.

"A whore, the wife of a prestigious man, and then a whore again. Only in Victory," Dolly said. "And now she's looking for another man with some money and some grit left in him."

Cody rose, taking a long swallow of his beer. "Well, ladies, we just came to check on you, though I see the sheriff is watching over you, too."

"That he is," Sherry Lyn said, smiling. "And the deputy. Victory isn't a bad place. Let's just pray we can keep it that way."

"Amen," Brendan said, dipping his hat.

They walked over to the poker table, aware that Cole had been watching them since they'd entered. "How is John Snow?" Cole asked as they approached.

"John is all right," Cody said as he and Brendan sat. "His daughter was…ill, though."

Cole frowned. "You didn't convince him to put a stake through her heart, did you?" he asked. "I don't want to have to arrest you for murder, you know."

Cody shook his head. "No, I believe she's on the mend. And John Snow understands the situation. He'll do what he needs to do."

"I left Dave in charge and rode out to a couple of the ranches today," Cole said as he set his cards down on the table.

Dave groaned. "A flush, ace high? Hell, I had a straight!"

"We're not playing for money tonight, Dave," Cole said.

"How were things out at the ranches?" Brendan asked.

Cole shook his head. "Pete Weathers thought I was crazy. But old man Dougherty out at the Red Mountain Ranch was ready to believe me. He lost a whole herd and three men just a week ago. They headed out one morning and never came back. He was ready to believe every word I said."

"That's good. Maybe he'll have some influence on his friends," Cody said.

"The town has been quiet. Mighty quiet," Dave said.

"That's good, but it won't last, not if there's no—" Cody broke off.

"No what?" Dave asked him.

Cole stared at Cody, then answered for him. "Food supply," he said.

ALEX WAS DOUBLY ANNOYED. She needed a good night's sleep, but knowing that Cody was at the saloon kept her up. She was worried—and, she had to admit—jealous. It was pathetic. He'd rejected her—nicely, of course—and yet…

She curled up in misery, thinking that it might literally kill her if…

If he chose to be with Linda.

As she tossed and turned, she heard the door open and close, followed by the twist of the bolt.

They were back, and they hadn't been gone long.

Of course, a tryst with a whore didn't have to last long.

It was none of her business, she told herself, but even so, the possibility of what he'd been doing twisted like a knife.

She heard him enter his room. Heard his footsteps, heard him hesitate near the connecting door, and waited, breathless.

Heard his footsteps move away.

She leaped out of bed and rushed to the door, tapping it lightly, then swinging it open. He was standing by his bed. He'd taken off his coat, hat and holster, and was in the process of unbuttoning his shirt.

"Alex, is everything all right?" he asked.

She let out a breath. "Yes, I suppose… I just wanted to make sure it was you."

He nodded. "It's me."

She tried very hard to sound casual and yet concerned as she asked, "Is everything all right over at the saloon?"

"Yes. Brendan and I went over for a drink and to talk to the girls."

"Just talk?" she said.

He laughed. "Yes, just talk."

She wanted to look indignant, but she found herself laughing instead. "Sorry, I didn't mean to be intrusive."

"Yes, you did," he said. "But it's all right." He stared at her. "One of the girls was married to your father?"

She shrugged. "Linda. I talked to her the other day. I believe she really loved him. I hope so, anyway. I don't really know what...what either of them really felt. I wasn't here when they got married. I never met her until I came back. I saw her at the meeting, but until Beulah told me, I had no idea who she was."

He looked as if he were about to say something, but he shook his head as if to banish whatever it was and said only, "Well, I guess we should get some sleep."

"Of course," she said, suddenly embarrassed to be standing there in her nightclothes. "Good night."

She retreated to her own room before the rush of blood to her cheeks could give away her embarrassment.

She lay down, drew her covers up and smiled.

He had gone to the saloon and talked.

Just talked.

She closed her eyes and slept at last.

WHEN IT CAME AGAIN, she fought it.

As always, she knew it was a dream. A dream, a vision—or a nightmare.

It started with a burst of wind. The French doors swung open, and the breeze entered as if it were a living being. The drapes billowed and fell, and someone whispered her name, and though she kept on trying to fight, she had no choice. She had to go.

She slipped out of bed, and though she knew, somewhere in the back of her mind, that she needed to fight the desire to go, she couldn't remember why. The breeze was balmy and delightfully cool. It played with the fabric of her gown, winding it around her legs, lifting it. The sensation alone was more erotic than anything she could remember.

Another voice was calling out to her from behind, commanding her not to go. She knew that voice. It was her father calling out to her, and she wanted to turn and run to him, but she couldn't. Whatever drew her toward the balcony was strong, and though she wanted to hate it, *did* hate it, she kept moving, anyway.

Suddenly she was jerked from sleep and realized that she was standing by the open balcony doors.

It wasn't a dream, wasn't a vision. It was real.

All of a sudden the connecting door flew open and Cody was there. He wrenched her into his arms, drawing her back. As he moved to close the French doors, a massive shadow seemed to descend. Alex looked up and screamed. Giant bats were sweeping toward the balcony.

Cody thrust her behind him and reached behind the drape. She hadn't noticed that he'd left a bow and a quiver of arrows there. As the first bat made a dive for the balcony, he drew the bow with muscle-crunching speed and let the first arrow fly. She heard a terrible shrieking, and the massive bat came crashing down on the balcony.

She stared at it in horror.

Cody didn't even spare it a glance. He was too busy taking aim again.

He hit a second creature, and it, too, let out that chilling, unearthly sound and crashed to the balcony beside its fellow just as the first disintegrated into a pile of black ash.

She looked closely and saw that the second…bat…had the face of a man, then watched as it curled into the fetal position, still screeching, as its limbs shook violently. Then it went still and dissolved into a pile of putrid flesh on its way to becoming ash, leaving her with the memory of something human—and yet not.

Cody closed the French doors at last and searched the room quickly. He grabbed one of her parasols and stuck it through the door handles, securing them against opening again.

A moment later they heard the sound of a bell clanging from the sheriff's office, and screams and shouts coming from the street.

"Come on!" Cody told her.

Gripping her hand, he was heedless of the fact that he was now shirtless and shoeless, and she was in nothing but a thin cotton gown. He pulled her along with him as he raced down the stairs. The others were already gathered in the entryway, Brendan gathering the stakes and bows and arrows that had been stored in the hall closet.

He tossed bows and quivers of arrows to Levy and Bert, and armed himself. Cody went for one of the stakes—his bow and quiver were already over his shoulder. "Stay here, and watch over the household," he told Levy. He threw open the front door and headed out to the street, Brendan and Bert right on his heels.

Alex looked around and saw Tess and Jewell huddled together in a corner, and Beulah standing dead still in the center of the entry hall. As Levy hurried to the window to look out, Alex hesitated for only a second, then raced to the closet herself, finding a bow and a quiver of arrows still hanging from a hook. She drew them out, not certain how accurate her aim might be, but determined that she was not going to be attacked and *not* fight back.

"Alex! What are you doing?" Beulah demanded with dismay.

"Guarding my home," Alex announced. *And avenging my father*, she added silently.

She opened the front door and stepped out onto the sidewalk. The shadows were coming from everywhere, shrieking with a blood-curdling intensity meant to instill terror, she thought.

She took aim as one came near, then loosed her arrow. She hit it, but only in the wing. It tumbled to the street, where it flopped around…

Then rose.

And headed toward the house.

It was some unnatural combination of man and bat, standing but winged, and as black as shadow, except for its eyes, which shone with a red so intense it was like the fires of hell. It came at her, stumbling at first, and then suddenly moving with terrifying speed.

She tried to nock another arrow, but her fingers fumbled. She realized with a sinking feeling that she wasn't going to be fast enough.

An arrow sailed by her and hit the creature dead-on. This time its cry was a death knell, and it fell and sizzled, and turned to ash and remnants of bone.

Alex spun around. Levy only smiled and shrugged, clearly pleased with himself.

She turned back to the street and saw Cody and Brendan standing back to back, shooting arrow after arrow. The shadows were falling all around them, some falling to dust and others remaining corpses, but all of them screamed and writhed in terrible death throes before finally going still. She looked around and saw Cole and Dave, along with a large number of the townspeople, all drawing courage and strength from one another as they shot their arrows.

One of the creatures nearly reached Dave, but someone shouted, and Cody turned and staked the creature before it could reach its target.

Another one swooped near the house, but this time, Alex didn't miss. She and Levy held their positions just outside the door and kept firing their arrows into the storm of black-winged shadow creatures.

She heard thuds, flopping, and shrieking and screaming. From the corner of her eye she would catch a flash of fire accompanied by a sizzle, and then there would be only ash…and bone.

Then, just as suddenly as they had come, the creatures rose into the sky in a giant black cloud, hovered there for a moment, and then were gone.

The street was still and silent. What seemed like forever passed as everyone stood dead still and silent, in shock now that the attack was over.

"Good work!" Cody called out at last. "But now we have to make sure they're dead. If there's a body, take off the head, because they can heal, if there's enough of a body left. We fought tonight, and we won the battle, so we don't want to let one of them in now."

Alex stood on the porch, suddenly shaking. She jumped when she felt Beulah's hands on her shoulders.

"You come on in now," the older woman said. "You did your part. Let the men finish it."

Alex allowed Beulah to lead her back in. Levy followed, shouting orders to Tess and Jewell, his voice firm and confident now, telling them to make sure that none of the windows had been breached. The girls ran off to do his bidding.

"Tea with whiskey sounds like a good bedtime drink," Beulah said, heading for the kitchen.

Alex had to admire her calm.

At last Bert, Brendan and Cody returned. Alex was still

standing in the entry hall, and Cody looked at her curiously as he locked and bolted the door.

As she heard the bolt snick into place, she snapped out of the trance that had seized her. "Beulah is making tea and added whiskey for everyone," she said, her voice calm. Then she turned and walked into the kitchen without looking to see if the men were following.

Tess and Jewell were all but inhaling their drinks. Levy was standing thoughtfully by the stove sipping his, and Beulah was busy preparing more cups.

"Thank you kindly, Beulah," Brendan said, taking one.

"Yes, thank you," Cody added.

"Pleasure," Beulah said, then set her hands on her hips and asked Cody, "Will they come back?"

He shook his head. "Not tonight. They took a beating. But they'll regroup. And when they *do* come back, they'll be looking for our weak spot, a way to slip in so that doors can be opened to them."

"Oh, dear," Beulah said.

"But not tonight," Cody repeated. "We took down a lot of the old and powerful ones tonight. Milo will need to regroup. I suggest we all get some sleep—while we can."

They finished their drinks without any more conversation, then dispersed to their respective rooms.

But Alex didn't stay in hers. She went straight to the connecting door and tapped lightly, then opened it without waiting for an invitation.

Cody was sitting on his bed, looking weary, wheaten hair drifting over his forehead, his broad shoulders hunched.

He turned swiftly, watching her.

"You're afraid," he said, smiling grimly. "You should

be. But you did well—even though I wish you'd stayed inside. So why are you here now?" he asked.

"I don't want to be the weak link that brings the town down. I dream, and then my dreams become reality, and I'm not fighting very well on that level," she said.

Cody rose. Moonlight seeped through the drapes, and a lamp was lit on his dresser, casting ripples of light over the skin of his muscled chest and arms.

"I'll keep watch over you," he promised. "You can sleep."

She met his eyes, her own open and honest. "I don't want to sleep. And I don't want you to keep watch. I want you to be with me. You say that you're not what I want, but I don't believe in forever anymore, and you're what I want *now*."

He stared back at her, eyes golden and enigmatic.

"Cody, please. I'm not some fragile creature, though I *have* learned just how fragile life itself can be. All I'm asking is for you to sleep with me."

Still he stared, those golden eyes on her. And then, at long last, he moved. Sleek and swift, he was at her side.

And then she was in his arms.

CHAPTER TEN

HE WAS EVERYTHING that she wanted.

She loved the way he held her, the strength in his arms when he swept her up. True, she wanted him on a purely sexual level, but there was more. She had fallen beneath the spell of his eyes, which were caring when he faced the travails of others, intense in anger, like the sun when he laughed. She loved the touch of his fingers, gentle when they stroked her face, strong when he held her. In his arms she was safe.

And dangerously wicked.

She felt no sense of fear as they walked through the doorway to her room.

She was almost preternaturally aware of everything. The feel of the sheets beneath her as he laid her down, the pressure of his body, the cotton of her gown brushing against her flesh. She felt his bare feet against hers and the rough fabric of the pants he still wore, the sleek, hot flesh of his chest burning against her, lighting a fire within her blood.

Moonlight, pale and mystical, bathed them. She saw his face and traced her fingers along the contours of his features, fascinated. She cradled his cheek and jaw when she saw his war with himself reflected in his eyes as he thought again that he should not be with her, and she whispered, "You have to believe me. I know what I want," praying that her voice didn't sound as desperate as she felt, and that he would not leave her.

He didn't. He only shook his head ever so slightly, and in a strange way, it was as if he were surrendering.

Then his mouth found hers, and in that kiss, it seemed as if the world around her exploded in a brilliance of wonder. Heat swept through her like a blaze in the desert, and she felt her body arching and moving by instinct, aligning with his lean and muscular form. His lips went from passionate to gentle, playing erotically against hers, and his hands cradled her face, giving him greater access to her mouth. Fevered, she returned his kiss, clinging to his bare shoulders, then exploring the length of his back with eager hands. She felt her gown tangle around her as they twisted and rolled in passion. They broke the kiss and laughed together, and then he lifted the gown over her head and held still for a breathless moment, before crushing her into his arms again.

They kissed again, clinging together, flesh against bare flesh, growing slick despite the coolness of the night air. His mouth ravaged over her shoulders as he cradled her breasts and groaned deep in his throat, and his hands ran down the length of her back, pressing her harder against him. She teased his skin with the tip of her tongue, drawing lines on his flesh, breathing in the essence of him, and with each breath, each touch, her hunger grew ever greater.

At last he rose to remove his pants, and for a moment she was alone, the air around her bringing a moment's chill. She saw him silhouetted against moonlight, and a rush of desire swept over her again. She knew, whatever he might think or feel, that she would cherish this night, this time together, forever. Life was so fragile. She had seen it slip away too often, but she herself was far stronger than he would ever truly realize.

He came down to her again, stretching out beside her, his body close, touching, one leg thrown over hers, his hands on her, brushing over her skin like an artist of the flesh. She moved into him, their mouths meeting and melding again, and she felt his vitality and power coursing beneath the skin. She moved against him, her lips traveled across his chest, and she felt his fingers threading through her hair, then moving along her nape and down to the small of her back. His hands cradled her buttocks, pressing her ever closer, until he shifted suddenly, and his lips and tongue began a tour down the length of her body, blazing a trail of liquid sensuality that made her writhe in an agony of need.

He was a practiced lover, she thought vaguely, and yet all that mattered was that he make love to her at that moment.

And he did, both tender and strong, bathing her with the touch of his hands and tongue, arousing her with his kiss on her lips and then the stroke of his tongue against her hips and thighs, and between. She gasped out a soft cry of wonder at the lightning streak of ecstasy that swept through her, her body shivering, shaking, trembling, as she rose to join the moon. And then she felt him inside her, and the desire that built within her then was like something maddening and tempestuous, burning out of control. A slow rhythm began to beat in her blood like a pagan drumbeat. She barely had time to savor the feel of him so completely within her when the fever sent her arching, writhing, falling into the rampant blaze he'd stoked in her.

The world shrank down to the feel of the mattress beneath her, the strength of his embrace, the damp sleekness of his body against hers. Finally, just when she felt she couldn't bear any more, they were seized as one by the power of climax, and their wild dance of tangled limbs became a moment of ecstasy frozen in time and then eased…down to a magical completion.

She grew aware once again of the gleaming moonlight, the air cooling her skin.

And his eyes meeting hers.

His touch was tender as he smoothed back her hair.

"You are…unique," he told her. "Incredible."

He started to pull away, and she shook her head. "Don't leave me, please. Not now. I'm not staking any claim on you, and when it's time, I will let you go, I promise."

A smile curved his lips, and he drew closer to her again. "You thought I was going to walk away tonight? Not a chance in hell," he assured her.

There was so much she wanted to know about him, so much she wanted to understand. But not at that moment. At that moment she was afraid of words. She just wanted to be with him, to revel in the moment and the feeling of being absolutely alive and vital and real.

The war was a world away, along with all the horrors she remembered.

Even the town and the plague that had descended upon it had been pushed to the back of her mind.

In his arms, the world was good and it was hers.

They lay together for hours, drowsy, half asleep. They brushed against each other, they made love again, and at last they slept.

And this time her dreams were only dreams, and they were good, for he was holding her tight as a benevolent moon shone down.

DOLORES! DOLORES, it's urgent that I speak with you. It's about Amy.

Dolores Simpson was awakened from a sound sleep by the voice.

She jerked up, clasping the covers to her breast, then looked to the side, thinking Bill must have spoken.

But Bill was snoring softly.

She frowned, certain she had heard someone call her name. And they had mentioned Amy. Precious Amy! Everyone said that Amy was dead, and yet each night she heard her daughter call out, her voice stronger every time.

That nice Mr. Vincent had come by to tell her that Amy was with God. That if she thought she heard Amy or any child—any voice—crying out, she had to ignore it. That it was very important to ignore it.

He had talked to Bill and the boys about locking the house and how to destroy the evil that was stalking the town, cutting out the heart or severing the head.

Brendan Vincent was a fine man, no doubt, but she was a good Christian woman, and she couldn't condone doing such terrible things to a human body, even the body of an enemy. Such brutality was positively pagan.

Dolores got up and slipped on her robe, then glanced again at Bill, who was still snoring softly. He was a hard-working man, and a gentle one. A good husband. She pulled the covers up higher around his shoulders, then walked down the hall and looked in on the last two children still living at home, Gary and Jared, their adopted sons, now fifteen and thirteen. She loved them so much. As much as she loved Amy. Amy had been her youngest daughter. Golden and sweet, so precious. Everyone had loved her.

The boys, too, were sleeping.

Dolores, please! It's urgent!

She walked to the window. A woman was standing outside. Dolores thought she knew her, but she couldn't recall from where.

She hesitated. They'd been warned...but the woman hardly looked dangerous. And her voice was so gentle, so compassionate and kind. And mesmerizing...

Dolores, come to me, I can help you. I can take you to Amy. Just come to me.

Dolores stopped thinking and gave herself up to her feelings. She loved her husband and she loved her sons, but Amy...

Nothing had ever before promised her such a sweet peace as the voice did now.

She walked straight to the front door and quietly slid back the double bolts, then carefully opened the door as quietly as she could.

She stepped out onto the porch and paused, frowning, rational thought whispering at the back of her mind that something was wrong.

Dolores...

The woman glided forward, looking for all the world like a shimmering angel wreathed in mist, and Dolores stepped off the porch.

I have a message for you, a message from Amy.

Dolores stepped forward eagerly, finding herself embraced by the same mist that surrounded the woman, lit by the gentle glow of moonlight. The woman embraced her and leaned down, eyes filled with compassion. *Come closer so I can whisper to you.*

Then the mist was gone.

And the reality that remained was pure horror.

Dolores saw, eyes wide-open at last, that she had been deceived.

Too late.

Oddly enough, there was very little pain. Like two little pricks.

The sound was far worse as the woman lapped against her throat, drinking thirstily, swallowing like a greedy animal, then sighing with ultimate pleasure.

I will not use you up. Not yet. But...you are mine, Dolores. Mine.

Again the slurping. But softer now. Careful, even.

When the vampire was done, she pulled away from Dolores and smiled. There was a touch of blood on her upper lip. Perhaps she felt it, or perhaps she saw it reflected in Dolores's eyes, but she extended her tongue, long and red, and lapped up the last drop of blood.

You will await my call.

Then she let go of Dolores, who fell as if boneless. When she looked up, the woman was gone.

Dolores blinked, confused, then realized she'd had a dream. A dream about Amy. And she had gone outside. She winced, thinking that Bill and the boys would be horrified, that they would worry about her common sense, even her sanity, if they found out, so she had to get back inside before they realized she was missing.

She tried to rise, but she couldn't. She was too weak.

Finally she managed to get up and practically drag herself to the porch and through the front door.

It took all her strength to relock the bolts.

Leaning on the wall for support, she finally made it back to her bedroom.

Trying hard not to stumble, she reached the bed and nearly fell back onto the mattress. She froze, praying that she hadn't awakened Bill, but he continued to snore softly.

She closed her eyes and—amazingly—she slept. She dreamed once again of the woman, of the voice in her head, and of Amy. Her little girl was within her reach, smiling at her. The woman was there, too, surrounded by mist, and her smile was benign once again as she waved to Dolores.

It's so, so beautiful here, with Amy and me.

So beautiful.

Dolores longed to join them.

In her dream, she moved forward as the shimmering mist grew dark, and the distant sound of shrieking rode the air as deep red clouds…rolled in.

But then she saw Amy again, and in her dream, Dolores wept, and real tears slid down her cheeks.

ALEX SLEPT LATE THE NEXT morning, and when she awoke, Cody was gone.

She smiled, though. He hadn't left her, she was certain.

Not yet.

He had simply risen for the day.

She was about to rise herself when there was a tap at her door. She drew the covers up over herself and called out, "Yes?"

"It's me. Tess. I've got hot water for you."

"Thank you. Bring it in."

Just as the door opened, she spotted her discarded nightgown lying in a heap on the floor. She made a dive for it and stuffed it under the covers with her, then pulled them back up over herself again.

"Miss Alex, you all right?" Tess asked, coming in and walking over to the dresser with the pitcher of hot water.

"Yes, thanks, just fine," Alex said, trying to sound completely normal.

"Beulah is getting worried down there."

"I'll be right down. I promise."

"All right, but you know Beulah. She says her fresh muffins aren't going to be fresh forever, and you'll be having chicken if you don't come eat your eggs soon."

"I'm on my way."

As soon as Tess left the room, Alex leaped out of bed and hurried to her washstand.

In the midst of washing up, she paused, closed her eyes and breathed deeply, wishing she could carry the scent of him with her always.

She opened her eyes and caught sight of the wild mane of her hair in the mirror, and quickly reached for a brush. It took several long minutes to undo the tangles and smooth it down into the semblance of a proper coif. Next she dressed hastily. Remembering the way the shadow-bats, the vampires, had descended the night before, she opted for riding breeches, boots and a tailored shirt, for mobility.

She couldn't resist the temptation to pause before she left the room and picked up her pillow, where a hint of his scent remained. She was being silly, she told herself.

Silly, and sad. There was something about him. But he wasn't going to stay in her life. He had made that clear.

And she would have no regrets over what she had done, the pleasure they had shared. Nor would she ever attempt to hold him back from whatever he felt his future demanded of him.

She bit her lip and set down the pillow.

She had been in love the proper way once. She'd met a man who loved her, who'd asked her father's blessing for her hand. She had loved him back, and she'd felt as if her heart and soul had been torn from her when he died.

And yet…she hadn't felt like this. As if every breath whispered of him, as if he had become one with her, body and soul.

She squared her shoulders in determination and left the room.

As some might say, she had made her own bed. And now she had to lie in it.

Downstairs, she found Beulah in a disgruntled mood, annoyed that she was so late to breakfast. Alex refused to go along with the other woman's mood. "Don't you think it's a lovely day, Beulah? Last night we fought against evil, and we won."

Beulah shook her head. "You're acting like it's all over, child. You mark my words. It's just beginning. Now, eat your breakfast."

Alex sat down at the table and tried to be casual as she asked, "Where are Brendan and Cody?"

"Up for hours, I'll tell you that," Beulah said, sniffing as she filled Alex's coffee cup.

"Do you know where they went?"

"Down to the sheriff's office, I think."

Alex thanked Beulah and ate quickly, and as soon as she was finished, she told the cook she was going to take a walk down to the sheriff's office, too, and find out what was going on.

Beulah stared at her gravely. "Wherever those men are, you be back here by dusk, Alexandra Gordon, you hear me?"

"Of course, Beulah. And I will. I swear."

Then she hurried out, her every thought of Cody and the incredible night they'd shared.

CODY AND BRENDAN HAD started early and reached what had been Brigsby by noon, which gave them an hour of full and advantageous daylight before they would have to head back.

Milo Roundtree had obviously found a hiding place to use by day. He had attacked Brigsby first, then Hollow Tree, which made those likely candidates but far from a certainty.

Cody felt weary, thinking of the many ways Milo could attack the target now in his sights: Victory.

He could choose an all-out assault, as he had last night, or he could approach using seduction and trickery. Vampires delighted in temptation, in pulling the strings of emotion and preying on the basic instinct of human desire. And no matter how proud the community might be of their success last night, if he didn't find Milo's hideout and destroy the vampires while they slept, eventually the creatures would find a way to infiltrate Victory.

And what really terrified him was that the way might lead through Alex....

Alex, whose father's grave was empty.

Which meant that Eugene Gordon was out there somewhere, and Cody didn't have the heart to tell Alex that her father had to be hunted down and destroyed.

He reminded himself that he had occasionally—very occasionally, it had to be said—seen cases in which a vampire who had truly cared for someone in life shunned harming them, even after "death." Such a vampire had been extremely strong-willed in life as well as afterward, and though he hadn't known Eugene Gordon, those who *had* known him referred to him as a man of strong will.

He thought of the way Alex had been drawn to the balcony.…

That hadn't been a call from her father.

He wondered if Eugene was somehow surviving on his own, hiding by day and feeding in secret at night, or if he was with Milo's gang, essentially hiding in plain sight while somehow managing to stay out of the attacks on Victory.

He shook off those thoughts for a later day as they stopped in the center of Brigsby's main street. The entire town was covered with a thick layer of plains dust. The door to the combination barber shop and dentist's office was slamming open, then shut, in the breeze, and the swinging saloon doors hung at odd angles, the lower hinges ripped free.

Cody dismounted and held very still, listening, closing his eyes and using his other senses. He felt nothing.

Nothing but emptiness.

"I'll check the saloon," Brendan said.

"We'll stick together," Cody told him.

They tethered the horses between the saloon and a general mercantile, then carried the tools of their trade inside, in case there was trouble.

The saloon was empty.

Empty except for the decaying, almost mummified, remains of a man who'd fallen over the poker table, his jaw at an odd angle.

He'd been holding a pair of aces.

Sadly, they had won him nothing.

Brendan looked at the corpse, then at Cody, and arched a brow.

Cody shook his head. "Dead as a doornail. Still…"

He walked over to the corpse, took the head in his hands and twisted. The dried flesh and bone broke easily. He set the head down on the table and said sadly, "We don't have time for decent burials."

"I know. Let's move on," Brendan said, his voice all business.

In the mercantile, they paused and stared at shelves of fabric, grain, feed and canned goods, all covered in fine cobwebs.

What gave them cause for concern was the fact that the floor was strewn with animal corpses—cats, dogs, rats, squirrels, one calf and one coyote—and the body of an elderly man.

This time Cody didn't need to remove the head. The body had already been savagely torn apart.

He signaled Brendan to be still and quietly moved to the end of the counter, his hand tightly gripped around a stake.

Something, someone, exploded out at Cody. He was ready with the stake and pierced the creature before so much as seeing its face or knowing its sex, race, color or anything other than that he was being viciously attacked.

The thing gripped the stake, casting back its head, giving the men a glimpse of wildly matted hair and a face so heavily bearded it might have belonged to a werewolf.

Cody pinned the vampire to the floor, where it thrashed furiously in its death throes.

Finally it went still, and the skin started to crackle and darken.

It was a young creature and stopped decaying before it became a pile of ash.

Brendan had stepped up behind Cody. "I knew him," he said softly. "His name was JoJo Grayson, and he was kind of a woodsman, kind of a gypsy. He made his money hunting rattlesnakes and trapping critters for fur. He came through all the towns around here when he felt in need of a night at a saloon. Always smelled to high heaven, but he was a harmless old coot."

Cody hunkered down and cut off the man's head.

Now he was harmless.

"So what do you think? Is the hideout here?" Brendan asked softly.

Cody shook his head. "No, this isn't it."

"Hollow Tree, then," Brendan said dully.

"Seems likely," Cody admitted. "We've got to finish here, see if there are any other wild cards, and get back to town before nightfall. Tomorrow we'll head out to Hollow Tree."

He retrieved his stake and stood.

They moved on. There were a lot of buildings in Brigsby and not much time to search them.

THE SHERIFF'S OFFICE was empty.

Alex stood on the wooden sidewalk and looked down the street. Jim Green saw her and waved, so she smiled and waved in return. A woman was sweeping out in front of the general store, and a man farther down the street was up on his roof, patching shingles.

She turned and looked out toward the cemetery. Though she couldn't tell who they were, she could see that there were people there.

Were they burying the dead from last night's battle?

Maybe Cole and Dave were out at the cemetery, she thought, and maybe Cody and Brendan, too.

She turned around and headed back to the boarding-house. She didn't feel like a lecture from Beulah, so she avoided the front door and walked around back, aiming straight for the stables.

She found Levy cleaning out the stalls and assured him that she could saddle Cheyenne herself, and also told him that she was only heading out to the cemetery.

He leaned on his shovel for a moment. "I figured you'd be heading out there soon enough. I was kind of surprised you hadn't been already."

Her heart flipped, and guilt ripped through her. She had desperately needed to see the place where her father had died; somehow, she had believed that seeing the site would tell her the truth about his death. But she had avoided the cemetery. The place where he had been buried. She had kept it out of her heart and out of her mind. If she didn't see his grave, she didn't have to fully accept the fact that he was dead, that he wasn't coming back.

She thought of the dream she'd had the other night. He would always be in her dreams. In that way, she told herself, he never would die.

"Right, Levy," she said softly. "Well, I won't be long. And it's perfectly safe—there are other people out there, and, anyway, you can see the cemetery from the sheriff's office."

Levy nodded. He looked as if he wanted to speak, but he didn't.

"I'll be back soon," she promised.

It was a short canter out to the cemetery. As she neared it, she saw that Cole, Dave and a number of other men were there. They'd built a funeral pyre safely outside the weathered wooden gates, and dug a pit, and she knew that the remains of the undead who had been truly killed last night would be interred in that pit.

As she dismounted, Cole spotted her. "Alex, what are you doing out here?" he demanded with dismay.

"I came to see my father's grave," she said, but guilt assailed her as she spoke. True, she *was* going to visit her father's grave.

But curiosity and restlessness were really what had brought her.

"Alex, this isn't a good time to be doing that," Cole said.

But she had already skirted the fire and entered the cemetery. "I know where he is," she said. "He always told me he wanted the highest point, dead center, because he'd thought of himself as the dead center of Victory for so long," she told Dave.

"Alex—"

"What in God's name…?" Alex murmured.

The graveyard looked as if it had been under attack, a number of graves standing open and empty in front of their silent headstones. She turned to stare at Cole for a long moment, then ran up the small hill at the center of the cemetery.

She found her father's grave right where she had expected it to be.

The ground was freshly dug, a giant hole gaping in the ground and her father's coffin lying beside it, open and empty.

CHAPTER ELEVEN

As HE RODE BACK INTO TOWN, worn and weary, Cody saw the group gathered at the cemetery.

And he saw Alex, standing by her father's grave, fists clenched at her sides as she stared wordlessly at Cole Granger.

"Oh, hell," Cody muttered.

"Maybe you should have talked to her, broken it to her gently," Brendan said.

Cody scowled at his friend. "You think I should have told her that her father might be a vampire, part of Milo Roundtree's gang?"

Cody kneed his tired horse and galloped toward the cemetery. Brendan urged his own horse to hurry and followed. As they approached, several of the people who had been tending the fire greeted them, but Cody only waved distractedly as he leaped off his horse, threw the reins over the fence and strode quickly toward the tense scene on the hill.

"What's the matter with you, Cole?" Alex was saying as Cody approached. "How dare you dig up my father? You had no right to disturb his grave—any of these graves. Why did you do it, Cole? Why?"

Cody knew the minute she saw him coming, because

she stiffened, her eyes narrowing in fury. His stomach took a dive.

"Alex," he said sharply. "Don't lash into Cole—none of this is his fault or even his doing. If you need to blame someone, blame me."

"Cody, it's all right, I can take care of myself," Cole said.

Before Cody could speak again, Alex walked over to him with long, hard strides and shoved him hard. "What the hell are you doing? Everyone has been so grateful for your knowledge and help, everyone has done everything you've ordered. But now you're taking advantage of this community. What? Did you draw straws, trying to decide who you should disinter and chop to pieces? What kind of a ghoul are you?"

She slammed his chest hard again to emphasize her anger.

He caught her wrists. "Alex, listen. We didn't choose anything. We only did what we had to do. I'm sure Cole would have explained—if you'd given him a chance."

"Why did you dig up these people? Why did you dig up my *father?*" she demanded furiously.

"Alex, we didn't choose to dig them up. They'd already dug themselves out."

"What?" Her eyes widened in shocked realization.

"You know what vampires are—you've seen them. When a person is bled to death by a vampire, *they come back*. How the hell did you think it happened?"

She shook her head. "But…they were in their graves! Cole said you had to decapitate them, like the man who died in the street, like the vampires we killed last night."

"Yes," Cody said.

She stared from him to Cole. "So you found them in their graves? But…why weren't they with Milo?"

"Milo doesn't want everyone he infects. He leaves them to stumble around like newborns, starving, desperate, deadly newborns. Alex, we let them rest in peace. We keep them from killing, don't you understand?"

"And my father? You did that to my father?"

Cody was silent for a split second too long.

"No," Cole told her.

"Why not?"

"Because he wasn't in his grave."

She stared at him for a long moment, saying nothing. Then she turned and raced down the hill to where her mare was tethered. She mounted in one smooth motion, and then, kicking up dust, horse and rider went racing off toward town.

"Where in hell is she going?" Dave demanded.

Cody didn't answer him. He was already halfway down the hill, intent on following Alex.

ALEX COULD HAVE HEADED straight to the lodging house. Beulah always kept alcohol on hand—for medicinal purposes, the cook said—and she could have chosen from brandy, sherry and perhaps some wine.

But she didn't want to go home.

She reined in at the saloon, sliding from Cheyenne's back and leaving the mare loosely tied at the hitching post in front. Then she strode through the swinging doors and walked straight to the bar.

Roscoe looked at her, hesitant. As if he was afraid of her.

"I'd like a whiskey, Roscoe," she said.

"Uh…pardon?" he said, blinking.

"I would like a whiskey," she repeated more slowly.

"Miss Alex…"

"A whiskey, Roscoe," she said.

He nodded, turned and poured her a drink. Alex took a long swallow, and a shudder racked her body. She grimaced. God, the stuff tasted awful.

But as it burned its way down her throat and into her stomach, she found that, oddly enough, it did give her strength.

They were all crazy, she thought. Her father was not a vampire. He was nothing like Milo Roundtree.

"Miss Alex?"

She spun around. Jigs was sitting on the piano bench, his back toward the keys.

"Hey, Jigs," she said glumly, then looked at him more closely. She frowned. He looked tired, ashen.

"Are you all right?" she asked him.

"I reckon I'm tired, and I know I'm worried. Dave Hinton right kindly been sleeping here the last couple of nights. He keeps vigil from midnight to 4:00 a.m., then I take over for a few hours, and then Roscoe."

She heard footsteps and looked up. Linda was coming down the stairs. Alex tried to watch her objectively. It was just so difficult, seeing Linda—Linda Gordon, that was her name now—so blithe and overt about her promiscuous sexuality when Eugene Gordon had done her the honor of making her his wife. When Alex had left after their conversation the other day, she had found herself actually liking the woman.

But right now, on top of what she'd just learned about her father, Linda, in all her skimpy finery, was the last person Alex wanted to see.

"What's the matter, sweetie?" Linda asked casually on her way to the bar.

"You watched them bury my father, right? I mean, you weren't out of town, seeking the future, before he was buried, were you?" Alex asked.

Linda started, then smiled slowly. "Ooh. Sweet little Alex has claws."

"Just answer me. Please."

The amusement on the other woman's features faded. "Of course I was at his funeral. Which you didn't attend, I might add."

"I didn't even know he was dead. You know damned well he was buried long before the letters ever reached me," Alex said.

Linda still seemed wary after Alex's initial attack. "I saw him buried, yes. Jim Green took care of him, and the pastor came over from Brigsby to make sure he was buried with a full Christian ceremony," Linda said. "Why?"

Alex didn't get a chance to answer. Cody, who was suddenly standing just inside the swinging doors, spoke for her. "Because he's not in his grave. That's why."

Linda looked from Cody to Alex. "Of course he's in his grave," she said, as if they'd both lost their minds.

"No, he's not," Cody said. "We dug up his grave the other day. The earth was already disturbed, and his coffin wasn't sealed. And he wasn't in it."

Linda shook her head, wrinkling her nose prettily. "I don't understand. Are you accusing me of stealing Eugene's body?"

"I'm not accusing anyone of anything," Cody said, walking over to join them. "I'm just stating a fact."

"Oh, yes, you are," Alex said, rounding on him. "You're

accusing my father of being a vampire. Like Milo Round-tree."

"I never said he was like Milo Roundtree," Cody argued.

"God in heaven," Roscoe breathed, pouring a whiskey into the shot glass and downing it in one swift movement.

"But they all have to be destroyed. They're all monsters, right?" Alex demanded.

Cody was stubbornly silent.

Alex looked at Linda again. "Tell me, have you seen my father? Has he been hanging around outside your balcony, calling to you—quoting from *Cyrano,* maybe. Or maybe Shakespeare. He always loved Shakespeare. Maybe he's playing Romeo, trying to entice his Juliet to come out and have her neck bitten and her blood sucked dry!"

"Alex," Linda murmured.

Alex was in a state verging on hysterics, and she knew it. She should have gone home. She *would* go home.

She turned and headed toward the door, pushing past Cody to make her escape.

Cole and Dave were just tethering their horses and stepping up onto the wooden sidewalk. "Alex," Cole said sympathetically. "One of us should have—"

"Not now, Cole," she said. Without another word, she collected Cheyenne's reins and led her horse home, walking her around the side of the house to the stable. Levy must have heard her coming; he was waiting at the barn door to take the horse from her.

"Miss Alex? You all right?" he asked her.

"What the hell does 'all right' even mean around here anymore?" she asked him.

It was Levy's look of sympathy that pierced through the

miasma of fear and dread that had gripped her and touched something in her heart.

She forced a smile. "I'm fine, Levy. How are *you* doing?"

"Good, Miss Alex. I feel good, and angry—and strong," he assured her.

"Thank you, Levy." She turned and started toward the back door of the boardinghouse, then stopped and looked back at him. "Levy, do you ever have dreams? Nightmares?"

He shrugged. "No, not really. Well, not that I remember, anyway."

"Have you ever dreamed about my father?"

"No, Miss Alex." He frowned, clearly confused by the question.

She shook her head, hesitating, as she felt tears welling in her eyes. She blinked them back. "If you ever should dream about him—if you think he may be calling to you, asking for help, or just looking for you—don't go to him."

"Pardon, miss?"

"Don't go to him. Promise me you won't go to him."

"I—I promise, Miss Alex."

He was staring at her, but not in a way that suggested she was crazy.

No, it was a look of helplessness.

She smiled sadly, shook her head and went inside.

She passed through the kitchen, where Beulah was preparing dinner, stirring something in a pot that bubbled over the fire. Tess was sitting at the table, peeling potatoes, and Jewell was next to her, snapping peas.

"There you are, Alex. I was about to get worried. I wonder if them fellows will be back for dinner tonight.

Well, you go ahead and wash up. Won't be long now till the food is ready," Beulah said.

"I think I'm going straight to bed tonight, Beulah. Feels like I just ate lunch," Alex said.

"What? You've got to eat," Beulah insisted.

Alex ignored her and headed upstairs, well aware that Cody and Brendan would be coming back soon, and not in the mood for conversation.

She headed straight to her room. There was clean water in the ewer, and she poured some into the washbowl, then doused her face. She prayed it would somehow make her feel better.

When she was done, she pulled off her boots and hose, and lay on her bed, staring up at the ceiling.

No one knew how her father had died. They had simply found his body.

He hadn't been torn to shreds, just lying there…dead.

Dead as if someone had sucked all the blood from him.

He had been prepared for burial and interred in the ground. Six feet under.

And now he was no longer in his grave.

She didn't feel angry anymore. She felt numb. She told herself that her father could never be a monster, and she thought about her dream.

He hadn't been about to hurt her. He had been trying to save her from Milo Roundtree. He had been *warning* her.

She winced, remembering how Cody had warned people that they mustn't be fooled by the cries of their loved ones.

Her father was different. Had to be different.

She rose and went over to her dressing table, where she sat thoughtfully brushing her hair.

She shook her head as if she could clear the awful implications of what might have happened to her father from her mind. Once the concept of vampires would have struck her as ridiculous.

But she had seen them, had seen them swooping down, black shadow-bats with death in their eyes, and she had seen what had happened when they were killed. She had seen April Snow.

She lay down again. If she could sleep, it might be possible to dream, and…maybe in a dream she could reach out and find her father. If her previous dream had truly been a vision, he wasn't with Milo Roundtree.

He hadn't become a vicious killer.

He…

He what? He was living alone, hiding out somewhere, fighting the blood thirst, that, according to Cody, had to be ravaging him?

Maybe it was true, maybe…

She closed her eyes, willing her breathing to come slow and easy.

CODY ENTERED THE HOUSE through the front and went from room to room, looking for Alex.

Returning to the entry, he found Beulah and demanded, "She's here, isn't she?"

Beulah nodded. "What's going on, Mr. Fox? Why is she so upset?"

There was no reason to honey-coat his words with Beulah, who always got straight to the point herself. "Her father's grave is empty. We discovered it the other day, but—"

"But no one wanted to tell Alex, and you were sure you

had the situation under control," Beulah said tartly. Cody stared at her, and she went on. "Well, you know what, Mr. Fox? I believe if anyone can control what's happening around here, it's you. But that don't mean you can manage Miss Alex."

"Where is she?"

"Up in her room, and you leave her alone right now, Mr. Fox. You can talk to Alex when she's had a chance to calm down a bit and think things out."

Cody frowned suddenly. "Beulah, you haven't had the sense that Eugene's been around here, have you?"

"Why, no!" Beulah protested.

"Beulah? This place is decorated with crosses and garlic."

She raised her chin and answered him with great dignity. "My grandmother was a wise woman, Mr. Fox. She was a slave in Haiti, but she came to the United States during the Haitian Revolution. She taught us things she'd learned back in Africa and things she'd learned from her French master. She knew all about the walking dead. Once Mr. Eugene was gone, I decided we needed to do everything we could to keep this place safe, what with the things going on in Brigsby and Hollow Tree." She sniffed. "Didn't help much the night those filthy scallywags came in here."

"This is a boardinghouse, a public place," Cody said. "But Brendan and I are here now, and we're prepared."

"Prepared?" Beulah said. "Maybe here, but the people of Victory are spread out all over the countryside. All the ranches, all the farms. And there's John Snow's place, and the Apache camp, and… Oh, Lord, Mr. Fox, what would happen if they got into the Apache camp, if they…made those warriors into monsters?"

Cody groaned; she was echoing his own thoughts.

"We won't wait for that to happen. We intend to find Milo and his gang, and exterminate them."

Beulah nodded. "I'm glad to hear that," she said. "For now, you come and sit down and have a nice dinner. You and Mr. Vincent, you're going to be needing your strength. Then you can go and talk to Miss Alex."

COLE AND DAVE PLAYED poker at the saloon, whiling away the time until sunset. The minute the sky began to don its nightly cloak of crimson, Cole grew wary and alert.

They were armed, just as he'd told the entire town to be. Eight bows, eight quivers of arrows and a stack of sharp stakes were at the ready, and garlic and crosses guarded all the doors and windows.

The girls, now that the men of the town were battening down their homes each night, had gotten bored with card games and gossip sessions, and gone upstairs.

Roscoe was sleeping behind the bar until an attack came or it was his turn to stand watch.

Jigs was up and alert, staring at the new saloon doors.

The new doors had just gone up an hour ago; the swinging doors with their implicit welcome had seemed not only inappropriate but an invitation to danger. The wooden doors that had taken their place were rough, not sanded or painted, but they had a bolt that kept them closed. Cole wasn't sure just how much good the new doors would do, given that the saloon was still technically open to the public, but he would take what he could get, and they were as ready as they would ever be.

He was restless, and he tossed his cards down on the table.

"Danged if you didn't beat me again, Cole," Dave said with disgust.

Winning a hand of cards had been the last thing on Cole's mind. He rose and walked over to Jigs. "Jigs, Dave and I are here. You look like you've been rode hard and put away wet, so go to bed and try to get some sleep now in case we need you later."

Jigs looked up at him. "Ain't right, Sheriff. Ought to be me, watching over the place. Me and Roscoe."

Cole set a hand on his shoulder. "Go to bed, Jigs. We'll wake you later, so we can catch some sleep. Now, get to bed or you'll be so tired, you won't be any good to anybody."

Jigs stood and arched his back, stretching. "I guess you're right, Sheriff." He shook his head. "Don't see how this can come to no good end. This town can't make it, everybody hiding all the time. This saloon, those girls... well, we can't survive without customers, you know?"

"We can hold out, Jigs. We got help when those other towns didn't. We'll win. You wait and see."

Jigs might not have believed him, but he was too tired to argue. With a wave of his hand and a muffled "Thank you, Sheriff," he shuffled on up the stairs.

He was so tired, Jigs thought. Dead tired.

He winced at his own choice of words and looked around as if afraid someone might have overheard his thoughts. "Dead" just wasn't a word to be using loosely these days, even in his mind.

He checked his window, which was securely locked, and rearranged the crosses and garlic around it. If anything happened downstairs, the noise would wake him, he knew, so he crashed down on his bed still dressed, boots and all. In two seconds, he was drifting off to sleep.

Jigs liked sleeping lately, thanks to the erotic dreams he'd been having. He didn't have any trouble finding women in Victory because of his mixed ancestry. Hell, not in a whorehouse. But finding love, that was something else again. Truth was, he was ugly, and women didn't cotton to that.

But in his dreams…

In his dreams, *she* would sneak right into his room, then kind of slink up to the side of his bed. He would open his eyes, and she'd be standing there, smiling. She would put a finger to her lips to warn him to keep quiet, and then she would grin mischievously and start to do things to him.

Not…everything.

But enough. Enough to have him panting like a schoolboy as she cuddled up beside him, all lean and sleek, and whispered in his ear. She liked to tease, to nip at his earlobes and caress his neck. He'd feel a pinch now and then, but then she'd start licking him, soothing his flesh, and he would be just about flying out of the bed.

"It's our little secret, Jigs," she would whisper as she left. "I wouldn't want the other girls knowing what a treasure you are. And I sure don't want anyone knowing that I come to you…on the house!" That always made her giggle.

And then she would be gone, leaving him alone in bed to relish the lingering arousal of that dream. He was always so tired afterward, but tired in a way that made him smile. What a fine way for a man to get so exhausted.

He knew they were just dreams…but every man deserved his dreams.

ALEX TRIED TO PICTURE her father. He was a good-looking man, and not so old, only forty-five. His hair was graying, but that only enhanced the character evident in his face. He was straight-backed, broad-shouldered and fit.

She pictured him out on the plain on the last day of his life.

She tried to feel the breeze, the touch of the sun, the glow of the sunset. She imagined the tumbleweeds.

Show me...

It was a thought. It was a prayer.

But no matter how hard she tried to conjure the image of her father, the picture kept slipping away.

It wasn't fair. He had already come to her once in a vision. Why couldn't she recapture that vision now?

But even as she tried, it was as if dark clouds came roiling through her mind, blocking both the plain and the image of her father.

The darkness was thick, with a life of its own.

Then it began to clear.

She saw a house. A pretty ranch house, and around it there were fields, some of them fenced.

The house was familiar, and she was sure it had been there a long time.

She heard a horse whinny, then another, and knew that there were stables just beyond the house.

And inside...

Inside there was usually the smell of fresh-baked goods and the laughter of children.

Not tonight.

She moved inside in her dream, her vision, and realized that tonight, while it was still early, the children and their mother had gone to bed, while her husband doused the lights. She knew them, she realized. Bill and Dolores Simpson. Poor couple, still mourning their beloved Amy, who'd been like sunshine in the house.

As she watched, Bill finally got into bed, and the house fell silent. Alex could almost feel the depth of their grief, something she knew far too well.

Then she sensed movement in the darkness, and in a moment she saw Dolores rise and get out of bed. She didn't bother with a robe, or even with slippers, just headed for the bedroom door, where she paused briefly and looked back. Bill hadn't moved and appeared to be asleep.

Dolores slipped out of the room, closing the door carefully behind herself, and walked down the hall. She almost seemed to…flow.

She reached the boys' room and stepped inside to assure herself that they were safe. After a moment she walked to the bed where the younger boy, Jared, was asleep and sat at his side.

A creeping feeling of unease swept over Alex, and she fought the dream, but it was no good. She had no choice but to watch as Dolores leaned over her son and clamped a rough hand over his mouth, then drew back her lips, baring her teeth.

No, her *fangs*.

She threw her head back with an animallike groan of pure pleasure. Then she ducked forward and sank her fangs into the soft flesh of her little boy's neck.

CHAPTER TWELVE

DINNER WAS ALL BUT OVER.

Cody and Brendan were drinking coffee, picking at the last of Beulah's cherry pie, when a blood-curdling scream sounded from the bedroom above.

Cody knocked his chair over as he leaped to his feet.

He raced for the stairs, bounding up the steps in seconds. He didn't knock, didn't hesitate, didn't go through his own room, only burst through the door of Alex's room, ready for anything.

But there was no intruder in sight. She was simply sitting on her bed, barefoot but dressed, staring straight ahead.

And screaming.

He scanned the room, seeking out any danger he might have missed, but no one was there and nothing had been disturbed.

He hurried to her bedside, clasped her shoulders and shook her gently. "Alex, what is it? What happened?"

She blinked and fell silent, staring at him.

"Alex?"

She gasped and grabbed his arm. "We have to get out to Bill Simpson's ranch. His wife…the boys." She stared at him, her eyes clear. "I saw it happening, but there may still be time."

She bolted off the bed, searching for her boots. Cody saw that Brendan had followed him and was waiting in the doorway, the rest of the household behind him. Brendan looked at him quizzically and whispered, "Did you tell her?"

Cody knew he was asking if Cody had told Alex about the Simpsons coming to the sheriff's office and wondering whether Alex might be having strange dreams because of that. He shook his head.

"Let's go," he said to Brendan. "We've got to get out there."

"You're not going without me," Alex said.

"Alex, there's no reason to risk—"

"There's every reason. It was my vision, and I want to help you stop it from happening. Levy, you and Bert keep a close eye on the house," Alex said.

"Alex, I'm telling you—" Cody began.

"And I'm telling you we're going to have another child to bury if we don't get out there—fast," Alex said, already putting on her jacket.

Cody was worried that he might be distracted from the fight at a crucial moment by the need to protect Alex, but since she was already heading for the door, he reckoned he had no choice.

"Bert," he said, following Alex, "get over to the saloon and warn the sheriff. This might be a ruse to get us out of town. Be on the alert."

Bert nodded gravely.

"Levy, don't leave the house," Cody said.

"I won't," Levy vowed solemnly.

"Let me lock you all out," Beulah offered. "Tess, Jewell, you girls be ready to defend yourselves."

Alex, familiar with the way out to the ranch, rode in the lead. Cody and Brendan raced just behind her, neck and neck.

Cody glanced up at the sky. Still a few days until the next full moon.

Still a few days before Milo Roundtree would make his final assault.

And still he watched the night sky, leery of what might be afoot. Did Milo know about Alex's strange dreams? Was this a ruse to get them out of town?

Or, worse, to get *Alex* out of town?

They pulled up at the gates of the farmstead, which had been chained shut. Bill had posted signs that warned, No Trespassing. Trespassers Will Be Shot on Sight.

Cody circled his horse away, then rode hard for the fence and sailed over.

Brendan and Alex followed suit.

As they neared the house, Alex called out, "Bill, it's Alex. Don't shoot. You're in danger, and we've come to help."

Cody didn't waste time waiting for Bill to open the door. He broke it down and strode inside, almost crashing into the man who stood in the hallway, shocked, a shotgun in his hands.

He was obviously debating whether he should be using it or not.

"It's your wife," Cody heard Alex say. "She's sick, Bill."

Cody left them to talk and started checking the rooms.

Dolores was in the second one he tried, sitting on the bed next to one of her sons, her face contorted and her mouth opened unnaturally wide.

Saliva dripped from her fangs as she leaned toward the boy.

Cody flew across the room, tackling her and knocking her off the bed. He straddled her on the floor while she shrieked in fury and swung her fists at him, twisting and turning, trying to sink her fangs into his flesh. By then the boys were awake, shouting, crying.

Jared, who had so nearly just been drained by his mother, raced up behind Cody and started slamming him on the back.

By then, however, the others had come in.

"Bill, get the boys out of here!" Alex cried, then managed to corral Jared, while Bill collected his other son in his arms, looking down at his wife with a combination of horror and fear.

Brendan moved quickly to help Cody, immobilizing Dolores's legs very effectively by sitting on them, leaving Cody free to grapple with her arms—and avoid her fangs. Just as the two men managed to get her under control, Bill burst back into the room.

"Oh, thank God! She's still alive. You can't kill her. But… what on earth is going on?" he demanded.

At the sound of her husband's voice, Dolores went off in another frenzy of rage, kicking, shrieking, trying to free her arms from Cody's grasp.

"Bill, damn it, I don't want to have to kill her," Cody said. "Get me some good strong rope. I'm going to do my best to save her, but I'm not letting her take anyone else down, do you understand?"

Bill nodded jerkily and disappeared.

A minute later he was back with the requested rope. Cody carefully tied her arms and legs while she struggled against Brendan's hold with a maniacal strength. Then the two men hefted Dolores onto the bed and tied her there. All the while, she was straining toward them, fangs snapping as she tried to bite.

"What should we do?" Bill asked anxiously.

"You should get out of here," Cody said softly. "You don't need to see her this way."

Bill stared at Cody, his eyes pleading. "She's my wife. We just lost our little girl."

"I know that, Bill, and I will try to save her. Now, go look after your sons. They need you." As Bill left the room, Cody turned to Brendan and said, "I need my medical kit."

"You're going to give her your blood?" Brendan asked, frowning. "It's too soon after last time, Cody."

"It's all right. I heal quickly."

"This quickly?"

"Yes. I think. Hell, Brendan, it's this woman's only hope."

Brendan left the room, and Cody leaned against the wall and watched Dolores as she began to slowly return to true consciousness. She closed her eyes and went still, then, a moment later, opened her eyes and looked around. She seemed absolutely mystified by the fact that she was tied to her son's bed.

She stared at Cody. "What—what happened?" she asked.

As he walked toward her, a look of alarm came over her features. "Where are my children? What have you done with my children? Where's my husband?"

"He's all right. The boys are all right. But you've been…infected. You nearly killed your son tonight."

She stared back at him in disbelief, shaking her head. "No," she whispered. But he could tell that she believed him. "No, no, no," she began to moan.

"Dolores, you have to trust me. You have to let me help you. I'm going to give you blood. My blood. It will fight the disease."

"Where's Bill?" she asked plaintively.

"He's right outside. I didn't want him to see you…until you were yourself again."

Tears suddenly filled her eyes and trickled down her cheeks. "Amy. I love my Amy so much. But my boys… how could I hurt my boys?"

"You weren't in your right mind, Dolores. Everything's going to be all right, but I have to keep you tied up for now. I'm going to give you some of my blood, and you can't fight me while I do it. Do you understand?"

"I won't fight you, Mr. Fox," Dolores said. "I promise. Please…" She was suddenly straining against her bonds again, not fighting, but desperate. "I'd rather die than hurt my boys. Please don't let that happen. If I…if I don't… well, if I don't come out of this right…then you've got to kill me. Don't let me put my boys in danger."

Brendan returned with Cody's medical bag. Cody quickly started selecting needles, while Brendan assisted him, arranging the tubing. "Blood transfusion is quite an amazing feat, Dolores," Cody said, trying to keep her calm. "In 1628, an English physician named William Harvey discovered the circulation of blood. Shortly after that, doctors tried the first transfusion, but it wasn't until 1665 that someone was finally successful, and it wasn't even on a person. A physician named Richard Lower kept dogs alive by transfusing them with the blood of other dogs. After that, there were several successes with humans, but because the doctors used animal blood, the law stepped in and it was a hundred and fifty years until we started being able to use human blood to save people's lives."

Cody wasn't sure she was paying any attention to his words, but she seemed to like the sound of his voice. "This is going to sting," he told her.

Dolores let out a little cry as the needle went in. Cody swiftly unstrapped the tourniquets he had tied around her arm and his, allowing his blood to flow into her, as she asked, "Am I going to be all right?"

"We're trying our best," Cody assured her.

Then her eyes closed, and she fell silent.

Cody took a deep breath, clenching and unclenching his fist to keep the blood flowing.

"Cody," Brendan said warningly. "Enough."

Cody nodded. As Brendan put pressure on Dolores's arm and withdrew the needle, Cody tended to himself.

"What do you think?" Brendan asked anxiously. "Does she have a chance?"

"There's always a chance," Cody replied grimly. "We'll just have to wait and see."

MILO ROUNDTREE PACED beneath the trees, his shoulders squared, his expression hard. Nasty.

The woman squared her own shoulders and approached him. "You sent for me," she said. "But you could have just come to me. You had no problem with that before."

He cast her a cold glance that sent chills racing through her.

"I'm not risking myself to come to you."

She stiffened. How the story changed. She remembered his original seduction so well.

She'd never stood a chance against his blandishments and promises. She had believed that he adored her, needed her, wanted her, and that she would be a queen among a new race, who were strong enough to take everything they wanted. To rule the world.

"All right," she said crisply. "What do you want?"

"Why is everything taking so long?" he demanded. "They'll be hunting—by day—very soon now, if they aren't already."

She laughed. "Cody Fox and Brendan Vincent. Two men, and you're afraid, when you've gathered so many around you?"

Milo looked uncharacteristically thoughtful for a moment. "There's something…Cody Fox isn't a normal man." He shook his head. "Never mind. That's my affair. What's happening in town?"

"In town? Things are going very well. I've already turned many people, and soon I'll have turned even more," she said proudly. "Now, as to the Apache camp…I've heard it's quiet now. And I haven't heard about the family turning on itself out at Calico Jack's, either. But I've already started infiltrating the ranches. I've done as you desired. I haven't failed."

He grasped her suddenly, his strength terrifying, and wrenched her to him. "I made you, my love. And I can destroy you."

"I have done as you desired," she repeated, trying not to shake. He was so powerful, and she'd seen the way, when he was displeased, he turned on his own.

He released her so suddenly that she almost fell, but she caught herself, straightened and stood very still.

"We'll see about the ranches," he told her.

"By tomorrow—"

"By tonight," he said. "I will know."

She kept her distance as she said, "If you don't want to come yourself, send anyone you want to check on me. They'll see that I can manage my end of any deal."

She saw that she had angered him. Good. She had meant to. She wanted to tell those foolish idiots following him that he was selfish, and a coward. He would cheerfully risk others' lives, but never his own, letting the townsfolk shoot down his minions, those he had seduced into doing his bidding.

And she was, she knew, expendable.

He walked over to her, but she held her ground, staring at him with hard, knowing eyes.

His arm shot out, and he slapped her. Hard. So hard that she fell to the dirt.

"Remember this, and remember it well. I made you, and I can destroy you. I made you, and I gave you power—I didn't leave you to rot, or survive off rats and vermin in the woods. Cross me, fail me, and I *will* break you."

She sat in the dirt, loathing him.

Loathing herself.

Then he was gone.

ALEX HAD GATHERED BILL and the boys in the kitchen, where she had Bill light the kerosene lamps and the gas stove, and she'd made hot chocolate. He had politely thanked her, but he seemed numb as he drank his hot chocolate.

Now he rummaged around until he found a bottle of whiskey he apparently kept hidden in a cabinet.

"I don't understand—what are those men doing to my mom?" Jared demanded suddenly, breaking the silence.

"You're old enough now to understand," Bill said. "Your baby sister—she was…diseased. And she managed to give the disease to your mama. It's vam-pire-ism, they said. Mr. Fox is trying to…to…"

"He's going to kill her!" Jared exploded. "He's going to kill my mother."

Alex looked at Bill, then walked over and hunkered down by Jared's chair. "Jared, you're wrong. Cody is trying to help her, to get her back to being the woman she was, the one who loves you."

"Hell, son," Bill said, "your mama nearly ripped your throat out."

Jared swallowed hard. "But she's still my mama."

Bill nodded and started pacing.

Suddenly, Cody appeared in the doorway. She thought he looked pale, and unsteady on his feet. How much blood could he give away in a matter of days and still survive himself?

"Cody?" she whispered.

She picked up a clean cup and filled it with hot chocolate, then handed it to him without a word.

"How's Dolores?" Bill asked, his eyes filled with fear.

"She's hanging in," Cody said.

"Can the boys and I see her?" Bill asked.

Cody nodded. "For a few minutes. But…I'm sorry. Don't untie her yet. We need to see if the treatment was successful."

Bill nodded as the boys shoved past him, already running down the hall.

Cody waited until they were gone, then practically fell

into one of the chairs at the breakfast table, his legs stretched before him.

Alex took a seat across from him, watching him intently. "Is she going to be all right?"

"I don't know."

"Is there…is there really a possibility?"

"Yes," he said, and offered her a half smile. But then his eyes grew serious. "If she *is* all right—same as this whole household—it's thanks to you. How often do you have these…dreams, or visions or whatever they are?"

Alex shrugged uncomfortably. "Not often, though… more often lately. In the past, I've tried to use what I learn to help people, but discreetly. I wound up in trouble when I was living in Washington. Arrested, actually. Luckily, both the president and his wife seem to believe in dreams, so I made it back out here."

"Abraham Lincoln is a good man. I feel sorry for Mary, though."

He leaned toward her. "Alex, you have to tell me everything you see. That you dream. It's crucial."

She nodded. "I do tell you everything."

"I'm not so certain. Alex, your father is out there somewhere."

She shook her head passionately, needing him to believe her. "I refuse to believe that he's a monster. Haven't you ever heard of anyone…having the disease and not becoming a killer? Ever? It's got to be possible."

He looked away so she couldn't look in his eyes and see the thought running through his mind, a thought he wasn't going to share with her. "Alex, there have been some unusual cases where a person hadn't fully made the transition into being a vampire—that's why we could save

April Snow, and why we may be able to save Dolores. But…your father was attacked weeks ago. We don't know who killed him, but we do know that he was buried and he isn't in his grave. Alex, you can't take any chances, even if he comes looking for you. That's a vampire's strategy. Amy was able to lure her mother out because she knew her mother loved her. I'm afraid that your father will do the same thing, and that you won't have the strength to fight him."

She straightened in her chair, drawing away from him. "And *I'm* afraid that you won't give me a chance to prove I'm right about my father. No one has ever seen him with Milo, you know."

Cody lifted his hands. "We haven't seen half of what Milo's got yet. We haven't found his lair. And he took down two whole towns, along with God only knows how many wagons and carriages and even wagon trains."

"My father isn't with him," she insisted.

"Alex, this is what I know. We killed a good number of Milo's men when they attacked Victory, but he *will* attack again. Right now he's trying to get to people through trickery and seduction. Look at what happened with Dolores. If he could have turned her, she would have killed her whole family. Or maybe she would have turned the boys—they would make fine soldiers for his army. And he's going to keep on doing the same thing, using whoever he can to infect the living. Then, when he's weakened the town, when he has it on its knees, he'll attack again. And this time he'll feast, just like a king enjoying the spoils of war."

Alex was about to reply when Brendan suddenly appeared in the doorway. "Cody, I think you need to come," he said.

Cody rose immediately, and Alex followed him down the hallway to Dolores's room.

The boys were curled up next to their mother on the bed, Bill Simpson on his knees by her side.

Dolores's eyes were open again, and when she turned her gaze toward Cody, she seemed to be clear and rational, but when she spoke, her voice was filled with tension.

"They're near…I can feel them," she said.

"I don't know what she's talking about," Bill said, looking at Cody with a worried expression.

"I do," Cody said, crossing the room to the bed. "Come on, boys. We've got to get you and your mother someplace safe."

"What?" Bill demanded.

"She can feel the vampires coming. We've got to get somewhere safe."

"You have to untie her," Bill said.

"Not yet," Cody said firmly.

"But…we're in danger!" Bill Simpson said.

"And there's still a thread connecting her and the vampires. I'm sorry, but we can't take any chances. Now, do you have a cellar? Anything underground with a good strong latch?"

"The storm cellar," Bill said.

"We've got to get your wife down there, along with the boys," Cody said.

"Okay, come on," Bill agreed. "I'll show you."

They had to leave the house to reach the storm cellar. Alex shivered as they walked outside. The very tenor of the night had changed since their arrival.

The wind had picked up and almost seemed to moan.

She stood on the porch, feeling the air and looking up

at the sky. A streak of red crossed that dark, star-filled canvas, like a warning written in blood.

"Alex!" Cody shouted to her.

Suddenly the wolves started to howl, sharp and shrill, like a wail of anguish in the night.

"Alex!" Cody repeated more loudly.

She hurried toward the storm cellar, frowning. Brendan was already beside the horses, procuring their weapons. He had a row of stakes lined up against the balustrade of the front porch and was armed with two revolvers, along with a bow and arrows, and he had laid out additional bows and arrows for Cody—and one more fighter.

She reached Cody. He'd carried Dolores Simpson into the cellar, still tied up. The boys were down there with her. Bill was standing next to him, like a man caught in the midst of a situation he still couldn't believe.

"You have to get down there," Cody told her.

"No, I'm better off up here. I can fight—I fought them the other night."

"Someone has to stay with Dolores," Cody argued.

"She has her sons."

"No. Milo still has influence over her through Amy, and they could be convinced to let her go," Cody insisted.

"Send Bill down," Alex argued.

"Bill will be just as vulnerable," Cody said, his tone growing more forceful as the wind continued to rise and the wolves to howl.

"Someone needs to get the hell down there!" Brendan cried out. "I can see them coming now!"

"I won't let her get to me, by God, I swear I won't," Bill Simpson declared. He was down the hatch and into the cellar in two seconds; the hatch closed, and they heard it lock.

Cody swore.

"Alex, get up on the porch—at least your back will be protected. Brendan, you go left, and I'll take the right," Cody commanded.

Alex saw the wisdom of his plan and raced to obey him. She saw that the two men were already taking aim, their arrows pointed toward heaven.

The sky…a deeper darkness was forming there. A darkness that moved, hiding the moon, whose light should have sifted down to illuminate the yard.

"Be ready. They're close," Cody said.

BILL SIMPSON HELD HIS wife's shoulders while the boys sat tensely, just feet away. He wished he could cover his ears against the howling of the wolves.

Suddenly, beneath him, Dolores began to move. She looked up at him, smiling, a coquettish look in her eyes.

"They're coming, Bill. You have to let me go."

He shook his head, instantly afraid.

"Oh, Bill. They can give us things you can't imagine. Virility and youth. If you would just let me go, Bill, you would know. You would remember."

He *did* remember. He enjoyed remembering the days when they were young, when they had kissed every chance they got. When they had first been intimate…. Somehow her words made him think back to hot nights, sweaty limbs and illicit ecstasy under the stars. They'd always intended marriage…but now he remembered, with a feeling of rather delicious wickedness, how they had dared to anticipate their vows.

"Dad?" Jared said worriedly.

Bill shook his head firmly. "It's all right. We do as Cody said."

"Cody!"

Dolores let out a cry of rage and rocked hard against him, baring her teeth, straining to reach him.

Bill drew back from her in horror.

He knew he had to do something, but he was frozen in horror, watching his wife twist and turn and convulse.

And seek to pierce him with teeth that had become fangs again.

"Dad!" Jared cried in horror.

Bill looked at his son. Amy was gone, and now the boys were seeing their mother turn into a monster.

"Forgive me, Dolores," he whispered, then gave her a good upward punch to the jaw.

A sigh escaped her, and all the fight drained from her body as she lapsed into unconsciousness.

CLOSER, CLOSER...

The wolves fell suddenly silent as the shadows drew near.

The men were ready. They had taken aim.

Alex followed suit.

Cody's arrow flew first. Seconds later, they heard a shriek in the night. Brendan fired off the next arrow, and Alex snapped into motion herself, nocking an arrow into place.

Another arrow sailed, followed by another thump and a scream, but Brendan's next shot apparently missed its mark. Alex let her own arrow fly, and a *thing* fell to the ground and started crawling toward them. One of the others hit it again, at close range, and it lay still.

She saw with a shudder that the monster had once been a man.

A smell of decay rose as the thing flapped around for a few seconds, then dissolved into a putrid mass of blackened rot.

After that the night came alive with a mass of screaming shadows, wings flapping and arrows flying so fast that Alex no longer had any sense of which were hers, and which were Cody's and Brendan's. Then several of the creatures managed to alight.

Cody tossed aside his bow and arrow and reached for the sword hanging at his side, stepping out to meet them as they approached. His swing was powerful, dispatching heads and cleaving through torsos.

Alex caught sight of movement and shouted, "Brendan!"

One of the creatures was slithering through the darkness by his side, seemingly a shadow and nothing more, so stealthily did it move.

Brendan swung around to face it as he drew a stake from inside his jacket and drove it into the shadow, all in one smooth motion.

A second later, there was nothing to see of it but ash.

The wolves began howling again, a terrible sound that rang in evil harmony with the shrill screams that cleft the night.

Then, as if a mass of migrating birds had suddenly taken flight, she heard the sound of wings beating the air, rising high.

Flying away.

The yard was strewn with…ashes. Body parts. Corpses in various stages of decomposition.

The three of them stood dead still as sounds of battle began to fade.

A lone wolf howled, and then that sound, too, faded away.

At last Cody said, "It's over. For tonight, at least."

CHAPTER THIRTEEN

ALEX WORRIED the whole way as they rode back to town, but Cody had insisted that they could do so safely, that there would be no more attacks that night.

The Simpsons were with them, because Cody had refused to leave them alone at the ranch. Bill had worried about his herd, but Cody had told him bluntly that if they didn't put an end to the vampires within the next few days, the herd was going to be the least of his problems.

For a while, as they rode, Alex checked the sky. But she never saw that strange streak of crimson again, and not a single wolf howled at the moon, so she finally had to agree with Cody's reading of the situation.

When they got back to Victory, Cody left Brendan to herd the others into the boardinghouse and walked over to the saloon to see how things had gone in town and fill the others in on the events at the Simpson ranch.

Beulah seemed to find nothing strange in the fact that they suddenly had four new boarders—nonpaying boarders, at that. She sent Tess and Jewell upstairs right away to prepare rooms.

Dolores, however, wouldn't be sleeping upstairs that night. She was going to lie on the couch in the parlor, and someone would keep watch over her until dawn. When, a few minutes later, someone suggested untying her so she could sleep more easily, Bill, his expression sad but his tone determined, was the first to protest. "No. We can loosen the bonds a little, but...she's not to be trusted yet."

"You need some rest, Bill," Brendan told him. "I'll take first watch."

"I can do it."

They hadn't seen Cody enter, yet there he was.

"Cody, damn it, you don't have to do everything," Brendan told him. "I'll take first shift."

"Second," Bert volunteered.

"And Lord knows, we won't need a third shift, 'cuz it'll be morning by then," Beulah said. "And with all these mouths to feed come sunup, I'm going to bed." She started to leave the parlor, then hesitated and turned, looking at Alex. "You need your rest, too. Brendan and Bert have this covered. The rest of us need to sleep. And that's that."

"Yes, Beulah," Alex said. She *was* exhausted.

Still, she couldn't help looking at Cody before she left. He was already looking at her.

"Good night, all," she said, and headed for the stairs.

In her room, she waited. She heard Cody enter his room and barely dared breathe as she heard something heavy being set down. His gun, she imagined.

She waited, tense, her hands clenched at her sides.

Then, at last...

There was a tap on the connecting door. She flew to it, opened it and threw her arms around him, drawing him in.

He kissed her. Hard and deep, and with no sign of weariness. His arms were strong and reassuring as he lifted her against him. She wrapped her legs around him as they walked over to the bed, where he fell to the mattress with her.

They rolled to face each other. "I was afraid…" she began, but then her voice faded.

"Afraid?" he asked gently.

"Afraid that you wouldn't come, that…oh, Cody, my father, everything that happened…the dreams…I know I'm not normal, and I know we don't have forever, you've made that clear, but I want what we have now. I—" …

He pressed a finger to her mouth to silence her and smiled deeply, as if she'd given him a tremendous gift. "Alex…trust me. None of us are normal. Some of us are just farther away than others. Nothing you can do or say could keep me away right now, unless you say that you don't want me—and even then, I'd still be here, protecting you, wanting you.…"

"I want you here," she assured him, breathless, then stroked his check, threaded her fingers through his hair and marveled that he was there with her, and that he felt the same fever she did. He leaned down, capturing her lips, and she felt his fingers fumbling with the buttons on her shirt.

Their kiss, damp, wild and sloppy, was broken by their desire to be rid of the clothing that separated them. They pulled apart, and in moments they were on the bed again, naked flesh against naked flesh. She reveled in the heat that filled her, the energy, the need to get even closer to him.…

It seemed like eons since they had been together this way. His eyes met hers with a sensual glitter. And tenderness. She reached out, capturing his head, drawing his mouth back to hers. Whatever inhibitions she might have had were swept away. She caressed his flesh and trembled at the erotic onslaught each time he touched her in return. His eagerness to savor each taste of her was palpable as he pressed his mouth against her, lips first, and then thighs, hips, abdomen, and *then*... She nearly howled like a wildcat in the night herself, but then she remembered that her house was full and bit down on her lip. She saw his shadow against the wall as he rose over her, then sank into her in a moment of ecstasy as he thrust fully and deeply home. The stars themselves seemed to enter the room, bursting in the night as she writhed and undulated to his rhythm, so close...reaching...easing...reaching...and finally climaxing in an explosion that was somehow both shattering and sweet, volatile and tender, as he wrapped his arms around her. His lips found hers again, and the kiss deepened as they eased down from the heights of sensual pleasure.

He rolled to her side, pulling her against him, but he didn't speak.

She was amazed when her eyes began to close. The feel of his hand, stroking her hair, was soothing and lulling. The warmth of his body, spooned around hers, was secure.

She drifted off to sleep. To sleep, and not to dream.

Just as she was reaching that nether region between the world of wakefulness and that of sleep, she thought she heard him whisper.

Just once.

And just a few words.

"If only it *could* be forever."

ALEX WOKE UP EARLY the next morning, but it didn't matter. Cody was already up and gone. She washed and dressed quickly, and hurried downstairs.

Bursting into the dining room, she was startled by the normality of the domestic scene that greeted her eyes. The

Simpsons were seated at the table. All of them. Cody and Brendan were there, too, and Brendan was talking to Bill about the situation back East, while Cody was telling Jared about his experiences in medical school.

The men all stood as they realized she had entered the room.

"Good morning, Alex," Cody said.

"Good morning, everyone," she responded, then walked to her chair, just as Beulah entered from the kitchen.

"Well, there you are. Breakfast is warm and ready to be served. It's lovely, having the table filled, now isn't it?"

Dolores Simpson was still pale, but her color was much better than it *had* been, and her eyes were clear. Someone had untied her and allowed her to clean up for the meal. She looked at each one of them in turn and said, "I can't thank all of you enough for what you're doing for me, for my family."

"It's a pleasure to have you here," Alex said. "And to see you looking so well."

"I—I only remember a little of what happened. It's all like a—a nightmare," Dolores said, flushing and looking downward to work her napkin nervously with her fingers. She looked up again. "I'm still so afraid." She straightened. "Not of dying. We're set on this earth to die. I'm afraid of—of turning into a monster."

Jared rose from his chair and hurried around the table to her. "You're not going to become a monster, Mother. We won't let it happen." He looked around the room, as if challenging anyone to disagree with him.

She hugged her son, and Alex smiled, then saw that Cody was watching them, too, something wistful in his eyes.

"Well, now, that's that, so let's eat, shall we?" Brendan suggested.

Just as they started eating, they heard a commotion in the street. Horses coming into town, lots of them, and that meant lots of riders. Milo's men? Alex wondered with a shiver.

Cody was out of his seat first, warning the others to stay back as he hurried to the front door, though Alex noted that he seemed more concerned than alarmed.

It was Tall Feather, she saw with relief through the open door as she stepped up behind Cody, ignoring his order to stay put. The chief had brought a party of nine warriors and two extra horses bearing packs made of blankets.

As Tall Feather slipped down from his horse to greet Cody, she saw Cole coming out of his office, with Dave just a few steps behind him.

In fact, all over town, people were coming out to stand on their porches or the plank sidewalk. Jim Green even came closer to watch the action.

"Tall Feather," Cody said, nodding in greeting.

"Fox," Tall Feather returned gravely. "We have been doing what you instructed. And we have brought something back for you. Last night, as dusk approached, they came. Different from what we had seen before." His eyes misted; Alex was sure he was thinking of his daughter. But he stood tall and proud as he spoke. "They attacked us in a large number, but we were ready. Laughing Man was killed, to our great sorrow, but we dealt with him as we must. But this…travesty we have brought you—these are two of those we killed last night," Tall Feather said, indicating the piles on the packhorses.

Cody looked at Tall Feather, then walked around to the packhorses. Cole arrived then, and greeted Tall Feather with respect. He set a hand on Cody's arm. "Go carefully," he said softly, nodding toward the gathering crowd of townspeople. "A lot of these folks had kin in Brigsby and Hollow Tree."

Cody nodded as he carefully moved the first blanket.

Alex had walked around for a better view, and she felt her stomach pitch downward.

The first corpse belonged to a young woman, just about Alex's age. She was missing part of her face, and her body was bloated and gray. She was lying next to an elderly man, and next to him, there was a teenage boy.

They heard a hoarse cry from down the street. Alex looked up to see Jim Green, his mouth opened in horror, running toward them.

"The boy. I have to see the boy!" he said. He pushed his way past them, grabbing the corpses, which fell to the ground.

The throats had been slit so deeply that the heads were nearly severed. Each corpse had been staked, leaving a hole through the heart like a double-barrel-shotgun blast.

Jim fell to the ground by the bodies, crying out, "No, no, no, oh, no. It's my nephew. I was afraid, but I didn't want to believe…."

Alex started over to him, then paused. Dolores was already on the way, a set and yet sympathetic look on her face. She rested her hands on his shoulders. "Come away, Jim. I know how you're feeling, and you know that—you know how I loved Amy. But this is the right and fitting thing for them. They're not under the control of that demon from hell anymore. Now your nephew can be buried in hallowed ground. Sheriff Cole will see to it that he's tended to. You come away now and have some coffee, and don't be looking at things that will just break your heart. Come on with me."

She managed to pull Jim away, and Beulah joined her, putting an arm around his shoulders and leading him into the boardinghouse.

"I am sorry for the pain this brings," Tall Feather said. "But we thought we must bring you those who were once your people."

"You did the right thing," Cody said.

Alex went up to speak to the chief as Cody walked over to talk to the sheriff. "Chief, do you—do you know any of the dead yourself?"

He looked down at her with his dark, wise eyes. "No, Alex, your father is not among the dead we have brought."

She stepped back. She saw that Cole and Cody had walked over to the second packhorse and lifted the blanket from the bodies. They eased the dead down to the ground, more easily than Jim had done. Alex thought she recognized a barber from Hollow Tree, but he was so discolored and bloated that she couldn't be sure.

She hadn't seen Dave leave, but he came down the street just then, driving a flatbed wagon. He stepped down and hitched the horses to the rail, and then he and the others began lifting the corpses, laying them out on the wagon bed.

"Tall Feather," she said, trying not to watch, "may we offer some refreshment to you and your men?"

He shook his head. "We thank you for letting us know we are welcome, but today we must go back to our people. We cannot leave the camp alone and unprotected."

"I understand," she said.

Tall Feather easily mounted his paint stallion by gripping the mane and throwing his leg over the animal's back. He was aging, but his agility was undiminished.

He bade a solemn farewell, and then he and his warriors turned, loping their ponies out of town.

When they were gone, Brendan turned to Cody. "We need to go," he said quietly.

"You have to go?" Alex asked. "Where?"

"We'll be back long before dusk," Cody promised. "No need to worry."

"Cody, you didn't answer me," Alex said. "Where are you going?"

"Out to the plain," he said. "There are some…signs I need to find. Signs that can lead me to Milo Roundtree's hideaway." He paused for a moment. They had an audience. Jim Green, Beulah and Dolores had gone inside, but Tess and Jewell were still hovering on the porch with Bert and Levy, and Dave and Cole were still standing beside the wagon.

Cody looked as if he wanted to say something to her, but he didn't speak.

"I should go with you," Alex said into the silence.

"No, you need to stay here," Cody said, and turned away. A moment later he and Brendan walked quickly toward the stables.

Alex started to follow, but Bert set a heavy hand on her shoulder and drew her aside, making certain none of the others could hear when he said, "Alexandra Gordon, what is wrong with you? Do you want to get that boy killed?"

She turned quickly to him. "Bert, I can help."

"You can help best by staying right here."

She turned and went into the house, furious but inwardly acknowledging that he was right.

THEY REACHED Hollow Tree in a few hours.

They had come heavily armed, but when they reached the center of town, Cody held still, a sinking feeling in his heart.

The town felt empty.

He turned to Brendan, who was looking haggard. This was where his family had lived. There was no doubt now. Hollow Tree was a ghost town. Tumbleweeds swept down the street, and nothing more.

Brendan dismounted in silence. "Let's do this. If anything is left crawling around, we've got to put it out of its misery—and prevent the same thing happening to anyone else."

Cody nodded, and Brendan started toward one of the buildings, his coat shoved behind his holster, a stake in his hand, his bow and quiver of arrows hung over his back.

"Brendan," Cody said, and Brendan stopped, his back to his friend.

"Maybe I should do this alone."

Brendan swung around. "I'll be all right. Really, what are the chances we'll find that my brother and his wife were the ones left here to…to feed on rodents? I say we move. Together. Come on."

Cody joined him.

Hollow Tree had been built according to much the same plan as Victory, Brigsby and dozens of other small towns that serviced the ranches and farms in the vastness of Texas. The sheriff's office was at one end of town, and the saloon was on the opposite side of the street at the other.

Hollow Tree had a small but fine church, however, at the corner of Main Street and what might have become a thriving cross street, had the town been given a chance to grow.

There was a barber shop right next to the sheriff's office, along with a general mercantile, a haberdashery and a place that had been called Miss Lola's Boutique. There were a pharmacy and a bank on the other side of the street. A fellow named Dr. Bernard Pritchard had set up his practice in town, along with James Jones, Esquire, Attorney at Law. Cody also saw a livery, a saddle maker and a blacksmith.

One by one, they started going through the buildings. Most were completely deserted, but a few contained corpses, *human* corpses, along with several decapitated vampires. Apparently someone in Hollow Tree had figured out how to fight the creatures, but if he had survived, he was no longer around.

Cody had been convinced that this was where Milo was holing up, so he searched every building with painstaking thoroughness. He looked for storm cellars, thinking of the way Bill Simpson and his family had taken shelter the night before, but they found nothing. He opened every closet in every building, businesses and residences alike, including the aptly called Hollow Tree Lodging House.

In small print beneath the name were the words Families Welcome. Not anymore, he thought grimly.

It was when they were nearly finished with the task at hand that they suddenly heard the loud slamming of a door. They stopped dead and looked at each other.

The sound had come from the church.

ALEX WAS CONVINCED SHE couldn't spend another minute in the house without going crazy.

In her effort to make sure that their guests didn't sit around dwelling on the troubles in their lives, Beulah had set the Simpsons to work; they were busily sharpening brooms, mops and any appropriate household utensil into a stake. The archery targets were still set up, and Bert had promised that when they finished with burial detail, he would be back to help the boys practice.

Jim Green had rallied quickly and was angry now. He wanted revenge. He, too, was happy to sharpen brooms and think about getting some target practice in, as well.

Alex managed to slip out to the stables. She didn't bother saddling Cheyenne; she leaped up on the horse the way Tall Feather had, then urged the mare along the carriage trail beside the house before hesitating. She didn't want to put anyone in danger—especially herself—and she didn't want to worry anyone, but she couldn't sit there in the house anymore.

She decided to help with the burial detail and called through one of the windows to tell Beulah where she was going, hoping to avoid giving the other woman a chance to protest.

Of course, Beulah tried to get one in, anyway.

"Alex Gordon, why on earth would you want to do that? You really ought to be—"

Alex didn't hear the rest.

She was already riding out.

She could see the men working as she rode closer, struggling because the ground out here was hard.

But a few of the townspeople had pitched in, and they seemed to be making as quick a task of it as possible.

Alex flicked the reins across Cheyenne's neck, and the mare took off, delighting in stretching her legs as she galloped across the open land between the graveyard and the town.

Cole looked up, resting his hands on his shovel as she drew near, slowing her mare.

"You should be at home," he said wearily.

"I came to see if I could help."

A flicker of amusement crossed his face. "What, you think you can dig faster than these men and me?"

She flushed. "No." She slid down from Cheyenne's back, tied the mare to the fence and walked over to him.

The corpses had been taken from the wagon and were lined up on the ground, covered with blankets.

The breeze blew a strand of hair into her eyes and she swept it aside, looking at Cole. "Did you know any of them?"

"Yeah," he said. "The doc is there, and a young fellow named Sam Birch, who was starting up a newspaper. But there's one corpse…no. He might have been passing through or something. Looks like a Latin gentleman. None of us knew him."

Alex sighed. "The doc—I remember him. I saw him a few times when I got sick…and when I broke my fingers once."

"He was a right fine man," Cole said.

"And Jim Green's nephew…" she murmured. "I really would like to help. I can't dig better or faster than anyone, but—"

Before she could say more, she noticed that Cole was looking past her. She heard hoofbeats and swung around to see who was coming.

Three riders were heading their way.

Three women.

Linda Gordon, Dolly and Sherry Lyn, from the saloon.

"Great," Cole muttered.

The women slid down from their horses and walked over. They looked awkward—except for Linda, who seemed to be in charge, even though Dolly was the madam.

Linda walked straight to the fence and accosted Cole.

"We need to see the corpses, Sheriff."

"Linda, please. No one needs to see those corpses," Cole said. "Go home."

Linda nodded toward Alex. "You let my stepdaughter in," she pointed out. "Girls, come on. It's our right to see the dead."

Cole's jaw tightened, and he shook his head.

"Cole, please…" Sherry Lyn said. "There was someone…I had a man, an old friend from back East, and he was coming out to see me. I…he didn't care what I'd been doing. Please."

"Sherry Lyn, if you cared about him, you don't want to see him," Cole said.

"I have to, Cole," she said. "His name is Carlos Ramiro, and…I have to know. I have to see…."

Cole fell silent then, and he made no protest as they walked around to the gate, where the other men greeted them politely, tipping their hats.

No one tried to stop them, only watched as Linda walked straight over to the row of bodies. She pulled back each blanket in turn until she got to the fourth corpse and went still.

Sherry Lyn suddenly let out a cry that was horrified, mournful, and full of the worst agony and loss imaginable. Then she fell to her knees and crawled over to the corpses.

"Sherry Lyn, no!" Dolly cried in dismay.

But Sherry Lyn wasn't to be deterred. She reached for the body of the man Cole had assumed to be a traveler and wailed, "It's him. Oh, God, it's him!"

She started to reach for the corpse, moving to hold him as if he were a soldier, dead in battle.

"No!" Cole called out, racing over to her.

But he was too late.

As Sherry Lyn clutched the body, the head went rolling away, and blank brown eyes stared sightlessly up to heaven.

CHAPTER FOURTEEN

LINDA DRAGGED the sobbing Sherry Lyn away from the body and held her comfortingly.

Everyone else stood there staring, clearly feeling uncomfortable.

Who would have guessed that a whore like Sherry Lyn would have been in love with a stranger none of them had even known existed?

Cole walked over to the girls, Alex at his heels, and patted Sherry Lyn on the back while she cried on Linda's shoulder. "There, there," he said ineffectually. "I'm sorry you had to see this. Linda will take you on back now. Roscoe can give you a double shot of whiskey, and maybe you'll be able to sleep for a bit."

Linda stared at him. "Whiskey and sleep. Think that will cure her, do you?"

"Please, Linda, take her back. It's no good her standing here with his…with the bodies…oh, come on, please. Let us get back to seeing them properly buried and have mercy on Sherry Lyn and get her out of here."

Linda glared at him but apparently saw his point. "Ladies, let's get home. Sherry Lyn, you need to lie down, and I want to check the place and make sure we'll be safe." She glanced at Cole. "Not that you don't make us feel safe. It's just that…seems like everything's on edge, like we're waiting for something to happen."

"It's always good to be alert—and do everything in your power to make sure you're not taken by surprise," Cole said.

Linda looked at him and nodded again.

"If Sherry Lyn is too upset to ride, I can take her back in the wagon, Cole," Dave said.

Alex opened her mouth, hoping to quickly distract Sherry Lyn from thoughts of the wagon—the wagon that had carried her lover's corpse to its final resting place.

But she was too late. Sherry Lyn took one look at the wagon and burst into tears again.

"What did I say?" Dave asked, as Alex stared accusingly at him.

"Come on," Alex said forcefully, slipping an arm through Sherry Lyn's. "I want to get out of here myself," she said. "Let's leave the men to their digging. I'd love a drink right now, a big swig of whiskey."

She walked to the gate, at first more or less dragging Sherry Lyn. But Linda helped, and between them, they managed to get Sherry Lyn out to where the horses were tethered, and she grew more malleable once they were outside the confines of the cemetery.

As they rode back toward town, Linda glanced over at Alex. "Very decent of you," she said.

Alex studied Linda's face. There was a curve to her lips that might have been a smile—or might have been a mocking smirk. The woman was difficult to read.

She nodded and rode ahead, not in the mood to try to figure out the stranger her father had married.

They reached the saloon and entered through the heavy new wooden doors—which weren't locked, Alex noted.

But it was daytime, and the fact that a saloon was open to the public meant, according to Cody, that it was more easily accessible to vampire intrusion than a private home, where only friends were invited in. Open to the public—just like her boardinghouse.

Roscoe was behind the bar, lining up shot glasses, and at the sound of the doors opening and the girls entering, he was so startled that he sent one flying into the air. He caught it swiftly, looking embarrassed.

"Hey, Roscoe," Alex said.

Linda laughed softly. "You could have locked the door," she told him.

"It's daytime, and someone might have come in. Someone with money who wanted to pay for a drink," he said, then frowned darkly when he noticed Sherry Lyn's tear-stained face. "More bad news?" he asked glumly.

"She knew one of the dead men the Indians brought in," Linda told him.

"Roscoe, we'd all like whiskey, please," Alex said.

He stared at her curiously for a moment, then shrugged. "Sure. Whiskey all around. On the house. What the hell else have we got to do?"

Like the others, Alex slid up on a bar stool. Once the shots were poured, Linda lifted her glass. "Cheers to us— at least we're still standing. And we might as well drink, just like the old Europeans as the plague swept away half the population."

"Linda!" Sherry Lyn said, horrified.

"Oh, Sherry Lyn, I *am* sorry for your loss, but we've got to remember that we're still alive. And if we've made it this far, we might just survive this thing all the way. Drink up, ladies!"

Then she looked at Alex, smiled mysteriously and downed her shot in one quick motion.

Feeling as if she were being challenged for some inexplicable reason, Alex did the same.

THE TWO MEN HURRIED toward the church, identified by a sign out front as the Plains Episcopal Church of Hollow Tree.

Cody, alert and ready, strode up the steps with Brendan at his heels. He strong-armed the door—and found that it was securely locked.

"Cody, something's not right here," Brendan said. "This is a house of worship. How could a creature like Milo Roundtree have gotten in here?"

"I don't know, but someone—or something—is in there," Cody said. "You heard the noise, same as I did."

"Maybe you shouldn't have started by trying to bang the door down," Brendan suggested.

"And how else were we supposed to get in?" Cody asked, but privately he was irritated with himself, because who- or *what*ever was in there couldn't help knowing about their presence by now.

"We could try knocking," Brendan said.

"Knocking? Why the hell—"

Too late. Brendan had already rapped heavily on the door.

Cody groaned and stepped back. There was a small casement window—stained glass, and bloodred in the sunlight on the second story, directly above the door, and someone was looking out, his identity hidden by the thick colored glass.

The window opened a crack, and to Cody's amazement, a man in ecclesiastical garments peered out at them. "Who are you?" he demanded.

"My name is Cody Fox, and this is Brendan Vincent," he said. "We're trying to hunt down the men who destroyed this town."

The priest glared at him. "Go out into the street and stand directly beneath the sun."

They did as ordered.

"This isn't a great test," Brendan called out to the man. "They don't go out a lot in daylight, because they don't have much strength then. But that doesn't mean they *can't* go out during the day."

Cody elbowed him. "What the hell did you tell him that for?"

"If we lie, he won't let us in, and it's important that we talk to the man, don't you think?" Brendan asked.

But from his vantage point above them, the priest was watching carefully, and he apparently had his own way of determining the truth about their alive-or-dead status.

"I'm coming down," he said, and the window closed with a snap.

"See? Honesty. It's the best policy," Brendan said.

They heard a rasping sound as they walked back up the church steps—evidently something heavy had been blocking the door. A second later, the door opened and the priest, a heavy cross hung around his neck, stared out at them.

He was about thirty years old, blond and blue-eyed, but his features, and the sharpness of his expression, indicated that he was intelligent and had great strength of purpose.

"Come in," he said.

A small group of people was standing behind the piano

in the nave: a blond boy of about sixteen, a man in his mid-forties, a woman of about sixty, and another who appeared to be in her twenties.

Cody stared at them for a moment, then turned to the priest and asked, "How the hell did you manage to survive?"

Brendan elbowed him. "Cody, this is a church," he whispered.

That brought a smile to the priest's lips. "A church in the midst of hell. I prayed that you would come…."

"You prayed that—*we*—would come?" Brendan asked.

"That help would come," the priest said. He offered his hand. "I'm Father Joseph. Back there we have Timmy Kale, Miss Mona Hart, Mr. Adam Jefferies and Mrs. Alice Springfield, our pianist."

"How do you do?" Cody and Brendan said in unison, then looked at each other and couldn't help grinning. The situation was terrifying, but it was also absurd.

And wonderful, Cody thought. Because somehow these people had survived.

"Have you ventured out at all…since this began?" Cody asked.

Father Joseph smiled. "Oh, yes. We've run out, but only at high noon. And only to bring back what the general mercantile had in canned food, what smoked meat we could find…to get water, and to raid the closest houses for some bedding." He paused.

"What about the people who were…killed?" Cody asked.

The priest spoke softly, "We dealt with them," he said flatly, his tone indicating that it wasn't something he wanted to discuss further.

"We'll get you back to Victory today," Cody said. "In fact, we need to leave as soon as possible."

"We're ready when you are. But you might have noticed, we don't have horses," he said. "What animals didn't run off…well, they're dead.…"

"There's got to be a wagon sitting around somewhere in town," Cody said.

"There's a livery down the street. You'll find something there. It's not like people realized what was going on in time to get out.…" He looked back at the frightened survivors by the piano, then turned back to Cody. "They came at night, like black birds from hell with burning red eyes and…and the result was carnage."

"And that night, you five were the only ones in here?" Cody asked.

Father Joseph shook his head. "I was in here, praying. Alice was at her piano, practicing for the Sunday service. But the others…a man brought them here as the attack started. A rather strange man. He hesitated at the door, then came in, dragging the others with him. He told me to believe in God and in the church, and to guard those he was leaving in my care. He said that if we had faith, we'd be safe in the church—the demons wouldn't be able to enter. And I reckon he was right. We've been safe, but we've also been careful. I'm sure they know we're here, and I'm sure they've been trying to devise a way to get us out." He smiled grimly at his own ironic choice of words.

"Okay, let's get right down to the livery, pick out a wagon and get the horses hitched," Brendan said. "And pray to God those horses will be polite enough not to fight us on the way back over to Victory."

"Right," Cody said, still staring thoughtfully at the

priest, wondering about the identity of the man who had brought these people here, then disappeared.

"Cody, the sun won't stay up forever," Brendan said.

"Be ready," Cody told the priest.

"We can walk over there with you now, if you think…if you think it's safe," Father Joseph said.

"No, wait here. Brendan and I can manage on our own," Cody said.

The livery was clear—they had been in it just minutes ago. But he didn't want to take the chance of having to protect the others any longer than necessary.

He unhitched his horse and strode after Brendan, who had already headed down the street, his horse's reins in his hands.

"What the hell do you think really went on back there?" Brendan asked, shaking his head. "Who would bring folks to a church, then go back out into the middle of the massacre? Why wouldn't he have stayed in the church?"

"That's something we can ask Father Joseph once we get them all back to Victory," Cody said.

"I'm more interested in finding out how they knew the way to destroy their dead."

They found a wagon and, with a little searching, harnesses for the horses.

Neither animal seemed enamored of the concept of becoming wagon horses, and they protested with rearing and neighing, but finally the men got the horses hitched together. Brendan led them down the street, getting them adjusted to pulling the wagon as one, stopping in front of the church.

Father Joseph was standing at the door, waiting for them.

He waited for the others to run out to the wagon, then followed, carrying a large portmanteau.

"Father Joseph, we need to travel light," Cody said.

The priest met his eyes. "My friend, this is filled with holy water and sharpened crosses. I see that you know all about these creatures and are armed against them, and I think it's a good idea for all of us to have weapons at our disposal, don't you?"

"You're right, Father. We'll find room for your bag," Cody said.

He looked up to the sky, judging the remaining hours of daylight, as he followed Father Joseph to the wagon. So far, the sky was clear and blue. But night would come, and it was going to take them much longer to return to Victory than it had taken to reach Hollow Tree.

"I'll drive, you watch?" Brendan suggested.

Cody nodded, and Brendan hiked himself up to the driver's bench, picking up the reins.

Cody jumped on the back of the wagon, his bow slung over his shoulder.

Father Joseph's four survivors were silent, huddled together. Cody smiled at the boy—Timmy, the Reverend had said. The boy stared back at him, not blinking.

"Shall we sing?" the older woman, Alice, suggested.

"I think we should stay quiet and not draw undue attention to ourselves," Father Joseph said.

Thank you, Father Joseph. Thank you, Cody thought.

It was going to be a long enough ride as it was.

ALEX STEPPED OUTSIDE the saloon and looked down the street. There wasn't a soul to be seen. She looked up at the sky and felt a moment's unease. The sun wasn't sinking quite yet, but it wasn't strong, either. The air had taken on the slight difference that came when sunset was near.

And Cody and Brendan weren't back.

The others had returned from the cemetery a little while ago, their grim task completed. Bert and Levy had headed back to the boardinghouse, and the others had gone home, ready to batten down for another long night—except for Cole and Dave, who were staying at the saloon, one of them always on guard.

She watched the street for another long minute, wishing that they would appear in the distance. But they didn't.

"Alex?"

She swung around. Cole was watching her from the saloon door.

"I'm coming back in," she told him. "It's still daylight."

"And you still shouldn't be out there alone," he said firmly.

"All right, big brother, all right," she teased him. "I just…"

"You're just worried. I know. I am, too," he told her. "But come on inside, anyway."

"Cole, where did they go today?" she asked. "I know you know."

He stared at her for a long moment. "Hollow Tree," he said. "They're looking for Milo's hideout. Cody says there has to be one."

She nodded. "Cole?"

"Yes?"

"Do you believe—do you believe that my father could be a monster?"

He lowered his head and sighed softly, then looked up at her. "Alex, I've seen lots of good people turned into demons by this—this disease."

"Don't you think that some people can fight it?"

"I don't know, Alex. But...but you can't let yourself be fooled, you can't take any chances. You know that, right?" Cole said.

"Yes, I know," she said.

He was still staring at her, and though he'd never said the words, he'd answered her question. No, he didn't believe that her father could be anything but a monster.

She glanced down the street in the direction of the distant town of Hollow Tree, then sighed and went back to the saloon.

Cole was still standing in the doorway. "Alex, your father was a good man. He was like a father to me, too. He was one of the most respected men in town. But the man you knew and loved, the man I loved, is dead."

"I know that, Cole."

He nodded. "We all just—well, we care about you, Alex," he said.

She smiled and gave him a brief hug. "I know that, Cole. I know that."

"Let's go in. And let's have some faith in Cody and Brendan, huh?"

"I have all the faith in the world in them," Alex said. "But no matter how much faith we have—well, they're only men, and there are only two of them."

"But they're two men who know what they're doing."

Inside the saloon, Dave was playing cards with the girls. Sherry Lyn seemed to have recovered. She sniffed now and then, but she also cried out with pleasure as she took a poker pot.

Roscoe was still standing behind the bar, drying the same shot glass he'd been drying when Alex had stepped outside.

"Hey, where's Jigs? I haven't seen him all day," Alex said, noticing the empty piano bench.

"Sleeping," Linda said. "He's been sleeping all day."

"I'll just go up and see that he's all right," Alex said.

Linda adjusted the cards in her hand. "Last door at the end of the hall, honey," she said.

Alex walked up the stairs and headed straight for the last room, then hesitated at the door. The poor man was probably exhausted. Keeping guard, on edge—all of them afraid that if they went to sleep, they might not wake up.

Or worse.

That they *would* wake up. As monsters.

She raised her hand, preparing to knock gently. But then she decided that if he was sleeping, she didn't want to wake him, only look in and make sure he was all right. She turned the knob carefully and opened the door.

The room was in shadow.

She stepped in, trying to make out the man on the bed in the dim light.

As she did, a cry like a bobcat's suddenly filled the room, coming from behind the door.

The door slammed into her, knocking her off balance, and she gasped for breath as Jigs came flying out at her, hands like talons, fangs dripping with saliva and anticipation.

"THEY'RE COMING," CODY SAID.

The priest stared at him.

"I can hear them. Get ready."

He heard Brendan swear, heedless of who might have heard him in back, and saw him flick the reins to urge the horses into a burst of speed.

They were still about five miles out of Victory, and the sun was going down.

Cody stood, balancing on the back of the wagon, stringing his bow, watching the sky.

The sun was a ball of fire in the west, and shadows were beginning to stretch across the plain.

The vampires came in a wave, but there were only a few so far, few enough that Cody could count them. Six.

To his surprise, he realized that the priest was standing at his side. He'd opened his portmanteau and pulled out a bow and arrows. Now he, too, was taking aim, gauging the distance as the creatures approached.

Alice was passing out stakes and vials of holy water to the other passengers. The boy slipped forward to take a position next to Brendan, a stake at the ready in his raised right hand.

The other two were braced against the side of the wagon so they could shove their stakes home without tumbling to the ground.

"Now?" Father Joseph asked.

"Wait…wait…hold…*now!*" Cody said.

They picked off the first two immediately. The third reached the wagon, flapping and shrieking, giant wings beating the air. The man surged forward, impaling the creature.

Cody nocked another arrow as, from the corner of his eye, he saw the monster's body fall under the wheels. The wagon shuddered, and they all struggled for balance.

Cody let his arrow fly.

The fourth creature went down without reaching the wagon. Father Joseph's arrow hit the fifth, which exploded in a burst of black powder, still fifteen feet from the wagon.

The sixth came diving toward them.

Alice rose. "God, let my aim be true," she prayed.

Cody reached for a stake.

He didn't need it. Alice splashed holy water at the screeching shadow, which let out a hideous wail and flopped into the back of the wagon. Father Joseph shoved it, and it fell into the dirt behind them, writhing as it turned to ash, which flew toward the sky like a tiny whirlwind.

The wagon kept rolling at a breakneck pace. Father Joseph lost his balance and fell backward, but the young woman caught and steadied him.

"Victory is straight ahead!" Brendan shouted.

ALEX SCREAMED, STUNNED and weaponless. She leaped away from the door, staring at the wild thing that Jigs had become.

He was ashen, with a day's growth of beard shadowing his face, and his eyes glowed with a red fire. Most terrifying of all, he was grinning at her with a madman's pleasure.

"Jigs! Jigs, stop!" she cried as he started toward her.

To her amazement, he paused for a moment, his expression uncertain.

In that blessed second of reprieve, she streaked past him out the door and slammed it shut, then leaned against it to keep Jigs from escaping. Immediately he began screaming and shrieking, hammering at the wood between them.

But by then Cole had come up the stairs, Dave on his tail.

"Alex, what in God's name…?" the sheriff demanded.

"It's Jigs—he's infected," she said.

"Jigs?" Cole said incredulously. "But…he hasn't left the saloon."

As he spoke, the door began to splinter.

"Dave, get something…anything. And hurry!"

Dave turned around, white as a sheet, and shouted down the stairs. Roscoe came rushing up, a sharpened stake in his hand.

Cole grabbed it from him and watched as the door shuddered and began to split.

With one final blow from the far side, the door shattered. There was not help for it. Cole gripped the stake hard and slammed it into Jigs.

The pianist let out a howl of pain, staggering back, gripping the stake, which had only gone through the shoulder, not his heart, as the momentum of his escape had nearly carried him straight past Cole.

But Jigs didn't come at them again. Instead, he staggered down to his knees, deathly white.

"Alex!"

She spun around, recognizing Cody's voice and feeling weak with relief that he was back. He was halfway up the stairs, his features taut with concern. Somehow she refrained from throwing herself in his arms.

"It's Jigs," she said.

Cole was already stepping forward, ready to rip the stake from Jigs's shoulder and impale him with it once again.

"Wait, please!" she cried. "Cody—can we save him?"

Cody stared at her, looking almost dismayed.

"We can give him my blood. Please?" Alex begged.

"Alex, what are you talking about?" Cole asked.

"Alex, no," Cody said.

"Cody, please. This is Jigs. We have to try to save him."

But Cody shook his head, then told Cole, "We'll get the

stake out. If he doesn't die, there's a chance for him. But be careful. Don't let him bite you. If he even scrapes you with his teeth, it will make you weaker and could end up killing you."

Alex stepped back, relieved that he was going to help Jigs, who was still wailing and writhing frantically as Cody and Cole closed in, as careful as if they were trying to pin a rattler.

She turned away, unable to watch, and saw that Roscoe and the girls were at the top of the stairs, watching with wide eyes.

And they weren't alone.

To her amazement, a priest stepped past them and headed toward her end of the hall. He was saying a prayer and carrying a vial of what had to be holy water in front of him. He went straight past her, to where Jigs was screaming as the men worked to remove the stake without getting bitten.

"In the name of the Lord," the man thundered, and sprinkled the holy water around.

To Alex's amazement, Jigs went silent, then began to sniffle. Cody and Cole quickly grabbed him and carried him back to his bed.

Cody looked at Alex. "I need my bag," he said. "It's at the boardinghouse."

"I'll go," the priest said.

"No, send Brendan. They don't know you. And priest or no, they might not let you in."

"I hear you," Brendan said as he walked along the hall toward them. "I'm going."

Cole asked, "Father, who are you?"

"Father Joseph, and I'd just come out to serve in Hollow Tree when this terror started," Father Joseph said.

"And you're…alive?" Dave asked skeptically.

"Father Joseph and a few of the others were holed up in the church," Cody explained.

"Others? Where are they?" Cole asked.

"Downstairs." Cody said.

Alex took a look at Jigs. His shoulder was bleeding, but Cody was stanching the flow with a wadded-up pillow-case.

Jigs had gone silent, but his eyes were open. He looked scared, and as docile as a lamb.

"Do we need rope?" Alex asked.

"Yeah, probably a good idea," Cody said.

"I think he still fears a higher power," Father Joseph said softly.

"And I'm afraid we still have to fear him," Cody said.

Brendan returned with the bag. Roscoe, who had come to the doorway out of curiosity and overheard the conversation, produced a curtain cord, which they used to truss Jigs.

"The rest of you might want to get out. Brendan can assist me," Cody said.

"I said that I'd give him my blood, Cody. You can't keep using your own," Alex protested.

"It's no good, Alex. Mine has a—a special coagulating power. Trust me, it will be all right. I know what I'm doing. Everyone, please, I need you to get out."

"Look, he can have my blood," Cole said.

"Or…mine," Dave offered, a little hesitantly.

"No. It needs to be mine," Cody said. "Out."

Cole took Alex's arm, leading her toward the stairs. The others turned and hurried down ahead of them.

Downstairs, Alex was stunned to see that the saloon was

now hosting two women, a middle-aged man and a boy of about sixteen.

"Hello," she said.

"Hello," the older of the two women said, stepping forward and taking Alex's hand. "I'm Alice. The boy there is Timmy, that's Miss Mona Hart, and that's Mr. Adam Jefferies."

"Uh—how do you do?" Alex said.

Alex hadn't realized that Linda was standing behind her until the other woman spoke softly into her ear. "Might want to get them over to the boardinghouse," she suggested. "At least the boy and the ladies."

"I own a boardinghouse across the street," Alex heard herself say. "I'm sure Beulah, our cook, has supper ready, and that it will stretch."

"A hot meal?" the boy said, smiling in a way that suggested he hadn't had one in a long time.

"Yes, so come on. We'll all walk over together."

"I'll escort you," Dave said.

"Thank you," Alex said, then glanced hopefully at Linda.

"I'll look out for Jigs," the other woman offered.

Alex nodded and headed across the street, her strange little posse following her.

"You can't keep using your blood like this," Brendan said.

"I know. But—this will be all right," Cody said.

"Are you sure he's not too far gone?"

"I don't think so. He reacted to the holy water like a child who's behaved badly. It didn't burn him, it cowed him."

"How did this happen?" Brendan asked, as Cody's blood started to flow into Jigs.

Cody looked at him. "You know how it happened," he said quietly.

Brendan shook his head. "You know what I mean. We see everyone in town, everything that happens, but somehow someone slipped in and attacked him."

"I don't think Jigs *was* attacked. I think he was seduced by someone he knew, someone he didn't know was dead."

"So you mean…?" Brendan asked, wincing, knowing what Cody was about to say.

"I mean there's a monster among us."

CHAPTER FIFTEEN

FULL DARKNESS CAME.

Even the sunset had looked ominous, streaking the heavens with crimson and gold, before darkening quickly. Unnaturally quickly.

And now, coming from all around them, she could hear the wolves.

Alex paced in the entry hall, waiting for Cody to come back from the saloon.

He couldn't keep giving so much blood.

She sensed someone behind her and spun around. It was the young priest from the Episcopal church.

He studied her gravely.

"I believe your friend will be all right."

She flushed. "I'm praying that all of us will make it, Father. I'm amazed—and glad, of course—that you and the others were able to survive."

"We had the church, and the church gave us comfort."

"Of course," Alex replied.

"A church is not just a building. It's consecrated, and we filled it with belief. That's what we all need if we're to survive, Miss Gordon, belief."

Alex frowned. "Belief, yes, but…still, some of the dead must have come after you. How did you know—I mean, frankly, not many men would suspect vampires, much less know how to kill them."

"It was the gentleman who led the others to the church who warned me. I thought at first that he was a madman, but when Timmy told me how his own father tried to rip his throat out, I believed, and quickly. The man explained to me that we had to rely on belief, on faith. He spoke like a scholar, and he explained to me how the vampires had to be killed. I begged him to stay, but after he explained to us how to melt what silver we had and form it into bullets, then dip them in holy water, he left. I never saw him again. No doubt those monsters killed him. And yet none of us would have survived without his help."

She stared at him.

The man who had saved Father Joseph and his small flock spoke well, almost like a scholar.

A man just like her father.

Her heart began to hammer.

"Father Joseph, you said that you were new to Hollow Tree. When did you come?"

"Six months ago."

"But Alice—she lived in Hollow Tree a long time, right?"

"Yes, why?"

Alex didn't answer. She burst through to the kitchen, where the women were making the final preparations to serve dinner. Alice was shucking peas.

"Alice?" Alex said, striding over to her.

The older woman straightened the pair of spectacles on her nose and looked up expectantly. "Yes, Miss Gordon?"

"The man who brought you to the church—"

"No, not me. I was already there, practicing my piano

for the Sunday services. Would have been mighty nice to have an organ, but out here, we make do."

Alex drew out a chair and sat down next to the older woman. "Please, this is important. Did you know that man?"

Alice inhaled and stared back at her, then shook her head. "No, no, I didn't."

"Are you sure?" Alex pressed.

"Yes, I'm certain."

Beyond disappointed, Alex stood, thanked the woman and left the room, returning to the front hall, where she posted herself at the window and stared out into the dark.

She wanted Cody and Brendan to come back. And she wanted to know what had happened. Jigs, a sweet, harmless man if ever there was one...

How had one of the creatures gotten to him? There had been sentries on duty at the saloon every night. The only way someone could have gotten to him was from...

...within.

It felt as if her blood suddenly froze in her veins.

Linda. It had to be Linda. Her own stepmother.

Linda, who hadn't been there the night of the first attack. Who came and went...

She had to get back over to the saloon.

But when she turned away from the window, she saw Adam Jefferies standing there.

"I know what you were trying to find out, Miss Gordon," he said.

"Oh?" she asked carefully.

"You don't remember me—you only met me once, when your father brought you with him to the bank where I work. Worked. Your father kept some extra funds with us, said that way he'd have something left if one bank got hit by robbers."

"I'm sorry," Alex apologized, wondering where all this was leading. "I—"

"Never mind," Jefferies said. "You want to know if the man who brought us to the church was your father."

She inhaled sharply, hope filling her. "And?"

"I'm not sure. He had a bandanna over his face, and he wore his hat low. And he was…so pale, almost ghostly, what I could see of him. But his voice…his voice reminded me of your father's. I didn't really think about it, though, because I thought your father was dead, but thinking back…well, I just don't know. It might have been your father."

Her father! And he had been saving people.

Poor Mr. Jefferies. She was pretty sure he almost fainted when she crossed the foyer toward him, grasped his head between her hands and planted a kiss right on his lips. At the very least, his blush was several shades deeper than sunset.

"I really can't say for sure," he told her.

"But it's something," she whispered. "Though…you might not want to mention this to anyone else…."

"As you wish," he said.

"Tell the others I'm going over to the saloon."

"Oh? Is that wise?"

"The others are still there, and they'll look out for me. But if you wouldn't mind…"

"Yes?"

"Would you watch me, see that I make it safely? Don't take any chances yourself, but—"

"Miss Gordon, I'll be happy to stand guard for you, and you don't have to be afraid. Father Joseph may be a gentle man, but he's proved to be an amazing warrior for Christ, and he's trained his small army quite well." With that, Jefferies walked her to the door, opened it and said again, "I'll be watching."

She smiled, then turned and raced across the street. He watched her all the way.

And they both watched the darkening sky.

CODY STAYED WITH JIGS for a long time after he had transfused him.

Brendan had gone down to join Dave, Cole, Roscoe and the girls.

Cody just sat and watched Jigs, and he didn't rise until he heard someone enter the saloon downstairs. He listened, frowning as he realized that it was Alex. He listened to her climb the stairs, opened the door to greet her, then paused. She wasn't on her way to see him.

She stopped at a door down the hall and pounded on it. "Linda!"

The door opened. Linda stood there, looking worn and disheveled. "What?"

"Where were you the night the town was attacked?" Alex demanded.

"What?"

"You heard me just fine," Alex snapped. "Where were you?"

"I wasn't out turning people into vampires, and I never touched Jigs, if that's what you're asking me," Linda told her heatedly.

Alex's hands were on her hips. "You married my father. And right after that, he died."

For a moment it looked as if Linda was going to take a swing at Alex, who looked as if she was barely hanging on to her self-control and no doubt would have swung back.

"Hey!" Dave called from below. "This isn't the time for a fight."

Linda managed to control herself. "I loved your father, Alex. But you go right ahead and think whatever you want about me." She started to close her door.

Alex slammed a hand against it. "If anyone else is hurt, if Jigs dies, you'll pay. I'll make sure you pay myself."

"Alex!" Cody strode down the hall and caught her by the arms.

Linda glared at them both, then closed her door.

"Alex," Cody said again, spinning her around to face him.

"What? It's Linda—it has to be Linda who tried to turn Jigs!"

"You don't know that," he told her.

"She married my father, and my father is dead!" Alex said angrily. "Or—or a *thing*. And you're going to try to kill him."

"Alex, we have to find Milo Roundtree and kill *him*," Cody told her.

She nodded. "Right. And after you've killed him, you'll have to go after the others. *All* the others."

"Alex…" He couldn't find the words to explain, not there. He called downstairs. "Brendan? Can you watch Jigs for a while?" he asked.

"Sure thing," Brendan said, already on his way up the stairs. He tipped his hat to Alex.

"Brendan," she said, and smiled at him as he kept going down the hall to Jigs's room.

At least the tension seemed to be easing from her, Cody thought.

"Let's go," Cody said. "Let's get some time alone, and

something to eat." For a moment he thought she was going to fight him. That she was going to protest and carry on trying to prove that Linda was a vampire.

But she only stared back at him, still tense, but reasonable. "All right. For now," she said. "But you've got to warn the sheriff, Cody. You've got to."

"Brendan's already warned him that...that someone here isn't exactly what they seem," Cody said.

They went down the stairs together. Cole looked up and nodded at Cody as they passed, the movement barely perceptible.

As they left the saloon, Cody stopped and gazed up at the sky. Night had fallen, but there was a red haze over the moon, which was almost full.

"Tomorrow someone needs to get out to John Snow. He and his family need to come into town for the next few days," Cody said, thinking out loud.

"Why?" Alex asked him sharply. "Because the moon is nearly full?"

He looked at her and nodded. "Yes."

"And Milo will be at his most powerful then?"

"Yes," he said simply.

They made it across the street without incident. The boardinghouse door opened as they neared it.

It was Bert, just keeping guard.

"There you are," he said, relieved. "Beulah was getting worried. Everyone else is in the dining room, eating, but Tess just took trays up to your rooms. Beulah figured you two might be needing some rest. She made up a sack of food for everyone over at the saloon, too."

"That's kind of her. Let me have the sack and I'll run it over right now," Cody said.

Alex frowned. "We just got back, Cody."

"Go on upstairs, Alex. This will only take me a minute," he said.

Her jaw tightened, but she didn't argue. Wearily, she started up the stairs.

"THIS IS GREAT—THANKS," Dave said enthusiastically when Cody showed up with the food.

"I'll run a couple of plates up to Brendan—and Linda," Cody said.

"We can handle it," Cole said.

Cody nodded. "I know you can, but I'd like to look in on Jigs, anyway."

Cody made up two plates and headed up the stairs. Linda's door was closed, so he passed it and went to Jigs's room first.

"How's he doing?" he asked Brendan as he handed over dinner.

"Hasn't moved since you left. But his pulse is strong, and his color is better."

"If he makes it through the night, he'll be fine. I think. When you get tired of sitting here—"

"I'll have Cole or Dave spell me," Brendan said.

Cody nodded and headed down the hall to tap on Linda's door. She answered it looking tired.

"I brought you some dinner," he said.

She flashed him a smile of gratitude, with nothing of her usual seductive air. "Thanks."

"Get some rest after you eat," he told her.

"I'm trying, trust me," she said, then closed the door in his face.

Cody stared at the closed door for a moment, then turned and headed back downstairs.

Linda took the plate of food and set it on her bedside table. It smelled delicious, and she was certainly hungry.

But she was also worried.

She looked at the man who stepped away from his hiding place behind the door.

"This isn't safe," she said.

"But it's necessary," he replied.

ALEX MEANT TO WAIT FOR CODY to start eating, but the aroma coming from her plate was too tempting. She hadn't realized she was starving until then, but now the only thing she could think of was eating. She sat down on the edge of the mattress and dug in.

She hadn't taken more than a few bites, though, before he arrived bearing his own plate, and a bottle of elderberry wine. He lifted it, and she shrugged.

"Looks good," she said.

He took the chair at her dressing table and started eating as if he, too, had suddenly discovered that he was ravenous.

"Cody, I think Linda is…infected." Before he could answer, she added, "Think about it. She's in and out of town, and no one really knows where she goes when she's not here. I get the sense she's conniving and manipulative. I think she killed my father. And you're wrong about him, too. I heard what happened in Hollow Tree. Someone saved those people in the middle of the massacre. Someone who *knew*. Someone who taught them how to deal with vampires. Cody, I think that man was a vampire himself, but he was strong and didn't turn evil. I talked to Mr. Jefferies, and he knew my father and thinks it could have been him. Don't you see? It had to be my father, and there has to be a way to reach him."

Cody stood, setting his plate down, and paced over to the window, where he stared at the drapes as if he could see through them.

She got up and hurried to join him. "Cody, it has to be my father. It *has* to be."

He set his hands on her shoulders, staring into her eyes. "No, Alex," he said sadly, "it doesn't."

"But—"

"Don't you think I understand how you feel? No," he said, shaking his head, "no, of course you don't, because…" He met her eyes, his own dark with the intensity of his gaze. "Alex, I keep thinking, praying, that it was *my* father."

She gasped, stunned, and backed away from him. "What?"

He let out a sigh, turned and strode toward the bed, where he stopped with his back to her. Finally he turned to face her. "You don't know," he said softly, "because I haven't told you. God knows I keep the truth from the world as much as I can."

"I don't know what you're talking about, Cody. What truth?" she demanded.

"I was born in New Orleans, Alex, but I was conceived out here, on a ranch near Victory. It still exists, and I still own it—the land, and what's left of a bunch of fallen-down, rotting buildings."

"But what does that mean?" Alex asked. She felt an overwhelming sense of dread, but at the same time, she wanted to know the truth, everything, no matter what he had to say.

He sighed. "This…war didn't just start. And this isn't the only place vampires have tried to take hold. It's just easier out here, where one of them can slip into a town and make a meal of the population."

"You've hunted vampires before. Obviously," she said.

He walked back to her and set his hands on her shoulders. He looked into her eyes, and when he spoke, it was sadly, his voice filled with pain.

"Alex, I *am* a vampire."

CHAPTER SIXTEEN

"WHAT?" SHE GASPED. He...must be crazy, driven mad by his continual search for monsters. "Cody, that's impossible. I've seen—"

"Alex, why do you think I can only use *my* blood for the transfusions?" He released her, stepping back, and his voice turned almost cold. "I'm an anomaly, as far as I can tell. The story I got as a child was pretty confused, but my mother didn't believe my father had been dead for very long. But he came home to her—when all the evidence says he was lying dead on the plain. The way I figure it, my father was attacked and...turned, but somehow he made it back to her, and that was the night I was conceived. He loved her deeply, and—I know she loved him. The idea of finding a new husband never once occurred to her. And, like you, she never believed that a man she loved so much could be evil. But as I grew up, it became apparent that I wasn't quite your usual kid. If I was injured, I healed. I was riddled with bullets during the war, and everyone was sure I was dead. When it turned out I was alive, I was discharged and sent home to heal. Except I already *was* healed. That's why I went to medical school, though. I wanted to help others heal." He paused. "I have some other unusual abilities, too. I can move like lightning, and if I concentrate, I can cloak myself, like a shadow. I have a superhuman strength. And my hearing and eyesight are acute. I really am—a vampire, Alex. Half vampire, anyway, which I guess is why I don't need an invitation to enter a house."

His story was insane.

"Cody, I know you believe what you're saying, but it's just because you've been doing this so long that you're… You're just strong, that's all, and you've got…you've got good blood," she said weakly.

"No, Alex, I am half monster," he said firmly.

"You don't drink blood!"

"Yes, I do."

Despite herself, she felt her hand slip to her throat. "But—"

He shook his head, turning away from her again and striding across the room. "I don't take human blood, Alex. Like anyone, I get most of my nutrition from food, and I learned as a child to subsist on any kind of blood when food just wasn't enough. And to go a very long time between…drinks."

"So what kind of blood do you…?" she whispered.

"Cow's blood, Alex. I've been known to hang around a slaughterhouse or two," he said dryly.

"Cow's blood," she repeated.

"Wild pigs did well enough when I went to war," he said.

Alex blinked. "Wild pigs."

"Right. Once, as a child, I bit the family dog. I really loved that dog, and because of me, he almost died. When he made it, I knew that I'd never touch a dog, or any pet, again. Or a coyote or a wolf, for that matter. They're too much like dogs."

"Chickens?" she suggested.

He turned around and met her eyes again. "Chickens—if I have no choice. They don't provide much blood, not like a cow or a horse."

"Oh."

"It's true. Every word I've spoken is true. I never wanted to come to Victory. I wanted to heal the injured—boys from the North as well as the South—as they straggled back into New Orleans. I wanted to deliver babies. But I'd gotten a reputation, I guess you'd say, and I worked for the government on a few cases before the war. And now I'm here because Brendan had heard about me, and he asked me to come out and help him with what was going on here. So you see, Alex, my father is out here somewhere, too. And I need to find him."

All Alex could do was stare at him. After a long moment he turned, went back over to her dressing table and picked up his plate.

"I'll take this to my room and leave you to your thoughts."

He walked away, closing the door behind him, and she couldn't even manage to move.

She couldn't—wouldn't—accept what he'd said. He was crazy. He'd been doing this too long.

And yet…

That first night…

He *had* moved like a shadow himself, slipped up behind Milo in a way that had seemed almost inhumanly effective. He knew exactly what he was doing. He…

It's true. Every word I've spoken is true.

He believed it. And after what she had seen…

She believed it, too.

She sprang into action, hurrying to the door, throwing it open—and then she froze, staring.

He'd set his plate down on the dresser and was at the washstand. His shirt was gone, and he was lathering himself up almost frenziedly. He scrubbed his face and chest, then drenched himself in cold water, letting it sluice over him. His back was to her, but when he looked up, she could see his face in the mirror.

And he could see her.

"What?" he demanded. His tone was sharp, as if he was trying to create a wall between them.

"I don't understand," she said.

"I think I laid it out simply enough. My father became a vampire. Then he went back to my mother—and I was conceived. Therefore, I am half vampire. Half monster. And I've figured out that I'll never get to go home and go back to simply being a city doctor—delivering babies and setting broken legs."

"So?" Alex said.

He turned around, mopping his face with a towel, frowning as he looked at her. "So…what?" he asked, scowling.

She strode into the room, facing him. Close. Almost backing him into the washstand. "I never took you for a coward."

"What the hell are you talking about?" His eyes narrowed.

"So you have a little quirk in your pedigree," she said, then smiled. "This is America. I'm some kind of Northern European mix. Between them, Tess and Jewell have Chinese, African, Mexican and Indian blood. God knows what Jigs is."

He allowed himself a small, grim smile. "Nice try, Alex, but that's not quite the same as being half vampire."

"It is for you, Cody. You use your birth, the abilities you inherited, for good," she said softly.

He pulled her against him for a long moment, and she could smell the clean scent of soap on his chest.

"Alex…"

"Even if you're going to hunt vampires all your life, there's no reason not to allow yourself to care—not have a home to go back to after you go hunting."

He cupped her face, lifting her chin. "You still don't believe me, do you? I'm a monster."

"And you still don't believe *me*, do you?" she whispered. "I don't see you as a monster. I see you as the man who saved my life. I see you as the man I want…for however much time I can have, whenever that time may be."

"No, Alex, I have no right. I *never* had the right…."

"Cody, for the love of God, will you please let me have the last word, just this once?"

He fell silent, staring at her.

She lifted herself on her toes, finding his lips, kissing them softly at first, then passionately.

"Cody, I need you tonight," she whispered against his mouth.

He wrapped his arms around her again, his chin resting atop her head, and he said, "I don't know what the future will bring, Alex. I honestly don't know."

"None of us do," she assured him.

And then he kissed her. Maybe, in his own mind, he felt he had to prove his humanity, because he was gentle, his kiss feather light. He lifted her as if she were precious and laid her down so tenderly that she was aware only of the softness of the mattress beneath her.

He stretched out beside her, stroking her cheek, staring into her eyes....

"Alex..."

She sighed softly, somehow knowing what was in his mind.

I'll stay here. I'll protect you. I'll be your strength against the night.

Overwhelmed by need and desire, she suddenly took command and straddled him, working at the buttons on her tailored shirt as she leaned down over him, her hair feathering against his chest, eliciting a soft groan that only fed her own hunger.

She threw the shirt aside and kissed him, her lips wild and hungry, her tongue passionate and demanding.

He rose to the challenge, returning her fever with his own, cupping her head, rolling with her, seeking to free her from her remaining garments. She helped, sliding her riding breeches down over her hips before shifting her hands to the buckle of his belt, then dipping her fingers beneath his waistband. His eyes met hers, and she bit back the words she couldn't say.

I don't care who or what you are. I don't care that we've only known each other a few days, the strangest days of my life. I know there will never be anyone else like you. I'm falling in love with you. No, I am *in love with you....*

No. She couldn't say those words.

So she made love to him instead, and she gasped in sweet pleasure as he returned each brush and gesture, as they turned into a tangle of stroking, touching, kissing and teasing, awakening an ever greater arousal. Finally they rocked into climax together, the moment seizing them with a sweet violence that swept them up into the wonder of the flesh, then allowed them to drift down still filled with the wonder of what could never be truly touched, truly understood, the power of the heart and the soul.

Afterward they lay together quietly for a while, just breathing.

"Alex," he said softly.

"What?"

"Neither of us can take the chance of being fooled."

"What?"

He was staring up at the ceiling, but his arm tightened around her.

"We both want our fathers to be…good. Not monsters. Not killers. But if they should come to us, we can't allow ourselves to be fooled. We can't let hope cost us our lives."

"Of course not," she whispered. "I can be strong. But we'll learn the truth. We'll bring down Milo, and then we'll discover that there can be such a thing as a good vampire. That shouldn't be so hard for you to believe. You say you're a vampire, and you're good."

"I *am* a vampire," he said. "And yes, I'm good, or at least I try to be."

"See? I told you that was the truth," she said.

He pulled her against him. "We'll find out soon enough, I'm afraid," he said softly.

And then she knew.

Tomorrow night the full moon would be here.

CHAPTER SEVENTEEN

IT CAME AGAIN. The dream in which she saw her father.

She was out riding, and then there he was, opening his arms to her, the essence of him still there, as strong and good as it had ever been.

There was a rumble in the sky, but it wasn't thunder, because there was no rain on the horizon.

Instead she saw a red cloud, billowing and rising, and blocking out the sun.

And even as the sun sank, the moon began to rise.

She could hear him, but distantly. He was calling her name, and he seemed to be warning her. Telling her to…

Run!

Suddenly he was by her side, and they ran together until they reached the caves, the same caves that had given Chief Tall Feather and his clan their name of Cave Warriors.

The caves where they interred their dead.

They ran through the caves, penetrating deeper and deeper into a maze, until suddenly her father stopped, his face twisted in horror.

A trick. It's a trap.

And then Cody was there.

Get away from her, Eugene. You might not want to, but you can hurt her.

No...she's my daughter.

Then he stopped, and Alex realized both men were listening to something past the limits of her hearing.

They're coming! Cody said.

Alex woke with a start. Cody was wrong about her father. She *knew* he was wrong. The dream might not happen just as she had seen it, but still, it was a foretelling.

Her father was out there. Her father, not Cody's, had saved the people who had survived in Hollow Tree.

She rolled over, anxious to tell him, anxious to make him understand that she knew—*she knew*—her father would never hurt her.

But Cody was gone, and daylight was streaming through the window.

She leaped up and hurried back to her own room, where she washed and dressed quickly, choosing breeches and a shirt again, thinking that this didn't seem likely to be a day requiring a ladylike ensemble. She industriously brushed her teeth with baking soda, then ran downstairs, but before she could get very far, she paused.

She could see out the front window.

And what she saw was Linda Gordon, in a shirt and breeches just as she was herself, standing out on the balcony of the saloon.

Linda took a look around, then slid town the drainpipe to the ground, kicking up a small clod of dirt as she landed. She hurried around back, to the small barn behind the saloon, and reappeared a moment later on horseback.

Alex started to shout for someone to come, but she

hesitated. It was broad daylight, and she wanted to know where the hell Linda was going. She wouldn't accost her; she would just follow her at a distance.

It would be completely safe.

She hurried out the door and around the side of the building, pausing beside the window of the dining room, because she could hear Bert talking anxiously to Father Joseph. "How can we be certain? Cody Fox plans to bring John Snow and his family in here by tonight, but how can he be certain he's not bringing in—a family of vampires?"

"We just have to trust in Cody—and God, of course," Father Joseph replied.

"We'd better keep a lot of holy water around, that's all I can say," Bert said worriedly.

Holy water.

As she passed the back door, Alex slipped quietly inside. She found the priest's portmanteau against the wall, where the weapons would be in easy reach whenever they were needed, and she hunkered down, opening it in silence. She grabbed several of the vials of holy water and slid them into her shirt pocket. She paused, then collected a bow and a quiver of arrows, too, grateful that there were plenty of people to keep carving weapons. If they ran out of broom handles and fence pickets, well, the banister could always be taken apart.

She hurried to the stables and slipped a bridle over Cheyenne's head, then leaped Indian-style onto the mare's back.

When she reached the street, Linda was gone, but she remembered the direction Linda had taken and leaned low against Cheyenne's neck, saying, "Speed now, Cheyenne. We'll slow down once we pick up her trail."

The mare pranced nervously, which was good.

She was ready to race.

CODY AND BRENDAN had started out at the crack of dawn, just as the first pale streaks of morning had cut across the darkness.

When they reached John Snow's, the man was excited to see them. His granddaughter had been doing very well. And though last night there had been vampires in the sky, there had only been a few, and they had simply been circling, watching. "I think they were like scouts, on a reconnaissance mission, or vultures, seeking out the dead. One or the other. But we brought down two of them."

"May we see them?" Cody asked tensely.

John nodded. "You're just in time. We have taken the precautions and were just about to bury the remains."

Outside, behind the house, John had the corpses under a tarp. He pulled it back.

He had indeed taken every precaution. The heads had been removed, and the hearts cut out.

Neither had been more than thirty at the time he'd been turned, and they couldn't have been turned long ago, since they hadn't immediately decayed into ash or a puddle of putrefaction. Cody didn't recognize either man. His father wasn't there, and neither was Eugene Gordon, or John would have said something.

And certainly not Milo Roundtree.

No.

Milo was biding his time, letting others go in.

He was letting his soldiers perish while he tested his prey.

"Go ahead and bury them, John," Cody said, replacing

the tarp. "But quickly. We need you to bring your family into Victory by tonight," he said.

John frowned, and Cody wasn't surprised. He had expected the other man to balk.

"We can fight here. We have proved it, Cody."

"John," Brendan said, stepping in, "we know that you and your sons—and your entire family—know how to fight. But there may be a mass attack tonight. It's the night of the full moon. And quite frankly, we need your help to save Victory."

Cody lowered his head, smiling slowly. Leave it to Brendan.

John Snow nodded sagely. "A united front… Yes, my sons and I will help. April owes her life to you. Perhaps the entire family, since we know how the infection spreads. We will come into town. It will take no more than an hour to finish with this refuse—" he nodded toward the corpses "—and ride in. We will be well ahead of the sunset," he promised.

Satisfied, Cody thanked him. "The boardinghouse is full right now. The sheriff has taken up residence in the saloon, and there's still room there."

"That will be fine, Cody Fox," John Snow assured him. "We will go wherever is necessary. We will come to fight."

SHE SHOULD HAVE KNOWN.

Linda was heading for the caves.

Alex had thought that she'd escaped the other woman's notice, but as she trotted past the entrance to the first arroyo, she was startled to see Linda waiting for her.

She had dismounted and was leaning against the rock wall.

"Alexandra. To what do I owe this honor?"

"I've caught you. Red-handed," Alex said flatly.

Linda smiled. "You've caught me doing what? Riding?"

"I saw you slide down a drainage pipe so no one would see you and ride out of town. That seems like proof of guilt to me."

Linda was standing, while Alex was still mounted. She felt it gave her an advantage.

But Linda was apparently not impressed. "I'm not a vampire," she said flatly.

"Then you're infected—and you tried to kill Jigs."

"I'm not infected," Linda said, sounding weary. "And I would never hurt Jigs."

"Oh?" Alex said.

She reached into her pocket for one of the vials of holy water, uncorked it swiftly with her teeth and poured the entire contents onto Linda's head.

"What did you do that for!" the other woman demanded, sputtering.

She was wet.

Other than that, the water seemed to have had no effect on her.

"Oh, my God! You brat," Linda said. "You dumped holy water on me, didn't you? I told you—I'm not a vampire!"

"Then what are you doing out here?" Alex demanded.

Linda sighed. "I'm here to see your father," she said.

CODY AND BRENDAN returned to the boardinghouse in midafternoon.

Cody was uneasy and had watched the sky the entire ride. Already it seemed that the usual blue of the Texas sky was turning to a bloodred shade. The sun had begun its descent. Even though there were still hours of daylight, he could see the pale orb of the moon, ghostlike, just beginning to rise.

He walked over to the saloon to tell Cole and Dave that John Snow's family would be coming.

The men had already prepared their weapons for that night. There were an abundance of stakes set in strategic places, and the men had been melting silver and casting silver bullets. Bows and quivers filled with arrows were lined up on the bar.

"Jigs?" he asked Cole.

"Weak as a kitten. I don't think he'll do us much good tonight, if the attack you suspect does come," Cole said. "But I don't think he'll turn on us, either."

"Someone in this house will," Cody said. "Be prepared." He looked around. Everyone was present and accounted for—except Linda.

"Where is Linda Gordon?" he asked.

"I don't know," Cole said. "I don't think she's come down yet."

He looked at Cody, then swore softly and ran up the stairs. Cody heard him bang on her door, then throw it open. A moment later he ran back down. "Gone," he said.

"Watch out for her return," Cody told him.

He strode across the street to the boardinghouse. He had to make sure, but his gut was certain Alex would be gone, as well.

He ran into Father Joseph—definitely the Lord's warrior—in the hall, inventorying their weapons.

"Have you seen Alex?" he asked.

Father Joseph frowned. "No, but I haven't seen her leave, either."

Cody swore and raced up to their rooms, bursting into one and then the other.

He had known he would be wasting time.

He hurried down the stairs, taking them two at a time.

Brendan called out to him when he reached the front hall. "Cody, wait. I'll go with you."

"No, you have to stay here. These people need your experience. I'll be back with Alex."

He hurried out with long strides, resaddled Taylor and followed the two sets of hoofprints leading out of town.

ALEX HAD DISMOUNTED and was sitting on a rock with Linda, sharing the canteen of water Linda had brought.

"He never wanted you to see him like this," Linda explained. "He didn't even come to me right away, only when he had no choice and it was time to warn me, and that's when he told me what had happened. Milo took him by surprise when he was riding back from Calico Jack's. He doesn't remember what happened to him, only waking up in his coffin with a terrible hunger—and an amazing strength. He dug his way out…and ran, trying to figure out what Milo had done to him. He took refuge in these caves, where he lived off bats."

"Oh, God," Alex said.

"He came to me, not long before you returned. I started bringing him raw meat and blood from the butcher's. He's not evil, Alex." She sighed. "A while back, he took to hiding out in Hollow Tree. He knew the town, and he felt safe there, less likely to be recognized. But then Milo and his men came, and he came back here again."

"I never believed he could be evil," Alex said. "But I'm sorry. I did think you were a bitch and a whore."

"I was a whore—until I met Eugene," Linda said quietly. "After his…death, I went back to the saloon because it was an easy place for him to come see me."

"I'm truly sorry," Alex said. "I shouldn't have judged you."

"I understand," Linda told her. "Your father…he's been afraid that you've been seeing him in your dreams. He told me that you have visions."

"Sometimes," Alex admitted.

"That's how Milo teaches his gang to get to people—in their dreams. That's how Milo tried to get to you. He knows that Eugene is out here somewhere, and once he's taken over Victory, he'll come for him. But he has a lot of power. He was able to tap into your father's mind, because your father was one of his kills, and could reach you. He tried to lure you out, and you were open to him."

Alex shivered, thankful for Cody—Cody, who had saved her.

She frowned suddenly, stood and looked out across the plain. "Linda?"

"Yes?"

"Over there. Is that him? Coming to meet you?"

Without waiting for an answer, Alex leaped up on her horse. "Forgive me, but I have to see him."

She slapped the reins against Cheyenne's neck, and the mare took flight across the plain.

She was vaguely aware that Linda was shouting something at her, but she was already too far away and couldn't hear the other woman's words, and she didn't care, anyway.

She reached the spot where he stood, reined in and dismounted.

He was wearing a long railroad frock coat and hat, standing with his back to her.

"Father!" she cried, but then the word froze on her lips when he turned, a smile on his face and a sizzle of laughter in his unholy red eyes.

Milo Roundtree's smile widened as he strode toward her.

CODY WASN'T FAR OUT of town when he realized that the red darkness was descending, and descending quickly. He looked up.

The sun was sinking far too rapidly.

He was suddenly aware of the shadows descending toward him, and he wrapped the reins around the saddle horn and reached for his bow and an arrow. He nocked the arrow, then let the arrow fly. A shrieking sound told him that he'd made a hit, though he had no idea whether it had been deadly or not.

A second shadow swept in with startling speed. He drew his sword from his saddle sheath in the nick of time, and the vampire's own speed became his downfall, as he flew directly onto the blade, then burst into a spray of ash and bone shards.

Cody kept riding, swinging the sword as the next vampire attacked. He didn't know if he killed it or only maimed it, and he couldn't stop to find out. A fourth creature shot down at him, and he drew his pistol and fired directly at the thing again and again. Finally the body fell with a heavy thud ahead of him, causing Taylor to rear. He was almost thrown, but he tightened his thighs around the animal just in time to keep his balance.

"Easy, Taylor," Cody said soothingly, urging the horse into a gallop again. Because in the distance he could see—

Alex.

And Milo Roundtree, descending on her.

Alex backed toward Cheyenne, hoping to make a run for it, but Milo laughed, raising his hands and calling down the sound of thunder. Cheyenne screamed in fear and bolted away at the speed of lightning.

"Why do I want you so much?" Milo asked himself, more than her, as he drew nearer. "I suppose it's just that there aren't many beautiful young women in these parts. Whores, yes, but you're a rarity, an educated beauty with spunk and style. I know you think you don't want me, but you will, I promise you that. When I finish with you, you'll be delighted to be with me. You'll be craving my company."

He was almost on her when she remembered the remaining vials of holy water in her pocket and reached for one.

What if it was worthless? What if Linda had fooled her and was really a vampire, after all?

She was wavering. Belief might well be everything.

Just as he was about to touch her, she pulled out a vial and, as she had earlier, opened it with her teeth.

"Only when snow falls in hell could I ever so much as *endure* your company!" she cried, splashing the water directly into his eyes.

She prayed…and then he let out a cry of agonized pain, staggering back.

She turned to run and saw another man approaching, and this time it *was* her father.

"We have to get to the caves," he told her as she raced up to him.

Linda, looking distressed, was right behind him.

"Hurry up," Linda urged. "Do you have more of that holy water? You're going to need it, because Milo's gang can't be far behind him."

"He'll come after her again—that splash wasn't enough to kill him," her father said, hurrying her toward the caves with his hand on her back. "I think the gang has been using the caves on the other side of the mountain."

Her father, she thought. Her father had a hand on her back. She stared at him, dizzy for a moment, unable to believe what she was seeing.

She had been right; he was a good vampire. There *was* such a thing. He had fought the evil inside him and won. He didn't need to kill.

"Eugene!" Linda cried. "Look!"

Alex spun around to look, too, and saw that Milo Roundtree had recovered, but instead of striding across the plain, he looked as if he were flying, floating.

Right in front of her eyes, he was turning into a winged shadow.

But even as he started to rise into the preternaturally early darkness, something massive raced across it toward him. The sound of huge wings flapping thundered in her ears, and suddenly the second shadow was descending on Milo.

The shadows met with a scream, writhing together and falling to the ground, and suddenly there were only two men, standing and staring at each other.

Milo Roundtree—and Cody Fox.

"Cody," Alex breathed. "We've got to go back. We've got to help him."

Linda caught her arm. "No, Alex. We can't help him, we can only distract him."

"Alex!" her father said sharply. "We've got to go. Now."

She heard another noise now. It was the sound of a hundred wings, rising on the far side of the cliffs. If the three of them didn't move, there was no doubt that the creatures would see them.

Eugene lifted his arms, as if to protect the women, and he urged them toward the nearest entrance to the caves. "Quickly!" he urged.

Still Alex turned back. Cody was racing toward Milo. He caught him in the midriff, and together they rolled across the ground, engaged in a vicious struggle. In the moonlight she caught the gleam of fangs, and what looked like talons.

What sounded suspiciously like a Rebel yell split the night.

KNOWING IT WAS LITERALLY a matter of life and death, Cody focused on Milo, but despite his efforts to close out everything else, he kept thinking of Alex.

He was grateful that she had thought to bring holy water, the only explanation for the burns on Milo's face.

Furious that she had come out here at all.

Scared to death…

He was sure that had been Eugene Gordon with her, but he still had a hard time believing there was such a thing as a good vampire—one who had been turned, anyway. He had never really trusted that it was possible, not even for his own father.

Milo rushed him so hard they both flew through the air, then fell.

Hard.

Milo had drawn a sword and was already swinging the blade toward Cody's neck.

Cody rolled just in the nick of time, then jump-kicked Milo as he leaped to his feet. Milo swung the sword again, but once again Cody was able to elude him.

"Fool," Milo taunted. "You could join me. You could rule the West."

"I don't want to rule the West," Cody said.

"No? Well, you could always join up with your old man. He's out there somewhere. But you know that, don't you?"

"I'll find him one day," Cody said, dodging the sword. "Without your help."

"So…it's the woman, is it?" Milo teased as he spun, his sword scything down, but Cody had anticipated the move and was already on Milo's other side. He slammed his fists hard against the other vampire's back, and Milo fell to his knees, but only for a moment.

"What? You think she'll accept you?" Milo laughed, back on his feet again. "You're a monster—an abomination. She'll never love you."

Cody got in a blow to Milo's jaw and grunted in satisfaction as he saw blood trickling from the outlaw's lip.

Milo paused, tasted it, then stared at Cody furiously.

"You could have had the world, but now you'll die like a dog in the dirt."

Cody smiled. Not all his tricks had come naturally. Some he'd been taught in the military.

Anger your opponent, because anger makes a man

careless. He himself had been careless, enraged, when he'd rushed to attack Milo barehanded. He wouldn't be careless again.

"You'll never have her, Milo," he said.

"Of course I will. I'll take her, and that will be that."

"I'd say 'over my dead body,' but actually, mine is a living body. Ever miss that? The pleasures of the flesh?"

"Sneer all you want, Fox, but while you're fighting me here, my children are sweeping into your precious town."

"Then your children will die."

Milo started to rush him, and Cody braced himself for the impact.

But Milo never hit him. He turned to shadow, then rose into the sky.

And headed for the caves.

STONES MARKED THE CRYPTS of warriors, those long dead and those newly lost. Her father led the way past them, deeper into the caves. "There's a place up ahead that must have been prepared for a warrior…who ended up interred elsewhere. It has a stone I can slide across the opening, and we can stay hidden there until morning," he said. "I have…stakes there. Protection."

But they didn't reach his safe haven. He drew back, forcing the women behind him, as the air before them swirled and coalesced into a menacing black form.

Milo.

Alex's heart sank. If Milo was here, then…

Milo let out a furious, gnashing sound, half growl, half howl, as he reached for her father and threw him across the cave to slump against the rock wall.

"Linda, get behind me!" Alex commanded.

"No…your father…"

Alex didn't waste time arguing. She thrust the woman behind her and prepared for what she knew might be the last fight of her life. The Milo she faced now was hideous. His face was contorted in a mask of fury. His lips were drawn back so far that they were almost nonexistent, revealing fangs bared and dripping with a viscous liquid.

Suddenly he was right on top of her. His arms were like a vise as he grabbed her, and she barely managed to reach into her pocket, grasp a vial of holy water and spill it on him.

His flesh sizzled, but he didn't let her go, only threw his head back and roared, preparing to thrust his fangs into her neck.

Just as she closed her eyes and said a silent prayer, Milo screamed and dropped her. She looked up from the floor of the cave and thought she was looking at a miracle. Cody was there—and alive.

He sent Milo crashing against the rocks on the far side of the cave, near her father's unconscious body. Loose stones rained down on him, but he shook them off and rose, growling.

Cody was prepared.

Before Milo could react, he half ran, half leaped across the distance between them and drove a stake into Milo Roundtree's heart.

Milo shuddered and writhed against the pain, teeth gnashing, a horrible animal sound emanating from his throat.

Then, in a sudden flash, he burst into flames.

The stake fell to the floor in a spray of ash.

Cody turned around, tension and rage contorting his face as he drew another stake and started toward her father.

"No!" Alex cried, running to protect her father, who was just regaining consciousness and trying to stagger to his feet. "Cody, no. Please, you have to believe me."

Cody stopped, and the tension in his features eased, leaving him the Cody she knew—and loved.

He reached out for her, and she rushed into his arms.

He held her for only a second, though, then dropped his arms and focused his attention over her shoulder at her father and Linda, who had rushed to her husband's side.

"We have to get back," he said. "Milo is dead, but the attack on Victory is under way."

"We've still got two horses," Linda said.

"Eugene, take the horses and bring the women. I can get there faster on my own. But if you—"

"Alex is my daughter, and Linda is my wife. I love them, and I'll guard them with my life—to my destruction," Eugene said firmly.

"Then let's go," Cody said, beginning to transform before her eyes.

She and Linda rode the bay, while her father rode Cody's stallion, Taylor. They rode hard, continually on the lookout.

But they didn't see any of the monsters until they reached the edge of town.

The townspeople, along with John Snow and his family, were more than holding their own. As they raced down Main Street, Alex saw that Sheriff Cole and Dave were leading the men as if they were a trained battalion.

Which, in a way, they were.

Target practice had worked wonders.

Arrows were finding their targets, and the screaming of the dying vampires filled the air.

They rode over a dozen of the downed creatures, the horses' hooves thudding into the flesh of the truly dead and dying, and those who were trying to rejoin the battle alongside their foul brethren.

Alex saw Father Joseph on the boardinghouse porch, splashing the creatures with holy water. Her father dismounted and headed for the porch, and the action slowed as she saw disaster descending.

She leaped to the ground and tried to throw herself between her father and the priest, but she was too late. Father Joseph had already flung holy water in her father's face.

She watched in horror as her father stood dead still and Father Joseph froze on the steps above him. "It's you," the priest said. "You're the man who…" His words trailed off as his eyes filled with remorse for what he had done.

Eugene nodded, then blinked in surprise. "I'm not burning," he whispered.

"Because somehow you've salvaged your soul," Father Joseph said in awe.

A wounded vampire suddenly fell at their feet, flapping and squirming.

Bert strode out from behind Father Joseph and slammed a stake into it.

"Have you seen Cody?" Alex asked anxiously.

"He's in the saloon," Father Joseph said.

Alex spun and raced across the street to the saloon, fearful of what she might find there. She threw open the doors and burst inside.

And there was Cody.

He was facing Sherry Lyn, whose pretty face was twisted into a vicious expression and whose fangs were gleaming in the light, and a host of seven vampires. He seemed calm, despite the fact that Jigs and Dolly were lying on the floor nearby, dead or at least unconscious, and God alone knew where the others might be.

"Sherry Lyn?" Alex gasped.

"Oh, please, you were all such fools!" the whore told them. "Of course it was me. You were all so easy to fool—especially with a few false tears. Milo gave me this incredible gift, and now he and I have succeeded. All your friends are out in the street, fighting, and here… well, we just have Miss Goody Two-shoes and one little man.

"Oh, sorry, Cody," she said, her voice dripping with false sweetness. "I'm sure you're not a *little* man, but you *are* on your own except for your useless little girl-friend here, and…you have no idea what I'm capable of, not to mention what my friends can do. And of course Jigs could wake up at any minute, a ravenous monster again."

She flew at Cody, but he was ready, catching her and throwing her back into her clustered friends.

She snarled, transforming into something big and ugly, and came at him again, and this time the others joined the fight by her side.

Alex drew the last two vials of holy water from her pocket, uncorked them and splashed the contents at the attacking horde.

She managed to strike three of the creatures, who screamed and flapped in agony, their skin sizzling and sparking.

Cody threw off Sherry Lyn, but she and the remaining creatures kept coming.

Suddenly Sherry Lyn stopped dead—literally—an arrow protruding from her chest.

More arrows flew, and more creatures fell.

Alex spun around. Her father and Linda were standing there, bows and arrows at the ready, but there were no vampires left to kill. Linda walked over to the body of Sherry Lyn, who looked like herself again in death. Her eyes were wide open. Blood trickled from her mouth.

"See if Dolly is all right," Linda said.

Dolly was only unconscious, and Jigs roused when Alex touched him. He immediately asked for a stake, and Alex smiled at this proof that he was all right.

"You sit tight," she told him. Then, taking one of the stakes, she rushed out to the street.

It was quiet and still. Everyone was looking around, wary, waiting for another attack.

But none came.

Cody, who must have rushed out while she was checking on Dolly and Jigs, was standing there scanning the sky.

The red haze was fading as she watched, revealing the full moon in all its brilliance.

In the distance, wolves began to howl, but it was a customary and oddly pleasant sound.

Alex stepped into Cody's arms and felt as if she'd come home.

EPILOGUE

THE NEXT DAY, John Snow and his family, although glad to have been of help, were ready to return to their lives.

Several of Tall Feather's warriors came in to report that the camp had been attacked, as well, but they had brought down all the creatures and dispatched them.

Thoroughly.

An equally thorough burial detail dealt with the dead in Victory.

A posse comprised of Apache and the men of Victory searched the caves and surrounding areas, but it seemed that the danger was over.

"For now," Cody said.

He and Alex were together on the balcony, savoring the breeze and the realization that the night was no longer full of danger.

"You're leaving, aren't you?" Alex asked him.

To her surprise, he hesitated.

A smile teased his lips.

"I don't know. There's still the matter of your father."

He had chosen to stay over at the saloon. People still weren't sure what to make of him, most of them settling on the story that he had been buried alive, then escaped and hidden out, fighting the vampires in secret.

"What about my father? You saw what he did. You know he's not a threat."

"Yes, I learned something from him. A vampire *can* fight evil."

"Just like you've been doing all these years?"

"But I'm half human."

"Very human," she said huskily. "So what about my father?" she asked again.

Cody pulled her into his arms. "He wanted to know my intentions."

"Oh," she murmured. "And…?"

"…And I found myself telling him how I felt about you."

"What happened then?"

"Then he mentioned that an Episcopal priest was living in the house."

She pressed a finger to his lips and told him earnestly. "I told you that I…that I would settle for whatever we could have."

"Yes, but I want more," he told her, pressing his lips to hers, his kiss both tender and urgent.

Then he pulled back and looked down at her again, his eyes glowing golden in the night.

"So much more," he said, his tone husky.

"I…I admit I'm more than a little in love with you," she said.

"Really? I hadn't anticipated such a surprising and amazing complication. You see, Miss Alexandra Gordon, I believe that I'm much more than a little in love with you."

"But…I know you want to find your father," she said.

"True, but…"

"But?"

"Every man needs a home base. And if he happens to be a vampire hunter, he could have no better wife than one who knows…all there is to know. The truth about that man."

She gripped his shoulders and rose on her toes to kiss him.

"You didn't actually pose the question," she whispered to him. "But the answer is yes."

He laughed and swung her up into his arms. In seconds they were tangled together, passionate and laughing, both question and answer spoken in the oldest language known between a man and a woman.

* * * * *

So you think you can write?

Mills & Boon® and Harlequin® have joined forces in a global search for new authors.

It's our biggest contest yet—with the prize of being published by the world's leader in romance fiction.

Look for more information on our website:
www.soyouthinkyoucanwrite.com

So you think you can write? Show us!

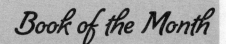

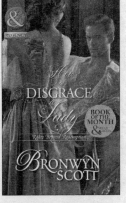

MILLS & BOON®
Book Club

Free Book!

Get your free book now at
www.millsandboon.co.uk/freebookoffer

Or fill in the form below and post it back to us

THE MILLS & BOON® BOOK CLUB™—HERE'S HOW IT WORKS: Accepting your free book places you under no obligation to buy anything. You may keep the book and return the despatch note marked 'Cancel'. If we do not hear from you, about a month later we'll send you 3 brand-new stories from the Nocturne™ series, two priced at £4.99 and a third, larger, version priced at £6.99 each. There is no extra charge for post and packaging. You may cancel at any time, otherwise we will send you 3 stories a month which you may purchase or return to us—the choice is yours. *Terms and prices subject to change without notice. Offer valid in UK only. Applicants must be 18 or over. Offer expires 31st January 2013. **For full terms and conditions, please go to www.millsandboon.co.uk/freebookoffer**

Mrs/Miss/Ms/Mr (please circle) _____

First Name _____

Surname _____

Address _____

_____

Postcode _____

E-mail _____

Send this completed page to: Mills & Boon Book Club, Free Book Offer, FREEPOST NAT 10298, Richmond, Surrey, TW9 1BR

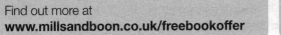
Find out more at
www.millsandboon.co.uk/freebookoffer

Visit us Online

0712/T2YEA